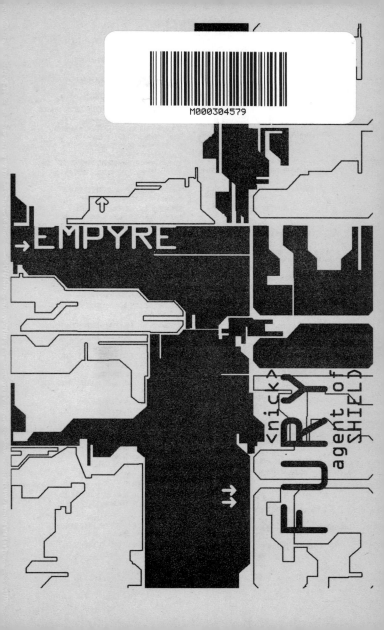

MARVEL®

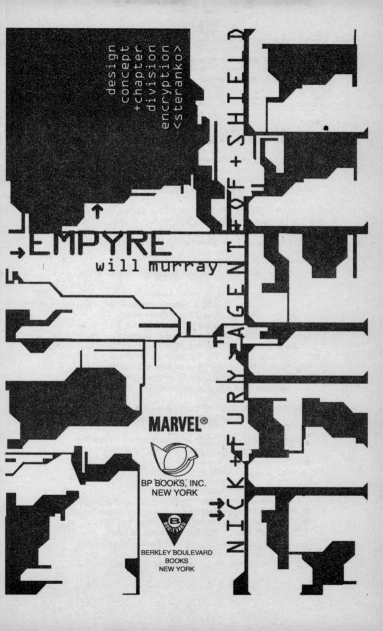

design
concept
+chapter
division
encryption
<steranko>

F OF + SHIELD

EMPYRE

will murray

A G E N T

N I C K + F U R Y

MARVEL®

BP BOOKS, INC.
NEW YORK

B BOULEVARD

BERKLEY BOULEVARD
BOOKS
NEW YORK

Special thanks to Ginjer Buchanan, John Morgan, Ursula Ward, Mike Thomas, and Steve Behling.

NICK FURY, AGENT OF S.H.I.E.L.D.: EMPYRE

A Berkley Boulevard Book
A BP Books, Inc. Book

PRINTING HISTORY
Berkley Boulevard paperback edition / August 2000

The Penguin Putnam Inc. World Wide Web site address is
http://www.penguinputnam.com

Check out the Ace Science Fiction/Fantasy newsletter,
and much more, at Club PPI!

ISBN: 0-425-16816-6

BERKLEY BOULEVARD
Berkley Boulevard Books are published by The Berkley Publishing Group, a division of Penguin Putnam Inc.,
375 Hudson Street, New York, New York 10014.
BERKLEY BOULEVARD and its logo
are trademarks belonging to Penguin Putnam Inc.

PRINTED IN THE UNITED STATES OF AMERICA

10 9 8 7 6 5 4 3 2 1

The future can be seen,
and because it can be seen,
it can be changed.

—J. B. Priestly

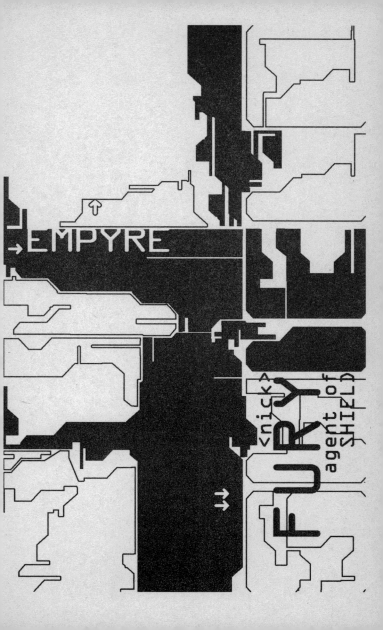

FURY

COLONEL NICK WAITED for the cold December moon to rise over the Colorado Rockies before lighting up.

Old habits die hard. In other times and other battles, he had learned never to light up under night combat conditions. The flare of a match, the red coal of ash burning at the end of a cigar, could turn a man into a target in an instant. And make him a dead man in the next.

A full hunter's moon came up over the eastern Rockies, washing Fury in stark light. Hunkered down in his rocky sniper's perch, his rangy body was sheathed in a midnight black S.H.I.E.L.D.-issue Neoprene-Kevlar-Nomex combat suit that absorbed light the way a sponge absorbs water. His unshaven features were corked black. Even the boxy molded polyurethane lines of his Stark Industries Elongatable Lateral Ballistic Offensive Weapon were a light-absorbing blue-gray.

Only one thing reflected light: his one good eye. The left was shielded by a black eye patch.

Fury reached down, extracting a blunt cigar from a capped tube on his combat belt. Without taking his good eye off the trail below, he severed the tip against the Randall Survival Knife tucked into its boot holster, then inserted the freshly cut end into his belt igniter. Ignition was shielded and silenced. The cigar came out, glowing ferociously.

Fury smoked with a preoccupied intensity as he fitted

the nightscope on the ELBOW. His quarry should be along any minute now. . . .

Some instinct made him look down. Movement. Hardly discernible. It was gone when his eye found the spot.

Laying the El Producto aside, Fury brought the padded scope eyepiece to his right eye. He touched the On switch.

The nightscope showed shadowy figures walking along in single file, one man taking point, three yards ahead of the others. They were rounding a boulder the size of an upended locomotive, rotating their upper bodies every few steps, sweeping the terrain with their jet-black AutoCobra machine pistols.

"Well trained, aren't you?" Fury muttered. "Well, all the training in the world don't mean jake when you walk smack into a high-vantage ambush."

Fury leaned into the ELBOW, thumbing a latch. The weird weapon's barrel extended with smooth precision, transforming into a rifle.

"Come to Uncle Nicholas," he growled.

Fury let the last man come out from behind the boulder, laid the laser dot in the exact center of his chest and fired once. The weapon whuffed. Recoil was nonexistent. The man went down.

Shifting his sights, Fury found the enemy on point. A single silent shot sent him corkscrewing away. Demoralized, the others broke for cover.

But he had to give them this: they deployed in complete silence. Even the casualties went down without a peep.

Scouring the terrain through his scope, Fury found no open targets. Taking a last puff of his cigar, he started down to hunt them.

From his belt, he extracted a set of stainless steel clamps, attached them to his gloves, and found his prepositioned nylon line. Rolling off his perch was like rolling out of bed. Fury accomplished it in a smooth, easy motion. The clamps bit into the nylon, and Fury rappelled down the line.

His boots struck hard ground seven seconds later—too fast for his quarry to get a bead. If he was lucky, too fast to be spotted at all.

Hunkering down amid tumbled granite, Fury found his lanyarded ELBOW, and waited. He crouched in a cup of stone, also preselected. And he had all night.

After all, he had counted only four survivors.

Ten long minutes crawled past. Fury inhaled and exhaled in shallow breaths. The plumes of cold condensation escaping his mouth dissolved in the bitter, still air. He listened for any sound of movement. There was none.

Retracting the ELBOW to short-barrel mode, Fury eased it out a little. He looked into the eyepiece, and saw only the empty trail and still, streaky shadows.

Rotating a dial, the scope angled left. This gave him a better view, one at an oblique angle to his position.

It took another six minutes, but an unfriendly finally ventured out onto the trail. Fury gave him a minute to reconnoiter. When the enemy thought it prudent, he signaled others to reemerge from hiding.

Two came out. Fury waited for the fourth, then muttered, "The hell with it."

Resetting his scope, he jumped out of concealment, shouting, "Hail Hydra!"

The ELBOW stuttered in short, decisive bursts. All three foes never knew what hit them. Fury had been that smooth, that lethal.

He withdrew too fast to draw return fire.

When Fury stole a look through the nightscope, his foes lay sprawled in the moonlight like a clutch of squashed spiders.

Retreating to full cover, Fury realigned his scope. The ELBOW was designed to cover tight positions, where its operator didn't dare poke his head out. But Fury was a soldier of habit. Poking his head out was ingrained.

Having only one good eye had its disadvantages, but Nick Fury found it easier to adapt than most. For one thing, staring into a scope for long intervals was a breeze.

He scanned the clustered boulders with concentrated patience.

"Just show me what I need . . ." he said softly.

And it came. A plume of cold breath condensation. Faint in the moonlight, but enough to show Fury where the sixth and last unfriendly crouched. He knew the lone survivor was pretty scared by now, that his breathing would be ragged and erratic.

Easing up from his chosen position, Fury picked his way toward the blind side of the concealing boulder. His boots were soft-soled, and made no sound. Everything on his combat rig was locked down tight. Big and brawny as he was, Fury could move like so much congealed smoke.

When he reached the boulder, Fury leaned into it. Easing around just so much, he played with his scope angle until he saw around the curve of the rock.

No sign of his foe. Fury eased forward. A boot heel showed in his scope. Holding his breath, he padded around, one inch at a time.

When the enemy's exposed back came into view, Fury laid the red dot on him.

It was going to be easy.

"Too easy," he breathed so softly he barely heard himself.

Reversing direction, Fury began stalking his quarry from the front. It was riskier that way, but a better field test of the ELBOW. And for that reason, he decided, worth the risk.

Creeping around, Fury kept his eye on the angled scope. He would see the man's face before the other had time to react. Plenty of time to get off a shot. It was going to be just like shooting pool. Eight ball in the corner pocket.

Something caused Fury to freeze.

He stopped dead in his tracks, the ELBOW up to eye level, his one good eye pressed tight into the eyepiece, free eye blind as a bat's.

There was nothing in the scope. But Fury sensed danger. He stepped around, suddenly. The face of his quarry was a smear of camo paint. It broke into a surprised explosion of patchy ochre-and-black slashes as narrow, hunting eyes spotted the leading lens of the scope.

"Freeze!" a commanding voice cracked out.

His quarry froze. So did Nick Fury. The voice was directly behind him.

"Whoever you are," Fury growled, "I got your boy dead to rights. Back off, or he's toast."

"Nice try," the unfamiliar voice behind Nick Fury said. "But I can see from here that you don't have a clean shot."

"Is that right?"

And Fury squeezed off a single round.

The man in his sights recoiled under the impact. Fury didn't take time to make sure he was down. Dropping and pivoting, he unleashed a stuttering spray in the general direction of the voice.

A satisfying scream of surprise came back as something with the force of a mule kick knocked Nick Fury back off his feet and into a punishing clump of loose rock.

"Oof!"

Fury landed hard. The ELBOW went skipping away, stopping when it reached the end of its belt-anchored lanyard. He lay there stunned, his teeth clenched in pain.

Reaching out blindly, Fury found the line, giving a hard yank as he fought for breath. His rib cage felt like it had been stove in. Executing a wild flip, the weapon jumped into the air, landing on his heaving chest. Fury cursed in agony as he snatched up the ELBOW, fingers searching for and finding the trigger and under-barrel handle.

Jerking half erect, he swept the area with the weapon. Beside the sheltering boulder, his quarry lay sprawled and unmoving.

And beyond it, lay another figure: a seventh, unsuspected enemy agent.

Beyond that, nothing moved.

Struggling to his feet, Fury reached into his belt. From a tube he extracted the unfinished cigar. Reigniting it, he brought the chewed end to his lips. The smoke didn't blunt the pain, but he felt better anyway.

Drawing in a deep, bracing breath of cold Rocky Mountain air mixed with cigar smoke, Fury called out, "All right, you goldbricks. On your feet!"

One by one, the fallen found their feet. They collected their weapons, falling into formation before him.

Pacing back and forth, Fury laid into them.

"You! Ellis! You are the biggest screwup on the planet! And you and you and you! I hope you got a good taste of what hard rubber bullets feel like when they hit your S.H.I.E.L.D. suits. Now imagine how you'd feel if I had aimed for your heads with hot lead!"

The individuals singled out hung their heads dejectedly. No one spoke.

Fury went to the person at the far end. A woman. Slim, willowy, she wore her tawny hair styled short. In the moonlight, green-gray eyes rimmed by a darker green gleamed. Her corked features had a set, almost feline cast to them.

Fury looked at the name tag: SPACEK

"That name strikes me as kinda familiar. . . ." he said.

"I'm Starla Spacek. You might remember me, although we've never actually met—"

Fury interrupted, "Starla. What kind of name is that?"

"Native American. I'm part Cheyenne. Spacek is my adopted name."

"Why weren't you in formation with the others?"

"I had gone on ahead. As scout, Colonel Fury."

"See anything interesting while your teammates were being picked off like ducks in a row?"

"I thought I smelled cigar smoke, and doubled back."

"Now that's very interesting," Fury said. "Seeing as how I was smoking a field cigar, which gives off hardly any odor."

"I'm very attuned to subtle sensory clues. The odor suggested possible danger. It seems I was correct."

"Your gold star will be presented at the funerals," Fury said sarcastically.

"I did avenge them. . . ."

"And got yourself shot in the process," Fury countered.

"Depending upon the objective," Recruit Spacek returned evenly, "that might have been seen by my superiors as mission accomplished."

"Well, I'm your ultimate superior, and I say you fouled up." Fury stepped back, bringing the others into the exchange. "You all fouled up. A fine lot of raggedy recruits you are. There I was smoking a cheroot with a tip as red as the planet Mars and none of you—not a one—had the presence of mind to scan above treeline and spot me."

"I had the drop on you, Colonel Fury," Starla insisted. "You should not have been able to kill Ellis. You didn't have the correct angle of fire."

"Here's a little flash for you, Recruit Spacek: expect the unexpected."

Lifting the ELBOW, Fury aimed it to the north. He fired. A round spanked off a rocky needle a hundred yards due west.

Reactions ranged from mild surprise to dumbfoundment.

Fury lifted the bulky weapon over his head. "This is what they're calling an ELBOW. That stands for Elongatable Lateral Ballistic Offensive Weapon. It's a multiprojectile hand weapon with rifle functions. Fires an array of rounds ranging from tonight's hard rubber bullets to what the technos call BLAM's—Barrel Launched Adaptive Rounds—with heat-seeking and guidance capabilities. One of the added features of the ELBOW is that it can be configured on a moment's notice to fire around corners, thus allowing the operator to keep his soft little head behind shelter."

Fury fired again for effect. This time, they saw the bullet speed true north, take an unexpected midair jog and explode against the cliff face. Rock and dust showered down.

Recruit Spacek said, "I noticed one other thing, Colonel."

"Yeah. What's that?"

"Before I signaled my intentions, you reacted to me."

"So?"

"You had your eye on your nightscope, yet you sensed my presence."

"You musta made a sound or something," Fury growled.

"I am part Cheyenne. I make no sounds."

"I beg to differ." Fury paused to remove his cigar. "Unless you got another explanation."

"You showed extrasensory awareness, Colonel. Clearly."

Fury grunted. "Tell me another one."

"I'm not just a field recruit, Colonel. I'm Special Powers."

Fury spat on the ground. "Special Powers. Just a fancy name for what we used to call the ESP Division. No, don't tell me. Let me guess: You're another psychic trying to qualify in the field. I've seen them come and go. Usually they come in cocky and go out feetfirst. What makes you think you'll be different?"

"I *am* different, Colonel. S.H.I.E.L.D. came to me. I've requested to be tasked to deal with the growing Hydra extrasensor threat."

"Let's see how long you last. In the field or out." Fury raised his voice to address the others. "All right. Listen up. We all got bloodied tonight. We get to lick our wounds to fight another day. But I want you to know I expect better in the field. We don't put the money and man-hours into training S.H.I.E.L.D. agents just to lose them to any old ambush they happen to walk in to."

"It wasn't just any old ambush," a recruit said.

Fury glared at him. "What's that?"

"It was *your* ambush."

"Come again?"

"You're Nick Fury. A legend. You fought in every major U.S. war over the last fifty years and a few nobody ever heard of, and you don't hardly look old enough to have fought in Viet Nam. You never rose higher in rank than full bird colonel, but they made you Executive Director of S.H.I.E.L.D. You're the best. But you went down just as hard as we did."

Fury hesitated. He ran his cigar back and forth from one side of his mouth to the other. He squinted one brown eye while absently scratching at the patch of white at his right temple, then opened it wide. He grinned.

"Look," he said at last. "There's two ways of looking at this. As recruits, the exercise flopped. As a test of the ELBOW, it was fair-to-middling. We'll call it even, and call it a night. Next stop for you Sorry Sams is Helicarrier duty."

Relieved grins broke out up and down the line.

They lasted only long enough for the roar of a heavy truck to come thundering out of the night.

Fury wheeled. Big headlights came funneling around a bend in the trail, causing night shadows to scoot and retreat.

"Grab rock!" Fury bellowed. "Unauthorized vehicle. Stay out of sight until I say so. This is not—I repeat—this is not part of the exercise."

DRAB

IT WAS AN OLIVE deuce-and-a-half truck, Fury saw. The vehicle rounded the bend. Door panels were emblazoned with the insignia of the U.S. Air Force.

Fury stepped into the headlights, ELBOW elevated, but ready to drop and fire, if necessary.

The truck screeched to a dusty halt and both doors exploded open. Fury brought the ELBOW down and made the tip of his cigar glow red.

"That's far enough," he warned. "This area is off-limits to non-S.H.I.E.L.D. personnel."

"Colonel Fury?" the driver called out.

"The same."

"We have emergency orders for you."

"The Strategic Hazard, Intervention, Espionage and Logistics Directorate don't take orders from airmen. You gotta know that. Now hands up."

The airmen obliged.

"Step into the light where I can see you," Fury ordered.

The airmen walked into the beams of their own headlights. They looked concerned, but not overly worried.

"Didn't you receive the transmission?" one asked.

"We're on radio silence out here," Fury shot back. "Training mission."

"Then I suggest, sir, that you activate your personal communicator."

"Sure. Just keep your hands where I can see them."

"We're unarmed, Colonel."

They seemed to be. Fury kept the ELBOW trained on the driver while he pulled his communicator from his combat belt.

"Saint Nick to North Pole," he chanted. "Saint Nick to North Pole."

"Copy, Saint Nick," an unfamiliar voice returned. It was half masked in static. Not unusual for a remote transmission. *"We have a global threatcon. Repeat, a global threatcon. Your immediate presence is required—"*

"Not so fast," Fury growled. "You know procedure. Password of the day."

The voice hesitated briefly. *"Juniper."*

Fury relaxed. "Copy that. Go ahead."

"Colonel Fury, you are urgently requested to proceed to Denver International Airport, where a first-class seat is being held on Empire Airlines Flight 666, departing at ten forty-five from Gate 4."

"Ten forty-five?" Fury barked. "That gives me a little over an hour to catch my flight."

"The Air Force has granted us the loan of a mobile launch system for your personal use. The system should be arriving any—"

"It's here," Fury interrupted. "What's going on?"

"Your briefing papers will be found in your airline seat pocket, Colonel."

"Briefing papers! That's a new one. Okay. We'll play it your way. Fury out."

The communicator went back into its belt pouch. Fury called over his shoulder, "It's okay. They're friendly."

The S.H.I.E.L.D. recruits emerged from their various points of shelter, curious. They surrounded the truck as the two airmen fell to preparing the vehicle.

Fury tossed his ELBOW to Starla Spacek, saying, "Hold on to that for me, Spacek. You others lend a hand."

"Colonel, I don't understand—"

"Just watch."

The airmen went to work pulling a canvas shroud off the back of the truck. It had covered a long shape that stretched from the back of the truck bed to project just over the cab. When the recuits started hauling it down, they all saw what lay in the truck bed—a stubby-winged A-4 Skyhawk fighter jet with standard Air Force markings, but painted in orange and white trainer colors. It sat on an angled launch rail, blunt nose poised over the cab's roof, tailpipe poking out of the rear.

The airmen popped the orange afterburner exhaust cover.

"Colonel, if you will," the driver said. "We're about ready to enable the bird."

"Right." Fury started climbing onto the truck.

Starla grabbed his arm. Her face was a tense mask of moonlight and shadows. "Colonel, I have a bad feeling about this. I sense definite danger."

Fury looked down. "You heard the transmission, same as me. Something's up. Something big. Headquarters wouldn't send a truck-mounted fighter for me unless it was urgent."

"That's not what I feel."

Fury clambered onto the fighter. He found the canopy latch and popped it.

"Yeah? Well, tune in and tell me what I'm flying into."

Starla half-shut her eyes. "I see a red flag. Danger. That's all I get—danger."

"I know that much. Let's hear some specifics."

"I'm a psychic, not a mind reader, Colonel Fury."

"Then stand clear. I got places to go and things to do."

"Colonel—"

Fury eased his surprisingly supple body into the cockpit, and began strapping in. An Air Force helmet went over his dark brown hair. He pitched his cigar away. It landed in a shower of sparks.

One of the airmen called up, "This will be a rocket-assisted takeoff, Colonel. You fire up the bird. We'll launch it, and the rest will be up to you once you're air-borne."

"Gotcha."

Fury gave the truck crew a thumb's up as the canopy settled over his head. The crew went to work on a side panel. Hydraulic machinery ground and the steel rail launcher erected the A-4 into launch position. At the rear of the truck, a fireproof steel plate hoisted into position, stopping just two feet from the cold afterburner.

"Back! Get back," an airman yelled. "Hot exhaust!"

Everyone jumped clear as the Skyhawk started spool-ing up. The whine grew to a roar and the entire truck shuddered and shimmied, its headlights dancing wildly. It looked as if the truck were trying to shake itself into large pieces.

Under the intense heat of the jet's building thrust, the exhaust deflector plate began to glow. Just on the point of going incandescent, one of the airmen lifted the red shield on an ignition button. He pressed it, then retreated to safety.

Shackles snapped apart, releasing the pent-up fury of the screaming fighter. Simultaneously, the JATO pack mounted along the undercarriage kicked off.

The Skyhawk leaped off its rail on a spike of white-hot fire, climbing into the night at a precise 30-degree angle.

The backblast of flame and noise and turbulent dust forced everyone on the ground to look away.

In what seemed like an instant, the scream of the A-4 and its fiery exhaust cone were far away and fading fast.

Starla Spacek was the first to emerge from behind sheltering rock. Others followed.

"This, I guess, is what it means to be a S.H.I.E.L.D. agent," Ellis muttered.

"No," said Starla slowly, "I think that's what it means to be Nick Fury."

They watched the afterburner dwindle to nothingness

as the airmen hosed down the deuce-and-a-half with portable fire extinguishers.

Nick Fury brought the borrowed Skyhawk down on Runway 2-R of Denver International Airport. Once he identified himself, they cleared him for immediate landing. Only Air Force One got that kind of cooperation.

A courtesy vehicle rolled up as he climbed down out of the A-4 cockpit.

"Somebody kindly return this kite to Uncle Sam's Air Force," Fury said as he brushed off the ramp agents. "Just get me to my gate."

At the gate, they asked Fury if he had any baggage.

"I'm wearing it," he said, slapping his combat rig.

They confiscated his utility belt contents, side and shoulder holsters, along with associated weapons. They were apologetic about it, but firm.

"FAA rules, sir."

"No problem," said Fury, letting them take everything but his side-mounted S.H.I.E.L.D.-issue plasma blaster. He gave the stainless steel barrel a twist clockwise, then counterclockwise. It clicked. He tossed it into the plastic container where his equipment lay in an unhappy heap.

With a *fwoosh*, the blaster turned to slag, taking everything else with it.

Security recoiled from the stink of burnt plastic and metal.

"S.H.I.E.L.D. rules," Fury growled. "Unauthorized personnel shall not have access to classified technology."

This was accepted with pained expressions.

A security agent gestured for Fury to step through the metal detector.

"You've got to be kidding. I got so much shrapnel in me, I'm liable to bust the magnometer."

The security team hesitated. A gate agent wearing an Empire Airlines blazer intervened, saying, "It's okay. It's okay. VIP passenger. This way, Colonel Fury. Your flight leaves in five minutes."

Fury strode on. "That's cutting it close."

"We held the plane for you."

"Much obliged," Fury muttered. "Sure would have been embarrassing if after all this, I missed my flight."

They hustled him down the jetway ramp. Fury was still garbed in his S.H.I.E.L.D. combat suit, still dingy with Colorado dust. The flight crew and first-class passengers gaped when he ducked into the cabin. Fury paid them no heed. He found his seat, sank into it, and buckled up as the airliner's engines began spooling up for takeoff.

Fury found the safety card in his seat pocket. It told him he was a passenger on a three-engine Lockheed L-1011 Tristar. It was an old bird, but extremely reliable. An accomplished pilot, Fury liked to know what he was flying, even when he wasn't the one at the controls.

The Empire Airlines jet left the gate, rolled into takeoff position, and vaulted into the air so smoothly the director of S.H.I.E.L.D. barely noticed.

It had been a long day. It promised to be a longer night.

Fury hit the call button and a stewardess appeared.

"I'm gonna catch me some shut-eye. I don't wanna be disturbed for the rest of the flight."

"Yes, sir. Anything else, sir?"

"Yeah. What in Sam Hill is our destination?"

"Sam Hill?"

"It's an old expression, not a place."

"Our destination," said the stewardess, snapping off Fury's seat light, "is Honolulu."

"Not bad. I'll bet it's nice this time of year."

"It's nice *any* time of year."

Fury set his seat back into the farthest position, gave his unlit cigar a chewing, and remembered the mission briefing papers.

Thrusting a huge hand into the seat pocket, he found

a dossier marked: S.H.I.E.L.D. The letters formed a semicircle around an embossed emblem—a heraldry shield surmounted by a gold spread-winged eagle, with a crossed pistol and dagger against vertical bars of red, white and blue.

Fury grunted. This was new. He hadn't seen a mission briefing folder like this since the days when S.H.I.E.L.D. had been inaugurated under its original name, the Supreme Headquarters International Espionage and Law Enforcement Division. A long time ago now. Back in the post—Cold War world. A world of trenchcoats, code-names and microdots. A world that no longer existed.

Fury opened the folder. There was only one page. Crisp laser-printed words stood out on white bond:

PRIORITY ACTUAL ONE

PROCEED TO HONOLULU

MAINTAIN RADIO SILENCE

YOU WILL BE MET AT GATE

"That's all?" Fury muttered. "Damn strange." Crumpling up the sheet, he slipped it into his belt cigar igniter, and closed it. He heard the muffled ignition and shut his eyes, confident the chemically-treated paper had turned to ash. Not that there was much of a security risk if the sheet fell into unfriendly hands, but procedure was procedure.

Even if the procedure was a decade out of date. Why the hell didn't HQ contact him by secure satellite line? Fury wondered.

He returned the empty folder to the seat pocket. There was no security issue in leaving it there. Practically everyone in the world knew who Nick Fury was.

The director of S.H.I.E.L.D. slept fitfully. Between the drone of the jet's three turbine engines and the stewardesses bustling about the passenger cabin, he gave it up.

It was well past midnight by Fury's wrist chronometer. That should put them over LA or San Francisco, depending on the air route to Honolulu, before dawn. Fury raised the window shade. Below, the golden lights of the Los Angeles suburbs were spread out in all directions. They looked like smouldering coals wrapped in thin smoke. It must have been a pretty bad smog alert for the stuff to hang in the air this late at night, Fury mused.

Catching the stewardess's eye, Fury asked, "We stopping over at LAX?"

"No. It's a through flight, sir."

Fury nodded. He reached into the seat pocket for something to read, pulled out the in-flight magazine.

"Empire's Sunset," he grunted. "Sounds like the title of a bad James Bond flick."

Upon opening the magazine, the S.H.I.E.L.D. dossier folder slipped out. Fury caught it. His good eye noticed the S.H.I.E.L.D. insignia on the reverse.

A faint chill touched Fury's mind.

"What the hell . . ."

Before his thoughts could organize themselves, the big aircraft's engines suddenly changed pitch. They had been humming along on a smooth lower key, now they grew into an ascending whine.

"Thought you said we weren't landing," Fury said to the stewardess.

The stewardess quietly took her jump seat and buckled in. Her face was strangely blank.

"I said," Fury repeated, "I thought we weren't landing at LAX."

"Emergency landing," the stewardess said, dull of voice.

"Emergency? The seat-belt light ain't come on."

At that moment, the Tristar started into a violent wingover. The airframe shook. Overhead baggage compartments flew open. In the back, passengers screamed.

Fury hit the seat-belt release and leaped out of his seat.

The jet rolled back, suddenly, unexpectedly.

"Who the hell's flying this crate? Evel Knievel?"

Using the seatbacks for leverage, Fury muscled his way toward the control cabin. The door was shut. Fury forced it open.

"What's the problem?" he bellowed.

The pilot and copilot were at the controls. The pilot was steadily pushing the yoke forward, throwing the nose of the craft into a steep descent. Fury had to grab on to stay upright.

"What the hell?"

When he looked again, Fury could see the lights of Los Angeles through the cockpit windows. They filled the glare shield. And the city lights were rushing up to meet the descending jetliner like an oncoming train.

"What the hell's the matter with him?" Fury raged. The copilot turned around and gave a weak, helpless shrug. He looked young. Almost too young to be copiloting a passenger airliner. Only his dark mustache lent him a touch of maturity.

Fury lunged forward, and took hold of the captain's blue-uniformed shoulder.

"Answer me!"

The pilot, his hand clutching the yoke with white-knuckled firmness, rotated his head in response. He had the same brush mustache and touch of olive in his complexion as the copilot. They might have been related.

Except the man's eyes were like glass—emotionless, unfeeling and very, very cold.

Without a word, he turned his attention back to the grim, silent business of committing suicide.

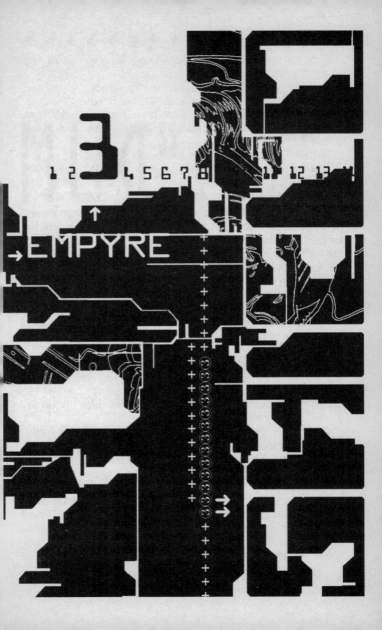

"DUM

TIMOTHY ALOYSIUS

Dum" Dugan believed rising with the sun and large doses of strenuous exercise were the main reasons for his longevity. He didn't like to think how old he was getting. He had stopped celebrating his birthdays around the time he had joined S.H.I.E.L.D. at the behest of his old comrade-in-arms, Nick Fury. They had fought in a few wars along the way. And between wars, life seemed empty and directionless. Joining S.H.I.E.L.D. made sense for a man who had been a professional soldier for so long civilian life was as alien to his nature as living in a fish tank.

Dum Dum rolled out of bed, swapped boxer shorts and drew on a S.H.I.E.L.D.-issue nylon jogging suit that had to be custom sewn to encase his gigantic frame. He slipped his gigantic feet into white canvas deck shoes resembling matched tugboats.

Giving his fierce shot-with-silver red handlebar mustaches a smoothing, the big Irishman set a battered and bullet-riddled bowler hat on his head at a rakish angle and exited his cabin, ducking every time he passed through a bulkhead door.

He whistled as he walked. Every day he woke up alive was a great day in Dum Dum Dugan's estimation. He had been a lot of things in his life: Dock walloper. Circus strongman. U.S. commando. But of all the strange careers he had undertaken, being second in command of the Strategic Hazard, Intervention, Espionage and Logistics Directorate beat everything.

Coming to a stainless steel door marked Barracks, Dugan burst in and lifted a voice that made the light fixtures in the room vibrate in complaint.

"Rise and shine! It's time for our little mornin' constitutional!"

There were thirty bunks in the long spartan room. At the sound of Dugan's voice, every blanket snapped away, virtually in synchronization. Feet smacked the steel floor. Clothes were hastily donned. Deck shoes discovered and laced up.

In twelve seconds, elapsed time, thirty new S.H.I.E.L.D. agents were standing at attention in a nervous row.

"Follow me!" Dum Dum barked.

He led them down a dimly lit steel-walled corridor to a circular dais emblazoned with the eagle emblem of S.H.I.E.L.D., taking a position in the center. The others made a perfect circle, facing inward, surrounding him. At their feet sat white-and-gold flight helmets.

"Helmets on," Dugan ordered.

They took them up, snugging them to their heads. Dum Dum reached up into his bowler—the incongruous hat was a good luck piece he had worn through more battles than he could remember—and pulled down a filament mike and headset rig.

"Radio check," he barked. And everyone in the circle winced in pain.

"Flight Deck," Dugan called out.

Amber safety lights lit up around the rim. The dais began lifting. It was a gigantic open elevator. As the transverse bands of black and zinc-yellow paint on the shaft walls fell beneath him, Dugan placed his fists on his hips and began lecturing.

"This is the way we start our day here at S.H.I.E.L.D. headquarters. Some of you have already been on a walkdown. Most of you ain't. For the benefit of those who ain't, a walkdown is nothin' more or less than a synchronized stroll combined with a little old-fashioned policin' action."

Some of the recruits exchanged uncertain glances.

"By policin'," Dum Dum continued, "I don't mean arrestin' litterbugs. I mean cleanin' up after them."

The uncertain glances grew even more puzzled.

Gigantic deck numbers rolled past their heads, until at last DECK 1 came into view, only to disappear below. On cue, the top of the shaft over their heads parted, exposing a gunmetal gray sky and indirect, but blinding, sunlight.

"Before we hit topside," Dum Dum said, "if anyone among you has a fear of heights, raise your hand now."

Two hands went up.

Dum Dum showed massive white teeth in a ferocious grin. His mustaches bristled like mischievous cat's whiskers. He jabbed a thick finger at the unlucky pair.

"You and you," he said, "get to walk the opposite ends of the line."

The two agents turned various shades of pale. One actually had a greenish tinge to his cheeks.

"All set now, boys and girls, we're comin' up on the flight deck."

Their heads emerged into thin early morning daylight. The dais elevator came flush level with the asphalt-black flight deck of what looked like the mother of all aircraft carriers.

As long as seven football fields, capable of launching and recovering planes as large as a B-52 Stratofortress, it was bare of conventional aircraft other than a single S.H.I.E.L.D. Orca class helicopter disappearing from sight down a deck-edge lift. Off to starboard, the windows of the tower island superstructure flashed under the rays of the rising sun. The immaculate white lines of the angled flight deck approach gleamed.

It might have been just an aircraft carrier. Except that the spires of Manhattan Island, smouldering a solar orange-red, showed about 20 miles due west and an estimated 3,000 feet beneath the flight deck's level. And set on either side of the port and starboard edges whirled six gigantic outboard rotors in massive strut-mounted housings. They spun in unison, creating countervailing vortices that played perpetually along the deck, yet somehow canceled one another out. Not exactly soundless, their eerie whispering verged on the subliminal.

"When S.H.I.E.L.D. was created as the strong right arm of the Free World, way back when before some of you were born," Dum Dum began, "the bigwigs knew that the organization needed a permanent headquarters as formidable as the agency. They considered a fortified island, a hardened hollowed-out mountain, and other ideas even wilder.

"You see, S.H.I.E.L.D. was created to deal with the international monster called Hydra. A monster we're still trying to stamp out. Hydra was everywhere, then just as now. If S.H.I.E.L.D. operated from a fixed location, that made us crushable. So a genius industrialist named Anthony Stark conceived a flyin' weapons platform in the form of an unsinkable aircraft carrier. He dubbed it the Helicarrier."

The sun, lifting higher in the sky, began peering over the flight deck, creating thin, lengthening shadows.

"Take a good long look," Dum Dum announced. "Because in a minute we are gonna walk from the bow here all the way to the stern. We go single file. Me in the middle. We walk with our eyes glued to the flight deck. We're lookin' for loose debris, empty shell casings, gum wrappers, anything that might snag a tire, get sucked into an intake, and otherwise interfere with flight operations. Or go tumblin' overboard to land on some poor civilian's head. All such complaints go directly to me." His voice crashed. "If any such complaint lands on my head, I will in turn land on yours. Is that perfectly understood, boys and girls?"

"Yes, sir!" they chorused.

"Say it like you mean it."

"YES, SIR!!!"

"Okay. Form up on both sides of me. The afraid-of-height types take the opposite ends of the line. Under no circumstances is anyone to fall overboard without my permission," he added dryly. "It's a long drop."

A voice quavered over his radio link. "Shouldn't we have parachutes?"

"You want parachutes?" Dum Dum grumbled. "You *earn* them."

The recruits fell in line and Dum Dum adjusted his headset and microphone.

"XO, do you copy?"

"Copy, deck," a mature female voice replied.

"We are commencing morning walkdown, Val."

"Proceed, deck."

"Hup, twop, threep, four," Dum Dum barked, setting the pace with swinging arms in an exaggerated gait.

They walked in a long wavering line, eyes fixed on the acres of black non-skid steel deck stretching before them.

"If you see anything out of place, do not think, do not hesitate," Dum Dum admonished. "Reach right down and grab it up. But keep movin'. I do not want this line broken. The record for a walkdown is thirty minutes. I've been tryin' to get it down to twenty-nine for the last three years. Let's see if you newbies can oblige me."

As they walked, Dum Dum offered additional background on the incredible vessel that served as S.H.I.E.L.D. mobile headquarters, multirole aircraft carrier and offense-defensive weapons platform.

"The Helicarrier was modeled on the Forrestal Class U.S. Navy supercarriers, with their straight and angled sections for round-the-clock air operations. It is powered by twin nuclear fusion generators. The six rotors turn perpetually. They have never been known to fail in flight. Naturally, they are shut down in rotation for periodic maintenance. The ship is designed so that it can maintain altitude, constant pitch and yaw, with only four rotors operational. Notice that even with all six rotors turning, all the breeze you feel is your hair gettin' a little mussed? That's because the genius who designed her, planned it that way. The rotor wash is what they call counterturbulent. In other words, they cancel each other out. They're as quiet as they are on the same principle that big-bladed helicopters like the Russian Hind or the French Puma produce a soft rotor sound, while small-bladed jobs tend to be noisy and clattery. By that measure, these gigantic babies just sort of whisper."

Dum Dum waxed expansive. No matter how many times he gave this orientation lecture, he never tired of it. He was an old soldier who never got past first sergeant in the regular Army. But long after his military career should have been over, he was second in command to the finest fighting force in the world.

"Any questions so far?"

A voice piped up. "Yeah. We hear a lot of rumors about Colonel Fury. Exactly how old is he?"

"That's classified. Next question."

"Yes. How old are you?"

"Old enough that my mustache has come in and out of style a couple of times that I can count."

Laughter rippled up and down the radio line.

Just then, an urgent voice crackled over their headsets.

"Deck, we have an airborne emergency."

"What kind of emergency?" Dum Dum barked.

"Commercial jet in distress. They're requesting emergency landing clearance."

"Are they out of their cotton-pickin' minds? This is a high-security installation. We don't grant civilian landing permission. Tell them to use Kennedy. It's just around the corner."

"Dum Dum, it's a fully-loaded Boeing 737. 130 passengers. They have smoke in the cabin and they report their

oxygen supply is not feeding properly. The captain is saying he doesn't put down soon, he might not be able to."

Dum Dum grabbed his bowler hat and mauled it in his big beefy hands worriedly.

"You know standin' orders, Val. Fury will have us skinned alive. And that's just for starters."

"If civilian casualties result, it could be much worse."

Dum Dum muttered, "Skinned alive if we do, boiled in oil if we don't. Okay, okay, clear the ship. My authority."

"I intend to take responsibility, too."

"Just do it." Dum Dum lifted his voice. "All right, you recruits. Break off, and follow me. Emergency landing in progress. You are all going to get a real eyeful. A controlled crash landin' performed by a passenger jet, no less."

As smooth and synchronized as a school of fish, the recruits reformed into three lines. Dum Dum led them at a trot to the nearest deck-edge lift. An orange-vested Safety Officer started the lift descending toward the belowdecks hangar as the 737 came thundering into view.

"That's far enough," Dum Dum growled. "I want to see this landing."

The lift stopped. Some of the recruits, crowded at the edge, looked down and quailed at the enormous drop into space.

"Don't sweat it," Dum Dum reassured them. "There are nets that will catch you if you happen to go tumblin' overboard. I neglected to mention that little fact earlier."

All eyes turned to the 737.

It was coming around from the southwest. The Helicarrier was reorienting itself to give the stricken aircraft a favorable angle of approach.

"They say that a carrier landin' is the trickiest landing any pilot can make," Dum Dum was saying. "That's because you're tryin' to land a screaming jet on the minimum amount of runway, with a rollin' and pitchin' deck to boot. It ain't like that here. Gyro stabilizers maintain absolutely perfect pitch and yaw. A Helicarrier landing is like settin' down on a regular airstrip. All you gotta do is stay clear of the rotors and hit the sweet spot between the first and second arrestor cables."

The Helicarrier completed its reorientation turn into the wind. The jet was coming in, wheels down. Its port wing engine was on fire and trailing smoke.

Dum Dum listened to the radio traffic between the captain and the tower.

"334 Heavy. I have your beacon. On approach."

"Drop your left wing, 334 Heavy," the tower was saying.

"Roger, S.H.I.E.L.D." The pilot sounded calm, as if he was certain of the outcome.

The jet leveled out. Along the deck, massive arrestor cables sprang into place. Breakaway cables, designed to slow the jet's landing speed. Commercial jet aircraft are not equipped with regulation Navy tailhooks, but provisions had been made for any type of emergency landing. At the broad stern, a gigantic Teflon-nylon net erected itself on folding pylons, poised to capture the aircraft should it overshoot the flight deck.

The jet touched down, rear wheels first. Rubber smoke spurted.

"Looks good from here," Dum Dum told the tower.

"Let's hope," Val said.

The nose gear assembly dropped slowly, almost touched.

It happened so fast, no one saw it coming. Just as the jet was about to execute a respectable three-point landing, the port wing engine came apart. One wing lifted without warning. The aircraft lifted, pitched, and began to slew wildly.

"Gangway!" Dum Dum bellowed. "Something's gone wrong!"

The nose wheel hit, skidded and broke off. It went screaming across the deck in one direction. Throwing up showers of sparks and peeling flaps of duralumin, the jet's nose careened in the other direction.

Directly toward the lift where Dum Dum stood watching with his recruits.

Dum Dum reacted instantly. Turning, he lifted his burly arms—arms that could almost bend railroad ties. Launching a mighty shove, he pushed the nearest agents away. They went down. The others fell like so many human dominos. Some at the outer edges tumbled overboard. Their screams were twisted and terrible. But it was either go into the nets or face the horror that was about to descend upon them.

As luck would have it, the Boeing plowed past their position, its underwing engine nacelles scraping and scouring the deck. Along the way, sparks ignited patches of grease and engine oil.

A dragging wing came off all at once, sending the jet plowing into an outboard rotor housing. It exploded in a furious paroxysm of Jet-A fuel.

In an instant, the port side of the flight deck erupted into an inferno in which human screams lifted over the spreading roar of uncontrolled fire, only to die away as if quenched by mounting flames.

The Helicarrier gave a great leviathan shudder, and started to lurch off its orbital axis. The shuddering continued, escalating. It seemed to go on and on in rolling, seismic waves portending a cataclysm yet to come.

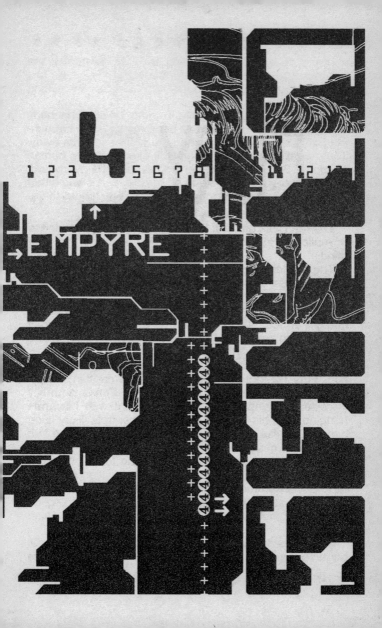

FURY

NICK READ THE LOOK IN the Empire captain's eyes in a split second.

The man was out of it. Whether due to drugs, madness or malicious intent, didn't matter. He wasn't in his right mind.

The copilot sat glued to the uprushing earth, his hands clutching his own control yoke. Paralyzed with fright, Fury figured.

Cocking a big battle-scarred fist, Fury uncorked a straight-armed punch that drove the pilot's head half around. The crunch of jawbone told Fury he wouldn't be coming out of it anytime soon.

Unbuckling the man's safety harness in a blur of action, Fury yanked him bodily out of the captain's chair. Desperation lent superhuman steel to Fury's normally Herculean strength. The pilot came out with his arms hanging limp, his feet dragging at the controls. Fury flung him around like an oversized rag doll, then dropped into the vacated chair.

Seizing the control yoke, Fury began to feel the controls. He was rated to fly most planes, civilian and military. But a commercial airliner was another matter. His right eye raked the controls, taking in airspeed, glide path, yaw, pitch, roll, and a host of other critical flying data.

Pulling back on the yoke, the director of S.H.I.E.L.D. began to haul the mighty Tristar out of its dive. The triple turbines, one mounted in each wing and the third inset in the tail, began to complain like murderous banshees.

Over the radio, a voice from LAX tower was calling.

"Empire 666, say your situation. Flight 666, what is your intent?"

Fury ignored the insistent voice. He had more important things to do. Ignoring the warning klaxon, he slammed the throttles to the firewall, bringing all three engines up to full RPM. If they stalled out, there would be no landing the plane intact.

There was one overriding reality about commercial passenger aircraft: they flew on the sheer power of their engine thrust. This was flying in the strictest, most unconventional sense of flying. Any prop plane could glide to an unpowered emergency landing. But there was no margin for error in the event of multiple engine cut-off in a jet. It was brute force or auger in.

And when it came to brute force, Nick Fury was a past master.

The altitude dial read 15,000 feet and falling rapidly. Airspeed was a violent 190 knots. But you couldn't tell that from the way the ground below was crawling by.

Fury pulled the yoke toward his chest. Sweat appeared on his brows, began running down his black eye patch and onto his grimy, stubbled cheeks.

Twelve thousand feet. Eleven. Ten. And all the time the copilot just sat there frozen, paralyzed by the imminent prospect of catastrophic impact onto the hard, unforgiving ground.

Slowly, inexorably, Fury brought the shuddering aircraft out of its dive. Gingerly, showing more craft than his rough exterior hinted, he found a level cruising altitude.

The altitude gauge now read 9,000 feet. Frighteningly low for non-approach flying. Fury throttled back, and tried to claw the plane up. No telling where the mountains were. Not to mention other planes. This was southern California. What commercial pilots called Indian

Country. By day, the airlanes were filled with pleasure ships—Piper Aztecs, Apaches, Cherokees, Seminoles and other aerial nuisances.

With any luck, the pleasure pilots were safely tucked in bed. If not, they would just have to stay out of his way. Fury stayed focused on regaining safe altitude. Thankfully, the big bird was cooperating.

At 15,000 feet, Fury felt he had the Tristar under control.

By this time, the LAX tower was frantic. The flight controller on duty had been talking all along, but Fury had tuned the voice out. Now the voice intruded back on his consciousness.

"Empire 666. Say intentions. Do you copy? If landing clearance is needed, say clearly, 666. Do you read?"

Heaving a sigh of relief, Fury looked over to the copilot. "Think you can take her in, pal?"

The copilot seemed to snap out of it. He blinked rapidly, several times. His white-knuckled fingers let go of the yoke with audibly sticky sounds. Then he took hold again.

His voice was thick when he spoke: "Yeah. Sure."

"You don't sound all that confident."

"I'm okay. Really."

"All right," Fury said guardedly. "You take her."

Fury released his yoke. The copilot squeezed his. He was as pale as some of the indicator lights—giving his dusky skin a weird bloodless pallor.

"Got it?" Fury asked.

"Got it," the copilot said.

"Take her out over the Pacific and back around. We gotta land this bird—fast. No telling what's shaken loose back there."

The copilot tapped his throat mike and said, "This is Empire Flight 666 Heavy. Request emergency landing LAX."

"Roger, 666. We were sure worried about you for a

minute. Take her around and come in on runway six Left."

"Roger."

The tide of smouldering lights that marked the California coastline dropped under their wings. The Pacific showed as a sparkling black blanket. Fury started to breathe normally again. If anything happened now, they were over water. No risk of causing ground casualties if the big bird gave up the battle now. . . .

Without warning, the copilot threw his yoke forward. Fury's went forward in perfect sync. Fury grabbed his yoke. The copilot fought him.

The jet lurched, dropped, and began surging for the moonlit Pacific.

Fury barked, "What are you doing? Pull up. *Pull up!*"

Grimly, his teeth bared in a wolfish grimace, the copilot pushed the yoke as far as it would go. The dive steepened. The airframe groaned and rattled under the stress.

"What the hell?" Fury unsnapped his harness, grabbed the copilot by the collar and inserted a silvery tube pulled from his boot into the man's neck. It was a TrikStik—a compact adaptation of a Taser. The twin electrodes were sharp. They bit into the man's flesh. Fury pressed the trigger button. The device buzzed and snapped. The copilot's head jolted wildly under an electrical assault that short-circuited the neural pathways of his brain.

The man collapsed into an inert heap where he sat. Fury left him there like a marionette with cut strings.

Back in the control chair, Fury hauled in the yoke. He had to pull carefully. There was a lot of play. And pulling too hard or too fast could exceed the Tristar's flight tolerances, shearing the wings clean off.

The aircraft began buffeting. Bad. Back in the passenger cabin, Fury could hear the racket. Everything that wasn't locked down and stowed away was becoming unglued. Passengers screamed. The world became a turning mass of confusion in which the L-1011 seemed to fight for its survival in screaming lurches.

"Back," Fury said through tight teeth. "Come on. Back."

The yoke wasn't designed to pull a jet out of a power dive. But it responded. Fury had no time to monitor flight information. He caught a glimpse of the altitude indicator. It read four thousand feet. He didn't dare look again. He didn't have the nanosecond to spare. His job now was to fly the unflyable and save the unsalvageable.

Under his breath, he uttered a prayer. If asked about it later, Nick Fury would have denied voicing it. It was an automatic response. Something from deep inside of him. He would never remember it.

At three thousand feet, the jet was once again level and skimming the ocean deck like a great seagull looking for land. But there was no land. The plane continued to shake. The turbines whined and hammered.

"Tower, this is Empire 666," Fury barked.

"Go ahead, 666."

"Got little problem here . . ."

"Say problem, 666."

"The pilot and copilot are out of it, and I'm flying the plane."

"Identify yourself, please."

"Nick Fury. Director, S.H.I.E.L.D. Listen, I can fly most anything with wings, but I ain't rated for passenger jets. I'm on a dead heading for Hawaii, and this bus doesn't seem like she'll make it."

"Can you come around for LAX?"

"Negative. I'm barely holding my altitude. I don't think I have time for anything fancy."

"Do not recommend you ditch in ocean," said LAX control.

"It wasn't exactly high up on my priority list either," Fury growled back. "Give me a better option."

"Divert to John Wayne Airport."

"Be glad to. Just point me there."

"Turning south-southeast, take up a heading of two-two-zero."

Fury fed the aircraft power and began executing a shallow turn. The Tristar started shuddering. He checked his indicators. Engines one, two and three were all operating. He hadn't lost any power. But she was handling like a ruptured duck.

"Tower, I think I have a problem with my stabilizers."

In another second, Fury knew it for a certainty. The plane began climbing. Hard. Completely on its own. The yoke was moving on its own. It resisted his attempts to wrestle it back.

Fury let it happen. He needed the altitude. Then abruptly, the Tristar started to level off, raggedly, fitfully, but manageably.

"So far, so good," Fury muttered. A glance at the flight deck displays updated him on the aircraft's status. All good.

Then the aircraft began sinking. Not hard. Not fast. But sinking in a slow uneasy slope like the big airliner was dying.

Fury touched his throat mike. "Tower, I'm losing altitude now. Stabilizer problem. I could use some fast advice."

"Hold her up," the tower replied urgently. *"Keep the aircraft in the air at all costs."*

"Thanks," Fury returned dryly. "I already figured out that part."

The coastline came sweeping in. A twinkling ribbon that could only be the Pacific Coast Highway hove into view. Even in pitch darkness, the waterfront area of Long Beach was recognizable. There was the *Queen Mary* at her berth, ablaze with light.

Too soon, it fell behind Fury's wings. He reached for his throat mike.

"Tower, where the hell am I?"

"Our scopes show you passing over the 405."

Fury looked down. A ragged line of moving lights, like lightbulbs in the thinning smog, told him where the 405 Freeway lay.

"Just follow it, 666. It goes straight to John Wayne."

Fury laid the nose along the highway and kept her there. He glanced at his altitude gauge.

"Sure hope I don't have to set her down on that," he muttered.

"Repeat, 666."

"Never mind. Talking to myself." Fury focused on the control he had available. A good pilot knew how to get the "feel" of any aircraft. It was an instinct, finding the envelope of comfort. Individual flying characteristics varied even among aircraft of the same make and model. It took time to learn the ropes. Trial and error was the only way. And Fury was having to lock in on the big bird's temperament under the worst possible circumstances. But by goosing the throttles and giving the yoke play, he began to feel his way toward understanding the Lockheed's unique handling quirks.

Then, the rules changed again.

She began to climb. The right wing lifted. The left dropped. It was the beginning of a vertical tailspin. Once centrifugal forces took hold, there would be no righting the lumbering jet. And it could only scream up into space like an ungainly rocket before it plunged earthward with the unerring instinct for hard ground. . . .

Fury tried everything he could think of. Trim tabs didn't help. The rudder only accelerated the spin. Altitude continued climbing like an August thermometer.

And all the time, the airframe body shook and shimmied as if straining to pop every last rivethead along its duralumin hull.

There are times when nothing works. When nothing can work. Fury had been in these situations before. By the manual, there was no way to fly the plane. No procedure that could fix or avert what was about to happen: a roller-coaster ride in the sky with just one gut-churning loop. Forty degrees up and back down at terminal velocity.

And Nick Fury, riding the top of the rocket, would be the first one to kiss mother earth.

Even with death staring him in the face, the S.H.I.E.L.D. director's crisis-honed mind wound into tighter and tighter focus.

"Gotta get control. Gotta get control. But how?"

The tail section began to yaw. Fury felt it—a sickening sideslip motion. That was the tail-root engine fighting the other two. If it got bad enough, the mountings might pop. Not that the loss of an engine would matter. Dead was dead. When they scraped up the pieces of the aircraft, it wouldn't matter to anyone but the National Transportation Safety Team if one engine struck hard ground miles away from the crash site.

Over the radio system, LAX tower was chattering.

"Empire 666. You are going to overshoot John Wayne."

In the split second interruption, something clicked in Nick Fury's brain. Some connection. An intuition, perhaps.

Angrily, he began snapping switches. He set the tail engine to a lower power setting. He brought the two outboard turbines up higher. Then with one hard, muscular arm, he pushed all three throttles forward.

It might have been a hunch. Or an inspiration. Maybe some half-forgotten memory coming to the surface. It might be worthless. It might be brilliant. But it was all Nick Fury had.

The differential thrust between the tail engines and the others straightened the L-1011 out. She started yawing. Fury dropped the nose, hoping for another miracle.

The airliner found an altitude she liked and stayed there. The stabilizers were out of the picture now. But so was John Wayne. Its blue and yellow runway lights flashed underneath the wings, off to port, and out of reach forever.

Fury's mind continued to work. Where to set down now?

"El Toro," he bit out.

"Say again, 666?" asked LAX tower.

"Marine Corps Air Station El Toro," Fury said firmly. "That's where I'm headed."

"El Toro was shut down three months ago."

"Just as well," Fury growled. "This could be a real messy landing."

"666, you'll have to come in on Visual Flight Rules. There's probably a skeleton staff still out there. We'll try to get them to turn on the runway lights for you."

"You do that little thing," Fury said, thinking that if he had to land without instruments, he'd take runway lights over nothing any day.

Fury had flown in and out of El Toro many times. He knew the area, knew the runways. It was a hell of a big difference between landing an F-14 Tomcat there and an overgrown flying bus, but knowing the field was the only edge he had left.

"It might just be enough," he told himself. "Now if I can just find the Santa Ana Freeway."

It was easier than he dared hope. A check of his cockpit maps told him the 405 merged with the Santa Ana immediately south of El Toro. Once he had a visual fix, Fury vectored toward it, noting with satisfaction that the big jet was reasonably responsive under the circumstances. Vehicles streaming south pointed the way. Searching his memory, he tried to recall the runway's exact configuration. It was a cruciform arrangement. Four runways laid out in a north-south and east-west intersecting cross. They were generous runways, too. Any one of them would do the job.

But first Fury had to keep his good eye peeled for obstruction lights marking radio towers and high buildings.

The area around El Toro had been cleared when the air station was first commissioned. But there were foothills here and there. The rest was pretty flat, and dotted with scrub chaparral and stunted trees, Fury recalled. He had to avoid those, too.

"Come on," he urged. "Come on. Where are you?"

Abruptly, a cluster of amber flashers sprang into life. That would be the runway approach lights. Then a double row of steady amber, marking one east-west runway.

Fury absorbed the layout, tried to match it against his memory, what he could see of the dark area ahead, and began setting the controls for landing.

"Flaps down," he said, tension rising in his voice. He found the landing lights switch, threw it. Two blazing funnels of incandescent light sprang into life, pointing the way.

Fury's mind flashed to the passengers in back. No one had stirred. Just as well. They were probably petrified, and still strapped into their seats.

Fury found the intercabin PA system, and announced, "This is your captain speaking. Prepare for emergency landing. I ain't gonna soft soap anybody. This is going to be rough. Anybody knowing any good prayers, trot 'em out."

The runway came up like an express train. With little opportunity to lose airspeed, Fury was coming in way too fast.

"LAX tower, this is Empire 666. On final approach. Let's all pray that it's not too final."

"Amen that," seconded the tower. *"Recommend you come in at 40 flap."*

"Way ahead of you, Tower."

Fury dropped the gear. The hydraulic whine was a welcome sound. Three telltale lights went from amber to a safe, reassuring Christmas green, indicating the gear had deployed and were locked in place. But his airspeed was still a hurtling 130 knots.

Critical cockpit indicators showed all systems were still within flight tolerances. Otherwise, he was flying blind. It was now or never.

Pushing on the yoke, Fury dropped the nose. He cut power, in effect slamming the wheels on the pavement in an aircraft-carrier style controlled crash-landing.

The aircraft bolted, flared, and the wheels hit—hard. The jet bounced, settled, hit again. On the wings, spoiler panels deployed, adding to the flaps' braking effect. The Tristar hugged the centerline.

Fury threw the engines into full reverse, drove both legs into the brake pedals. The whining bark of burning tires mixed with the screaming of the brakes taking hold.

Skipping and skidding, the big steel-belted 28-gauge tires clawed runway like a skimming eagle. Biting hard on his cigar, Fury leaned into the brakes. Everything else was superfluous now.

The brakes would save them, or they wouldn't.

The scream of stressed tires held its note for an unmeasurable eternity before finally diminishing to an ongoing rumble. But the big bird kept skipping along. It slewed. It shimmied. Cabin luggage bins shook and rattled the length of the cabin. A few let go. Fury could hear luggage tumbling and thudding.

Without warning, the Tristar bucked around and lurched out of the landing path, bumping off the apron, breaking safety lights as it careened out of control toward a wide swatch of chaparral.

And smack dab in the middle of the chaparral was a lonely eucalyptus tree.

The nose of the Tristar aimed for the tree like a semi-guided missile.

Fury's white teeth bit down in a pungent Anglo-Saxon curse. They cut his cigar in two.

Then the tree was filling the windshield, and it was all in the hands of the Almighty.

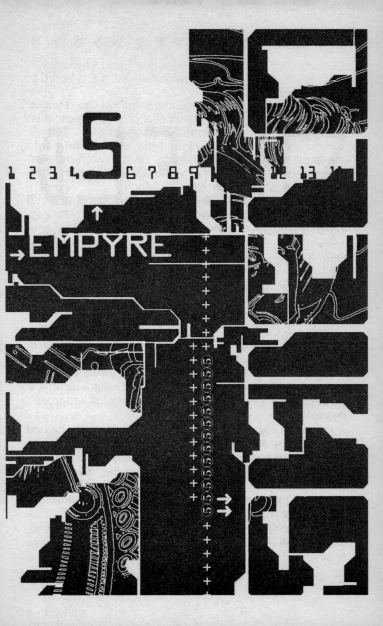

S.H.I.E.L.D.

Special Powers Agent Starla Spacek was looking forward to being stationed on the Helicarrier. It was considered a plum posting. But her excitement was colored by concern. It showed on her face, in the way she narrowed her gray-green eyes. Her lean features—sans camouflage paint—were an unusual tawny hue very near her hair color. It was a face that evoked impressions of a female tiger. Today, a worried tiger.

Ever since Director Fury had blasted off into the Colorado night, on to a rendezvous with who-knew-what, Starla had felt an oppressive feeling of dread. There was nothing she could do about it. Special Powers protocols were clear: Psychic agents were not to volunteer PSINTEL—psychic intelligence—except through approved channels.

In the old days of the ESP Division, even highly-trained psychics sometimes cried wolf without meaning to. The program had been shut down several times, each time reconstituted in another guise. For a while they were calling it the Anomalous Cognition Sub-Directorate. No matter what they called it, the problems remained the same.

The chief trouble was that nobody understood how so-called Extra Sensory Perception actually worked. And nobody could figure it out. Every tasking was strictly operational. Research went by the boards, and because there was no research, no one was mapping the psychic terrain.

Without maps, psychic agents got lost in what they came to call the Zone—that altered-state netherworld where dreams seemed real and reality took on the semblance of dreams. Even the most grounded of them inevitably became drifty, spacey, unfocused. The less grounded started bouncing off the walls.

By the late 1990s, S.H.I.E.L.D. had just about given up on psychic intelligence. The Army and the CIA remote viewing programs were also crashing.

As an operational reality, the entire concept was on the verge of extinction.

Then the first Hydra Remote Vipers were detected by remaining reclassified S.H.I.E.L.D. Anomalous Cognition Agents. No one saw them. No one heard them. But psi operatives still on the S.H.I.E.L.D. payroll sensed unexplained presences, and there were strange, impossible intelligence leaks.

That was where Starla Spacek came in. A civilian psychic consultant to the CIA Stargate program in its final crazy days, she was orphaned when Stargate was defunded. Quietly, she returned to private consultations. That had been the end of it.

Except for the book. Once CIA remote viewers were furloughed from the program, they began to open up—some because they felt free to talk about their experiences, others bitter that a critically important, intelligence-collecting methodology had been shut down because of narrow-minded politics and a growing number of unfortunate psychic casualties.

It was absurd, Starla thought. CIA field agents are often compromised, and even killed. Nobody talked about shutting down field operations. But when some of the more talented remote viewers, after years of pushing the psychic frontier, started losing contact with reality—a few

ending up in mental institutions—the outcry grew too strident to be ignored.

A dead CIA agent was a hero. A crazy one, an embarrassment.

So Starla had written a book about her experiences,
Psi Spy. It flirted with the bestseller list, then sank from
sight. But she had made her point. She hoped.

One rainy April day a man had come to her home. He
showed her a S.H.I.E.L.D. ID badge.

"We need your help," he said, blowing cold rain off his
thin lips.

"I'm very interested in what you propose."

"I haven't proposed anything."

"You don't have to," Starla had told him.

The man recovered quicker than most. "Can you stand
up to a background check?"

"The CIA thought so."

"This is S.H.I.E.L.D."

The background check completed, Starla found herself
driven to a secret location where several stiff-faced men
interrogated her in a blank, windowless room.

"Tell us everything we need to know about remote
viewing," one demanded.

She laughed. They were so intent, so earnest. And so
clueless. She could visualize their Beta waves dancing in
their heads. She met their concerns in Beta.

"I can tell you there is no defense, no shielding, no
countermeasures except launching your own program,"
she said flatly.

They frowned. Beyond the long one-way glass mirror,
she sensed other presences, observing her. She gave
them a little wave. If they waved back, she didn't sense it.
She had only an impression of tense grimness.

"I assume you gentlemen have read my book."

"You hinted at a lot of things. It's obvious you know

more about how these talents work than you let on in print."

"I paid attention to my experiences, and learned a lot. Achieving and maintaining Alpha brainwave states are how you access the function. The temporal lobes of the brain are the key. But Psi isn't strictly a brain function, or a mind function. Yet subtle temporal lobe variations and certain personality traits make for superior psychics. I can identify these candidates for you. And I can teach any ordinary human being to be intuitive and any intuitive to be operationally psychic."

This impressed no one. "Working psychics are a dime a dozen. You can find them in tea rooms and 900 lines in all fifty states."

"Not disciplined psychics," Starla returned. "Not remote viewers. Not the kind of talent S.H.I.E.L.D. needs to deal with the new kinds of threats the next millennium will bring."

They exchanged worried glances. And Starla knew she had hit the bull's-eye. They were already dealing with psychic attacks. She could read it in their eyes.

She decided to go for broke. "I think I'm the best person to head up your program."

One tried to bluff. "What program?"

Starla fixed him with her steady green-gray eyes. "Have you forgotten who I am, and what I can do?" She let a beat pass before she pointedly dropped his name: "George."

The man flinched. He had not offered his name. No one had.

"You'd have to become a S.H.I.E.L.D. agent," George said hastily. "Go the whole route."

"I'm willing."

"You don't understand. This isn't Central Intelligence. For security reasons, we don't employ civilian consultants. Assuming you're invited to join S.H.I.E.L.D., you will have to pass rigorous physical and psychological tests."

"Try me. Or cut me loose. I've cooperated as much as I care to."

They looked helpless. From somewhere beyond the one-way glass, a gravelly voice growled over a concealed loudspeaker:

"I got a hunch about this one. She gets her chance."

A flash image of a black eye patch impressed itself upon Starla's mind's eye, and she knew she had been approved at the highest level of S.H.I.E.L.D.: Nick Fury.

That had been six grueling months ago. Six months in which her muscle-to-bodyfat ratio had been burned down to the prescribed S.H.I.E.L.D. tolerances. Six months in which she had learned to shoot a variety of weapons, live off hostile environments, resist strenuous interrogation, and exceed her physical limits in ways she had never thought possible.

It had been exhilarating. And frustrating. After the first six weeks, Starla had not been allowed to practice any psychic skills. She had not remote viewed now in months. And here she was returning from the last day of training to take her place in the S.H.I.E.L.D. organization, her Alpha skills rusty as untreated roofing nails.

Still, she couldn't wait to begin.

But in the back of her mind was a nagging dread. Fury. Was he all right? She considered reaching out to him mentally. Fear stopped her. If caught, she would be washed out for sure.

The pilot came over the intercabin PA system.

"We are diverting, people. There's been a problem on the Helicarrier."

Starla sat up. Throughout the cabin, other new agents began buzzing among themselves. *Let them buzz,* she thought. *I'm going to find out what's going on.*

Dropping her seatback, she slipped into an Alpha state. Letting her mind go completely blank, she visualized the Helicarrier as she last saw it.

She saw a red ball. That was all. Just a blazing ball like a Colorado sunset. "Damn. I think I'm getting analytical overlay."

Starla tried pushing the image. It wouldn't push. A ball of fire floated stubbornly in her mind's eye, and that was that.

Green-gray eyes snapping open, she gave up.

The seat-belt sign came on. Starla restored her seat-back to the landing position. The S.H.I.E.L.D. jet began losing altitude for its approach.

They were flying into the rising sun. The wingtips were burnished an orange-gold. The fiery color was the same hue she had seen clairvoyantly. Interesting synchronicity. Maybe that was what she had picked up.

A moment later, she got confirmation of her first impression.

The Helicarrier came into view, hovering ponderously off on the starboard side of the aircraft.

Its deck was bare of the usual complement of neatly-arrayed warplanes. The entire portside, opposite the island radar tower, was awash in pools and rivers of burning fuel.

"Oh my God!" Starla gasped.

She had been the first to spot it. The others came out of their seats to lean into the port windows.

Through the flames, they saw the tail section of what looked like a passenger jet. It was blackened under the heat and boiling smoke. But through the soot, patches of the livery of a commercial airliner was clearly visible: a burnt orange ball like a setting sun. As mounting flames ate at it, it steadily turned black.

"What's a passenger jet doing on the Helicarrier?" someone wondered.

"Look! One of the rotors is out of commission!"

It was true. Amid the flames, they could see the tangled and mangled blades of a gigantic rotor hanging in fronds like a thin, wilted flower. It was a sorry sight.

The Helicarrier was listing drunkenly. Even as they watched, it began to right itself. Streamers of chemical foam and high-pressure water were playing about the wreckage. No S.H.I.E.L.D. aircraft were orbiting the vessel. The accident must have caught them all belowdecks, in the hangars. Maybe that was good. Maybe that was bad. It depended on where the flaming fuel had spilled.

From the cockpit came the voice of the pilot:

"You know as much as I do, people. Prepare for landing. Let's see what they tell us on the ground."

A S.H.I.E.L.D. courtesy van was waiting for them at their gate. They were loaded in and whisked across the Triboro Bridge into Manhattan. That took the better part of an agonizing hour. During that time, the Helicarrier crossed the island overhead, heading out to sea.

"Maybe they're going to attempt to put down in the water," the driver theorized.

Starla mentally scanned the stricken carrier. She shook her head.

"No. They're just repositioning for mop-up."

"How do you know?" the driver asked suspiciously.

"I know," Starla said absently.

The driver noticed her purple-backed shoulder eagle, and fell silent. Even among S.H.I.E.L.D. personnel, being psychic was sometimes seen as a mark of mental instability. Too many old ESP agents had lost it over the years. Psi ops had a reputation to live down, as well as its operational worth still to prove, Starla realized.

S.H.I.E.L.D. Central Headquarters in lower Manhattan was a blue glass tower on Seventh Avenue in the Chelsea district. The basement garage received them in silence.

A Special Officer, his midnight-blue combat suit distinguished by pale orange uniform strapping and shoulder insignia, met them.

"This way," he said.

"What's going on?" a recruit asked. "What's the latest on the Helicarrier accident?"

"No word. Is Special Powers Officer Spacek here?"

Starla stepped forward. "Here."

"Come with me."

She followed the security agent to the elevator. It whisked them to a processing room on the 13th floor, where Starla submitted to a fingerprint scan and retina check.

"Pass," the system chirped. *"Spacek, Starla B."*

"Why am I being segregated?" Starla asked the SO.

"Orders from on high. This way."

Starla passed through a succession of iris-style and vertical doors, each one more imposing than the one before. They took her to a spacious conference room where she recognized several Level Two Special Directors.

The SO waved her to an empty seat around a circular table. She was startled to see it was reserved in her name. The plate said: SPACEK, SPECIAL POWERS DIRECTOR.

"This is the first I've heard of this," she breathed.

"Quiet. Security briefing begins in five minutes."

Taking her seat, she composed herself. The room was shielded, she saw. Copper mesh walls. A Faraday cage. She had sat inside them during her CIA days, while they were testing psi-function limitations. Faraday cages were designed to block electromagnetic radiation. For a time, the CIA assumed psychic energy was some form of extremely low-frequency electomagnetic radio waves. It was a good theory. Psi behaved like a signal phenomenon.

The trouble was nobody could isolate the signal. And it couldn't be blocked. They ran tests sending images to submerged U.S. Navy submarines deep in the Pacific's Mariana Trench where no radio signal had ever successfully penetrated.

Nine times out of ten, psychic "transmissions" got through. Sometimes there was distortion, confusion, but they got through. The CIA gave up trying to understand ESP, and just used it.

Starla hoped that the Faraday cage was intended to foil electronic eavesdropping. If Level Two thought they were protected from psychic spying, they thought wrong.

The room was hushed. As they waited, the special directors looked tense and drawn.

After an unbearably long time, the S.H.I.E.L.D. emblem showed on the big four-sided Jumbotron monitor. It was replaced by the sooty face and walrus mustaches of S.H.I.E.L.D.'s second in command, Timothy Dugan. He looked like a man who had been through hell. His voice reflected Starla's impression.

"You've all been waitin' for my report. Well, here it is: At approximately 0500 hours this morning, a Vinegaroon passenger airliner requested emergency landing privileges on the Helicarrier. I personally waved them in. Me. No one else. Got that? It's my responsibility." Dugan seemed to catch his breath. His voice was hoarse, raspy. From the soot on his face, it was plain he had inhaled his share of hot smoke.

"Something went wrong on approach," Dugan continued. "The airliner blew the landing and plowed into port rotor assembly Number Two. We sustained manageable damage. Zero casualties on our end. Which is more than I can say for the passengers and crew." He paused. "So far there's been no survivors. We don't expect any, either."

The special directors absorbed this in tight-faced silence.

"I can report that we have moved Helicarrier operations to a point over the Atlantic in order to facilitate Hazmat and decontamination detail. And body processing. The NTSB and FAA have been notified. And Washington. Technical tells me that they can have the Number Two rotor replaced within two days' time, tops. Until then, we are on stand-down status."

Murmurs of relief went around the room.

"There's more," Dugan broke in. "And this is the tough part. In a separate incident, an Empire airliner carring S.H.I.E.L.D. Director Nicholas Joseph Fury crashed while attempting an emergency landing at Marine Corps Air Station El Toro in California." Dugan paused. "He didn't make it." His voice cracked on the last two words. Half of it was inaudible.

Stunned silence gripped the room.

"That can't be," Starla gasped under her breath. She looked around. The others were stiff-faced, but outwardly unperturbed. Weren't they getting it? It was too much of a coincidence.

She raised her voice. "Are the two incidents connected?"

Dugan looked down from the screen like a looming giant. "Who are you?"

"Spacek, Starla. Special Powers Directorate. I'm new."

"We have no reason to assume anything at this point," Dugan said tightly.

"No reason! Don't you see? This is too coincidental. They *have* to be connected."

"We don't operate on hunches in S.H.I.E.L.D.," the Director of Security admonished her. "Hard facts. We proceed on hard facts only." He pounded his fist on the table as if taking his contained grief out on her.

Starla swallowed her indignation.

"What about the mission Colonel Fury was undertaking when he was killed?" she asked Dugan.

"That's need to know," the Director of Intel said. "Don't you agree, Dugan?"

The big Irishman looked down at the circle of S.H.I.E.L.D. heads and growled, "That's the briefing. Now if you'd pardon me, I have funeral arrangements to make."

The screen returned to displaying the static S.H.I.E.L.D. insignia.

It took a full minute for the others to gather up their folders and things. One by one, they stood up. A thick, dazed silence clung to them like visible auras.

The head of Intel sidled up to Starla and in a low-key voice said, "Arthur Skindarian. Welcome to the Second Level."

Starla said tightly, "This was not how I envisioned it happening."

"Colonel Fury selected you personally to head the new Special Powers Directorate. Over my objections, I might add. With him out of the picture, no telling what will happen to your unit."

Starla swallowed. "You don't have to be psychic to see what's coming."

"Well put," said Intel Director Skindarian. He gathered up his portfolio and quietly left the room.

The last one out, Starla found herself with nowhere to go. She found a wall directory, looked up Special Powers Directorate on the alphabetical listing, and found to her surprise it occupied the top floor. She had expected a basement suite of offices where no one went. At CIA, they had been segregated in a ramshackle windowless building.

The elevator whisked her to the top floor. Her eyes were hot, but dry. S.H.I.E.L.D. agents did not cry, Starla told herself. But she felt like crying anyway. Too much was happening too fast, too furiously for her to process it all.

Special Powers had the entire top floor to itself. A skeleton staff was manning it until the arrival of the new director.

Starla found the security desk manned by a serious-faced black man of about 28. He wore the usual S.H.I.E.L.D. uniform, but his shoulder patch and strappings were purple.

"Can I help you?" he asked.

"Who here knows how to run a remote-viewing session?"

"We all do."

"Fine. I need some help. Follow me."

"Who are you?"

"Your new boss. Starla Spacek."

The black agent's sober manner changed instantly. "We've been expecting you. I'm SPO Mark Youngblood." He cracked a self-conscious grin. "One of the last of the Anomalous Cognition dinosaurs."

Starla walked past a room where purple-strapped S.H.I.E.L.D. personnel sat before banks of computer screens, bodies in unnaturally fixed postures, faces pressed to their screens.

"They're our first line of defense, psychically-speaking," Mark explained.

"They're in Alpha trances?" Starla asked.

"Right. We found that meditating on a screen saver gave them the tightest focus. If any extrasensors infiltrate the building, they'll pick them up."

"Good. Now find me a quiet office where I can remote view. One with a couch, preferrably."

"I can do better than that," Mark said. "This way."

Starla followed him to a wing marked RE-VUE.

"Re-Vue? That was my name for—"

"Colonel Fury had them built according to your exact specifications," Mark said, coming to a round door boasting a single porthole-like window. He punched a code into an adjacent keypad. The hatch rolled open. He waved her in.

Starla stepped inside. "Fury knew who I was all along," she breathed.

"Excuse me?"

"Last night. In Colorado. Colonel Fury was playing with me. All the time I was in training, he was setting this up. And now, he's . . . gone. . . ."

The Re-Vue chamber was custom designed to promote easy access to Alpha states. There were three of them, Starla discovered, all built along the lines of the interior of an egg. Walls and rugs were the same robin's egg blue.

So was the padded platform waterbed in the center.

"I'll be your monitor," Mark said, shutting her in.

Starla walked across the deep-pile carpeting and lay on the mattress. Reaching down, she found the expected dimmer switch. Indirect lighting softened, making the blue interior melt into one seamless azure blur.

Mark reappeared in the elevated control room recessed into one wall of the chamber. He looked down through a long sheet of Plexiglas. Behind him were video cameras, their lenses converging on the center of the chamber where Starla lay.

"Can you hear me?" Starla asked.

"Loud and clear."

"Good. Punch up the longitude and latitude of the El Toro Marine Base, California."

"Give me a minute," Mark said, going to his terminal.

"Am easing down into Alpha."

"Okay."

"I'm there." Her voice was thin, like spider silk made audible.

"Okay. I have target site coordinates for you."

"Proceed."

"Go to 33 degrees, 36 minutes North Latitude, 117 degrees 40 minutes Longitude West."

No one had yet figured out how it all worked. The crazy part was that any assigned address would work. Pick a target to be remote viewed, give it a name, a computer generated random number or longitude and latitude, and eight times out of ten, the tasked remote viewer could send his or her mind there, and accurately perceive what was going on at the site in real-time. Starla found she was most comfortable with unencrypted real-world coordinates.

Before her eyes, the seamless blue blur of the Re-Vue chamber seemed to recede.

"Tape rolling," Mark called out.

Starla could hear him only dimly. "I see scrub."

"Keep going."

"Burnt scrub. Smoke. I smell burning plastic, rubber, heated metals. A salty tang, like fresh blood."

"Push past the smell. Tell me what you perceive."

"A jet airliner. It's flat on its belly. Cockpit is wide open. It's all black and sooty. The controls have been carbonized. There's been a fire."

"Can you see anyone alive?"

"Rescue workers. EMTs. Examining three bodies on the ground. They are laid out in a row, covered by Red Cross sheets."

"Can you pick up what they're saying?" asked Mark.

Starla was staring at the ceiling, her eyes wide open. But they were seeing a faraway place. She concentrated her attention on her left temporal lobe, where language is processed. Mentally, she listened. It was the hardest part of what she did. A natural clairvoyant, she was only intermittently clairaudient. For her, it was easy to ride the right temporal lobe, painfully difficult to make the switch. But she had to try.

"One is them is uncovering the face of one of the dead," she murmured. "He's saying something like, 'This is the captain.' I see the pilot. Ugh. The face is raw and black, like a charred pork roast."

"Stay with it," Mark encouraged.

"The second body, he's saying, is the copilot. They're leaving that one alone. I can sense the body has been horribly disfigured."

"So far, so good. What about the third body?"

"They're conferring on that now." Starla listened. What she heard was exactly what people hear in their minds when they imagine or remember sounds. Only it was not the product of imagination.

"'This is the man who tried to save the plane,' one of them is saying. 'He probably saved the passengers' lives.' The other man is saying, 'It's a damn shame he didn't make it.' I sense a great sadness about them."

"What are they saying about the third man?"

"They don't know who he is. Wait. They're throwing back the sheet." Starla took a deep sip of breath. She held it in. "His face is as black as a lump of coal. I can see his teeth. They're drawn back over shriveled lips. The teeth are brown like scorched porcelain. One of them is cracked from intense heat."

"Anything else?"

Starla fought back a sob. "Yes. He's still wearing his eye patch. It covers his left eye. They're wondering how his eye patch survived the inferno."

From the control booth, Mark Youngblood's voice said, "Colonel Fury's eye patch is fireproof . . ."

Starla Spacek closed her eyes in pain. It didn't shut out the sight three thousand miles away. In fact, it made it that much more real, and terrifying. . . .

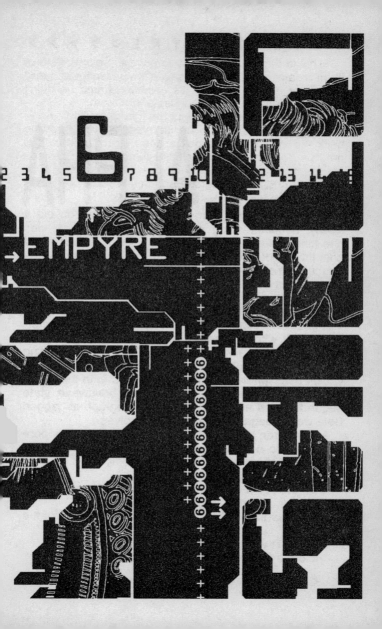

ALPHA

COMING OUT OF DEEP was like coming up from a deep-sea dive. You did it slowly, decompressing mentally. Going non-local was one kind of mental leap. Returning to local space-time orientation got harder and harder the more often Starla Spacek remote viewed. It was one of the chief occupational hazards of psychic work: coming back to mundane reality perceptually unchanged.

Lying on the platform waterbed in the womblike Re-Vue chamber, Starla focused on her breathing, recentering herself within herself. She knew from the CIA CAT scans that her cranial blood flow was slowly shifting away from the intuitive right brain to the logical, analytical left hemisphere, seeking to reconnect with the physical world. Her slow, rhythmic Alpha brainwave state began to pulse and jump like a seismograph as jagged Beta waves began reasserting themselves.

A shrill siren broke through the transitional state, popping her into Beta. Starla came up off the couch, clapping hands to her ears.

"Owww!"

Over the PA, a voice sounded. *"Special Powers Director Spacek, report to the motor pool. At once!"*

"Who was that?" Starla demanded, coming out of the chamber.

"You don't want to know," Mark said guardedly.

"Hold the fort until I get back, SPO Youngblood."

"*If* you get back," Mark said.

Starla took the elevator down to the car pool. A gray-strapped Technical Officer was standing beside a metallic silver Lamborghini Diablo. It sat with its gullwing doors lifted as if poised for flight. "I'm SPD Spacek," she told the Techno.

"You're wanted on the Helicarrier."

"Fine. Take me there."

"You're driving."

"Me? I've only driven—I mean flown one of these things in a simulator."

"This is the way we do it at S.H.I.E.L.D. Learn as you go."

"I keep hearing that," Starla muttered, climbing in behind the wheel. The Techno took the passenger seat. The doors folded down automatically.

Starla gave the dash a quick, refamiliarizing glance. It was a nest of digital readouts and touch-sensitive displays.

She pressed the ignition pad. The plate recognized her fingerprint and the engine roared to life.

"Let me get the lift," the Techno said, snapping a roof switch.

The floor began hoisting upward.

"This is the roof-door control," he added, pressing the red button beside it.

Overhead, the plate-steel ceiling parted. The hood blazed with reflective light. A touch of a button changed the shiny color to a matte-finish gray.

"Thanks," Starla said. "Now I can see."

The lift came flush with the roof and Starla initiated the conversion process, calling out the sequence.

"Hydraulics."

Beneath the front and rear bumpers, steel feet dropped, made contact with the lift, and under growing hydraulic pressure began hoisting the chassis off the ground until all four tires hung low off their suspension mounts.

"Converting wheel orientation," she said, tapping a floorboard stud.

To the whining accompaniment of servo motors, the tires began folding out of their wells as DRIVE TRAIN DISENGAGED appeared on the heads-up display.

"Switching to flight mode," Starla called out.

FLIGHT MODE ENABLED, flashed on the display.

Each armored hubcap split apart, revealing bladed turbines. They began spooling up. The whine grew and grew in quadrophonic stereo. Loose grit began kicking up.

Starla unlocked the steering column, converting the wheel into a universal flight yoke. Her feet found the control pedals. Her right hand took hold of the throttle array emerging from the seat divider compartment.

"Take her up slowly," the Techno suggested.

"Exactly my plan."

The four turbines lifted the Diablo—it was really a Lamborghini shell mounted on something far more than an exotic sports car—perpendicular to the roof. Despite the strident sound, takeoff was surprisingly gentle.

"Just like the simulator," Starla said.

"Don't get too comfortable."

"I've driven in Manhattan traffic. This is nothing."

Goosing the throttle, Starla sent the S.H.I.E.L.D. Mark V multimode vehicle out toward the Atlantic. The car handled smoothly. Rear-deck thrusters provided vectored push. But it was the wheel-rim turbines that did most of the flying. It was a lot like piloting a helicopter, only infinitely more stable. There was no balancing the torque of a main rotor against tail rotors, no struggling with the collective and cyclic stick that made helicopter flight so tricky.

They cleared Manhattan Island after five minutes of

easy flying. On-board navigational computers guided them out to sea.

"A child could fly this thing," Starla marveled.

"Try to keep in mind maximum airspeed is 700 miles per hour. This is supposed to be a short hop."

Starla eased back on the throttles. "Sorry. Overexcitement, I guess."

The Helicarrier came into view ten minutes later.

A long intestine of black smoke, shading to gray at the end, continued to uncoil from the portside of the carrier. Signs of fire were minimal. The remains of the 737 lay splashed across the angled flight deck jutting out portside. The fuselage was mostly intact, Starla saw. The nose had been popped open like an aluminum bag of instant popcorn. There were bodies, black things with outflung limbs scattered here and there like charred starfish.

"What do we know about this?" Starla asked.

"You'll be briefed," was the stiff reply.

The flight deck, so small five miles out, grew and grew in size until its full breathtaking scope became evident.

The tower came in over the on-board com link.

"Hel-1 Control. Ident, Mark V vehicle."

Starla hit the Ident button. The transponder relayed the vehicle's S.H.I.E.L.D. IFF number.

"Capture," said the tower. *"Cleared for landing. Main runway."*

On the dash, a three-view wireframe display of the Helicarrier popped to life. Runway One, the only one clear of debris and blowing smoke, flashed red on the dorsal view.

"Copy, Hel-1 Control," Starla said crisply.

"There's your locator beam," the Techno said, pointing to the heads-up symbology painted on the windscreen. "Just center it and ride the beam in."

Starla jockeyed the Mark V until the floating green circle captured the X of the beam. "Got it."

She took the multimode in flat like a plane, clearing the

stern deck lip by a comfortable twenty feet. The uneasy sense of being suspended over miles of ocean vanished as the massive flight deck rolled on and on under them.

"Set it down any time you feel like," the Techno said. "We have the flight deck to ourselves."

Starla tapped the nose retros, sending the car into a flat spiral that bled off forward momentum. She dropped the undercarriage feet, setting the craft onto the deck in a perfect two-point landing.

"Tower, we are down," Starla announced.

"Copy."

On the display, the runway lines stopped flashing, and a rectangular square turned red in outline.

"That means drive to that lift," the Techno indicated.

Starla waited for the turbines to finish spooling down, then hit the Restore sequencer.

In short order, the hubcaps closed up, wheels retracted into their wells, while the hydraulic feet withdrew. The car settled. Tires touched the deck with a single soft bump that shook the suspension only slightly.

Returning to drive mode, Starla tooled toward the lift as if looking for a parking space at Disneyland. There was no longer any sense of sitting on a vessel floating four thousand feet over open water. That was how gigantic the flight deck was.

They passed the downed jet. Hoses were still playing here and there on the wilted aluminum carcass. Hazmat teams in orange bunny suits walked around, toting their portable oxygen tanks. Here and there, patches of flame smouldered. Grease fires. The predominant smell coming through the closed windows, oddly enough, was of burnt rubber.

Starla shuddered.

The Techno offered laconically, "You get used to death working for S.H.I.E.L.D."

"I get a creepy feeling off that jet," Starla said thinly. "Fear has nothing to do with it."

The Techno grunted. Starla read him as pure Beta. He had the intuition of a brick.

Sending the vehicle into a smart S-turn, she parked it. The lift began dropping before the car fully stopped. Watching the black-and-yellow striped walls rising over the roofline, Starla had the feeling she was being swallowing by a great steel whale.

On the deck below, rank after rank of white-and-gold S.H.I.E.L.D. fighter aircraft stood in their hangar spaces. They appeared intact and untouched by fire. That was a relief.

Three decks down, the lift shuddered to a stop. They got out.

The Techno led the way. "Follow me."

Starla followed the man down a bewildering maze of stainless steel corridors. Surprisingly, there were no security checks. This seemed to be a little-used section of the ship.

He left her in a room marked CONFERENCE PRIVATE. The door shut, and the lock clicked ominously.

There were no lights. But there were presences. Starla could sense them. They read as neutral—unthreatening.

"Hello?"

A gravelly voice said, "Light switch to your immediate left."

Starla hit it. Fluorescents popped to life. She found herself looking down a long cherrywood conference table.

At the other end sat a man. He stood up, all six feet, one inch of him. He fixed her with a single smouldering brown eye.

"Who authorized you to remote view me?" he barked.

Starla blinked. "Colonel Fury? You're alive!"

"A little louder," Nick Fury growled. "I don't think they can hear you on Hydra Island."

FURY

S.H.I.E.L.D. DIRECTOR NICK removed his trademark El Producto cigar from his tight slash of a mouth and exhaled a cloud of fumes pungent enough to fumigate a barn.

"I asked you a question," he growled.

Starla Spacek fought back conflicting emotions. "I—I—"

"Out with it!"

"I'm very sorry, Colonel Fury. I was concerned about you. As the new head of Special Powers—"

"I know your rank. I authorized it two months ago. Had the Re-Vue chambers built to your specs and everything. Gave you everything you asked for. And for all my pains, how did you repay me? By blowing my cover."

"I don't understand."

"Sit down and we'll explain it to you."

Starla sat. She laid her hands flat to the cherrywood tabletop. They didn't shake so much that way. Fury's voice was like a battering ram. She felt every word punching into her psychically-sensitive solar plexus. But she took it.

"Understand you remote viewed the crash sight out in California," Fury said.

"I know it was unauthorized, but I—"

"You saw a dead man wearing my eye patch."

"Correct."

"A body from a local morgue borrowed for the occasion," Fury explained. "I survived the crash-landing. Which is more than I can say for the two jokers who tried to spread my flight all over Los Angeles. The plane's nose clipped a tree, and split open like an overcooked hotdog. Passengers and crew all got out alive. By the time I crawled out, I had a plan. I needed to smoke out the people who tried to assassinate me. So I contacted S.H.I.E.L.D. LA, and we rigged us a little subterfuge."

"I know I was wrong. But—"

"Stow it." Stabbing a desk stud, Fury said, "Dugan, get in here."

A concealed door hummed open and a flame-haired human mountain decorated with a fierce walrus mustache lumbered in. He was taller than Fury by nearly half a foot, which made him very tall indeed. He dropped onto a seat with all the grace of a crashing rhinocerous.

"You know Dum Dum Dugan, my second in command," Fury said. "Anything that comes out of his mouth might as well have come out of mine. Got that?"

"Yes, Colonel."

"Dum Dum, chew her out for me."

Dum Dum leaned forward. "With pleasure. It's like this. That little teleconference speech I gave an hour or so back? It was a ruse."

"Ruse?"

"Designed to foil any Hydra Remote Vipers that might be lurking at Manhattan headquarters."

Starla blinked. "I don't understand."

Fury said, "Those two airmen who came to collect me last night? Fakes. They weren't sent by S.H.I.E.L.D. If they hadn't bulldozed me, I would have remembered the A-4 Skyhawk is a Marine plane. My mistake. And that commercial flight out of Denver was piloted by a pair of kamikazes. It was all I could do to wrestle them and the aircraft out of a suicide dive right into the heart of LA."

"If the airmen weren't legitimate," Starla asked, "why did S.H.I.E.L.D. verify them?"

"S.H.I.E.L.D. didn't. It was a faked transmission. A decoy. Calculated to lull any suspicions so I'd fall into their neat little trap."

Starla frowned.

"I know what you're thinkin'," Dugan inserted. "How did they know the password of the day?"

"I guess I'm not the only psychic in the room," Starla said. Neither man smiled at her mild attempt at humor. She swallowed her own tentative smile. They were very serious.

"Remember how the joker on the other end hesitated when I asked for the password?" Fury reminded.

Starla nodded. "I do."

"I don't know, but I have me a hunch he took advantage of that pause to read my mind. What do you think?"

"Are you asking my professional opinion, or do you want me to scan the situation?"

"Whatever works for you," Dum Dum said gruffly.

"Alphanumeric information is the most difficult to send or receive telepathically," Starla said. "But a crack clairaudient can apprehend single words or short word strings with excellent clarity. A password could be obtained clairaudiently. No doubt about it."

Fury and Dugan exchanged unhappy glances.

"My gut also tells me that's exactly what happened," Starla added. "For whatever it's worth."

"I wouldn't have made you Director of Special Powers if it wasn't worth something."

"Thank you, Colonel."

"Don't relax yet. I ain't done chewing you out. That performance Dugan gave was designed to buy us time until we could assess the threat. Thanks to you, it may have tanked."

"I'm truly sorry, Colonel."

"Save it. Sorry don't splint broken bones. Reason we called you here is not just to chew you out."

"Although you should consider yourself chewed out," Dugan interjected.

Fury eyed the glowing tip of his cigar. His single visible eye reflected it like a dim coal. "Like I said, we gotta do some threat assessment. Here's what we know so far: We have two airline crashes on our hands. Looking past the PR problem, it's a rip-roaring mess. Topside, we have a Vinegaroon Air 737 splashed all over our flight deck, with who knows how many dead civilians spilled every which way. And the NTSB and FAA screaming for access."

"Which we've so far denied on the grounds of national security," Dugan inserted.

"It could be just one of those coincidences that Mr. Ripley used to make a lot of hay over—except for the Empire Airlines jet I smeared all over Orange County."

"Was it a legitimate flight?" Starla asked.

"I looked into it," Dugan said. "It's legit. The passengers were, too. We're runnin' background checks on the pilots. Empire is a new carrier. Ever since deregulation, airlines have been breakin' up and mergin' and consolidatin' like there's no tomorrow. Pilots float from system to system. These guys may have quite a history."

"Meaning?"

Dugan said, "Meanin' that they could have flown for anyone from AeroMexico to Hydra along the way."

"So what we have," Fury elaborated, "is two different crashes involving two unconnected carriers. The common thread is both incidents seem designed to immoblize and demoralize S.H.I.E.L.D. on two fronts. The question is: are we dealing with sabotage and a coincidental air accident—or a coordinated two-pronged attack?"

"I sensed danger when you left, Colonel," Starla reminded.

"I remember that," Fury said, his gruff tone growing subdued. "And there's another wrinkle." He pushed a dossier folder across the table. "This was waiting for me on the plane. Notice anything funny about it?"

Starla picked the folder up. It was empty. She examined it, front and back. "No, I don't."

"It's an old folder," Dugan explained.

"That means the person or persons who lured you into the death flight had access to S.H.I.E.L.D. files at one time," said Starla. "Could be a mole."

"That's my worry, too," Fury said.

Silence hung in the room.

Fury ground his cigar out in a steel ashtray. "What's your hunch, Spacek?"

"What's yours, Colonel Fury?"

"My hunches don't count. You're supposed to be the psychic."

"Everyone has psychic potential. The difference is aptitude, practice and of course, training. I doubt you would have come this far in life unless you had highly developed instincts."

Fury seemed to consider this. "Fair enough. But I asked you first."

"My hunch is that both crashes are connected. I could go further."

"Be my guest," Fury invited.

"Both crashes appear deliberate. But were designed to pass for accidents. If the people who wanted you dead didn't care about appearances, it would have been far simpler to booby-trap your Skyhawk than to lure you into a doomed commercial plane. For some reason, they wanted it to appear that you died in a commercial aviation accident. That was important to them."

Fury and Dugan swapped satisfied glances.

"Moreover," Starla continued, "the attempt to knock out the Helicarrier was also designed to look like an accident. The force or agency behind this dual attack intended to cripple and demoralize S.H.I.E.L.D."

"Why would that be?" Fury asked. "Why not go for

broke? Strike a double blow and show the world they're not afraid of us. What do they have to gain by playing coy?"

Starla considered. "They fear retaliation. That's the only logical answer. Striking a blow against S.H.I.E.L.D. was preemptive, not punitive. These people are planning something. Something big. Something they feel they can pull off more easily if S.H.I.E.L.D. is overwhelmed by organizational problems."

Fury massaged his perpetually unshaven chin. "That's my read, too. Now we gotta prove it to our satisfaction and figure out who and what's behind it."

"And what they're plannin'," Dugan added gruffly.

"That's the proverbial devil in the details," Starla admitted. "Getting good PSINTEL is one thing. Verifying it in Beta is another."

"PSINTEL is your bailiwick, Spacek. Verification is ours. I want you to get right on it. Pronto."

"Which aspect?"

"You're Special Powers honcho. Attack it your way. Just remember, Special Powers is probationary. If you can't deliver consistent results, you go the way of the old ESP Division. I don't have to tell you that Intel would be happy if you and your whole unit took a tumble overboard without a chute."

Starla made a face. "I've met Director Skindarian. He as much as told me so."

"Skindarian is old school." Fury paused. "Come to think of it, I'm old school, too. But I ain't stayed alive this long by not changing with the times. S.H.I.E.L.D. was the U.S. agency that pioneered psychic counterintelligence. Along the way, we kinda dropped the ball. So I'm handing it off to you."

Dum Dum cocked a reddish thumb in the S.H.I.E.L.D. director's direction.

"Until such a time as we tell you different, Fury here died in California," he said.

Starla nodded. "I doubt that will remain secret for very long. Hydra Remote Vipers can go anywhere and see anything. One may be in this room even now."

"What you're saying we already know. That's why you've gone from raw recruit to SPD without any of the usual pit stops. For all practical purposes S.H.I.E.L.D. is unshielded. Your next job will be psychic countermeasures. But right now, I want to see results. Dugan will hand you your briefing folder."

"Not neccessary, Colonel. I will conduct an open search. I want to go in with no preconceived ideas or theories. The key to solid PSINTEL is objectivity. That means no front-loading."

"Go to it, then. Dismissed."

"Thank you, Colonel. Uh . . . Mr. Dugan. How do I address you?"

Dugan grinned lopsidedly. "I've had so many titles over the years, I plum forget which is current. Dum Dum works."

"Dum Dum?"

"Like the bullet. Goes in like a hot poker and comes out the other side of you like a hobnailed boot."

Starla shuddered. The image Dugan's words conveyed may or may not have been clairvoyant, but it certainly was vivid.

After she left the room, the big Irishman turned to Fury and said, "What do you think, Nick?"

"My gut is telling me she's got the goods."

Dum Dum grunted. "Yeah. But can she deliver them in time to pull S.H.I.E.L.D.'s fat outta the fire?"

"Come on, let's see if they're done processing the last of those poor souls off the airliner."

"You forgettin' something, Nick?"

Fury hesitated. "Oh, yeah. Thanks for reminding me that I'm supposed to be dead."

Fury went to a wall. Out swung a concealed apparatus. Taking off his eye patch, which revealed a dull brown eye that looked whole but lacked the gleam of sight, Fury sat down at a high-tech chair before a curved console that was padded.

"Don't just stand there, you old walrus. Give me a hand with this ridiculous contraption."

"Smile when you call me that, you ornery war horse," Dugan returned.

With Dugan's help, Fury clapped two halves of the curved console together. They encased his head. An automatic sequence kicked in, and the device warbled and whined. Fury sat, his head out of sight, with his arms straining as his head was subjected to unknown forces.

A double beep signaled the procedure had completed its cycle.

When Dugan broke the device in two, Fury gave his head a shake, growling, "Feels like that thing scrambled my brains for sure." He stood up. "How do I look?"

Dum Dum grinned. "Twenty years younger, and if possible uglier than ever."

Fury felt his face. It was unaccustomedly smooth. The FACE—short for Facial Anatomy Contour Equalizer— had given his bestubbled jaw a laser peel as well as laying in a new set of computer generated bony contours.

Fury checked himself in the console mirror. "Not bad. I make a fair-to-middling redhead."

"Just remember who's the real deal in that department," Dum Dum reminded.

OFFICER

AS EXECUTIVE of the Helicarrier, Special Director Contessa Valentina Allegro de Fontaine had seen a lot during her term with S.H.I.E.L.D. She had witnessed acts of sabotage that had ripped apart entire decks. Missile attacks that had been turned by the ship's incredibly violent offensive-defensive array.

One hellish day, green-suited Hydra boarding teams, like modern-day buccaneers, had descended on the Helicarrier in a swarm of Harpy-2 hovercraft. For an entire day a pitched battle raged on the carrier deck. It had been like trying to fight off a horde of voracious locusts. They appeared relentlessly single-minded, determined and unstoppable.

Until Nick Fury, at the last-ditch, had authorized the fire-control systems switched to Repel Mode.

In an instant, strategically-placed nozzles and hoses configured to dispense fire-suppressing chemicals and good old-fashioned H_2O, began gushing flaming fuel and naplam instead.

The Hydras were incinerated like many green locusts. Those not caught in the initial counterattack either jumped overboard to a less unpleasant death, or evacuated to their retreating Harpys.

That had been an ugly day. The memory refused to fade. The stink of burnt flesh sometimes still troubled Val's sleep.

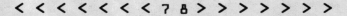

Somehow, in an eerie way, this was worse. A Hydra attack was, after all, an expression of warfare. A war S.H.I.E.L.D. and its chief adversary had been locked in for over thirty years now.

But to watch a commercial airliner, filled with innocent men, women and children, come thundering in, almost make it, only to go plowing into a giant rotor in a boil of flame and carnage—somehow, that was far, far worse.

Val's heart was still pounding as she oversaw the extraction and processing of the dead.

Most had been incinerated, still strapped in their seats. The stink wasn't the same, though. It was mixed with the stench of burning chemicals.

They say that most people who perish in airline cabin fires succumb to inhaling toxic smoke generated by melting plastic bulkheads and synthetic fabrics. This conglomeration of odors was almost as bad. Despite herself, Val kept expecting to catch a whiff of that awful roast-pork stink under the lingering fumes. But she smelled nothing of the kind. Mercifully.

A white-haired black man came running up. He wore the red strapping and insignia of a Special Field Officer. Soot and sweat made his fleshy, care-worn face a smear of dark hues.

"What is it, Gabriel?"

"We got through to the president of Vinegaroon Airlines. He confirms they are not missing a flight."

"What!"

Gabe nodded grimly. "I ran it all the way up to their C.E.O. before bringing it to you. But that's what they're saying all the way up and down the chain of authority. There was no Flight 334 on Vinegaroon Air bound for Kennedy International. They are not missing a flight, crew or passengers. They plain don't know what we're talking about."

Val frowned darkly. She was a beautiful mature woman with classic European features. A white streak of hair ran back from her smooth brow to separate her lustrous up-swept raven hair into two unequal parts. Her lips looked as if they were sculpted out of some soft sweet clay. Her eyes were very, very gray. Almost clear.

"Isn't that the Vinegaroon livery?" she asked, pointing to the jetliner's charred remains.

Gabe admitted, "Hard to say, I'm not familiar with that carrier. Aren't they a regional line out of the Southwest?"

"I guess we can scratch accident off the list of possibilities here," Val said grimly. "How many dead?"

"We count 133. Including crew. There may yet be a few not accounted for."

"Well, these people belong to somebody."

"A missing flight has got to show up."

"If it doesn't," a bear of a voice announced behind them, "then we got an altogether other kind of wildcat on our hands."

Val and Gabe Jones turned in unison.

Dum Dum Dugan loomed over them like a tower of gristled meat. His blazing blue eyes held a fierce light.

"You overheard?" Val asked.

"Yeah. Doesn't make sense."

"It makes more sense if this was deliberate. First, someone lured poor Nick to his death, and now this."

"Watch how you speak of the dead," a gravelled voice growled.

Val gasped. "Nick?"

The man who walked up wearing a standard issue S.H.I.E.L.D. flight suit was tall, muscular and red-haired. His blue eyes sparkled with the steely glint they half-recognized. Otherwise he was a stranger.

"Who else wears this brand of cologne?" asked Nick Fury.

Gabe Jones broke out in a grin. Val started toward the disguised S.H.I.E.L.D. director.

Fury held her off with upraised hands. "Not so fast. I'm still deceased. Officially."

The pair composed themselves. Grins kept cracking their faces. They fought them down to relieved smirks.

Fury growled, "Out with it."

"We don't know who this aircraft belongs to, or who all these people are," Val explained.

"Let's look over the dead."

Fury stalked off toward a long row of sheeted forms. He whipped back a shroud.

The body was nude from the waist up. A cheap blue polyester shirt had melted to the skin, merging with it. The face was intact, but it was just a lifeless mask now. It could have been anyone.

The next body belonged to a woman. Her shape told them that. They couldn't tell from the head. A charred stump sat where the head should have been.

"Any ID on these people?" Fury asked.

"None found so far," Val reported.

Fury frowned tightly. "Kinda funny, don't you think? All these people, and not a wallet or a purse between them?"

Gabe shrugged. "Not so surprising. Clothes were burned. When the wing fuel tanks ruptured, the fire swept the length of the cabin. Everything and everyone got scorched to the bone. Some were completely car-bonized."

"Let's see one of those," Fury suggested.

Val winced. A yellow-strapped Landing Signal Officer took them to a pitiful little sheeted thing that might have been a child—or a full-sized human being curled up in a fetal position.

The sheet came off like a sail cracking. Fury looked down. His face registered his disgust only a particle.

"Looks like a blamed blob," said Dum Dum. "Can't tell if it's man or woman."

Fury knelt. Taking a steel penlight from a pocket, he probed the still-hot bundle of tissues.

An eyeball rolled out of the mess. It hit the deck with a thin click, rolling away like a loose marble.

Dum Dum stopped it with one size 15 shoe. It made a distinctive sound in stopping. The sound was not organic.

Fury reached over and claimed it. Coming to his feet, he held it up to the blazing noonday sun.

Outwardly, it looked like a human eye. It was mostly white. There was a gray iris and a black pupil. But the back of the eyeball, where the controlling muscles should have been, looked more like an aperture or socket.

Fury snapped, "Somebody cut this thing apart. I think we got a Life Model Decoy on our hands."

Dum Dum stepped in, and gave the mass a hearty kick. It flew apart. The pieces were not organic.

"No doubt about it," he announced. "This here's an android."

They went back to check the headless woman.

Fury and Dum Dum knelt, facing the charred stump. They used their fingers to probe, at first tentatively, almost squeamishly, then with increasing confidence.

Pulling out a tendril of multicolored wires and fused circuitry, Fury held it up for all to see.

"Anyone want to bet when we're done processing all these corpses, we find they're all LMDs?"

Nobody seemed eager to take that bet.

"They're not ours," Fury announced grimly. "So they can only belong to Hydra."

Dum Dum reared up and scratched the unruly red hair under his trademark bowler hat.

"Well," he mused. "I guess that answers the question of the day. We're up against a blamed Hydra offensive."

"Yeah," growled Fury. "But which active branch of Hydra? That's what I want to know."

Val said, "I much preferred it when we were fighting a cohesive enemy force. All these splinter groups with their own agendas defy tracking and objective analysis."

"Hydra is Hydra," Fury growled. "'Cut off a limb and two more will take its place.' That's the way it's always been and that's the way it always will be—until the last head is chopped off and we drive a stake through the monster's twisted heart."

The quartet exchanged glum glances.

Cut off a limb and two more will take its place. This had been Hydra's credo, indeed its boast, since its inception. Through three decades of struggle, S.H.I.E.L.D. had tried to crush the beast. The enemy had more arms than a human. And it was completely, reptilianly, ruthlessly inhuman.

Their minds went back to what they knew of their implacable foe.

The roots of the international criminal organization known only as Hydra took seed in Imperial Japan during World War Two. It had been a secret society then, under the control of Japanese militarists. Late in the war, a fugitive Nazi war criminal named Baron Wolfgang Von Strucker had seized control of the nascent organization and in the post-war years had built it up until it was wealthy and powerful enough to send out its evil tentacles to capture and control individuals, corporations and even small nations.

No one living knew why the originators of Hydra took their inspiration from Greek myth—other than the obvious fact that, like the many-headed Hydra the demigod Hercules once battled, no matter how many heads were chopped off, the Hydra monster refused to die. Always, a new head grew to replace the old.

By the 1960s, Hydra had mushroomed into a globe-girdling, neo-fascistic cabal with its talons in virtually every major country on earth. It was worth billions. It commanded an advanced technology. And it was single-mindedly devoted to one overriding goal: world domination.

To meet this threat, the United States of America had constituted S.H.I.E.L.D. Conceived by military industrialist

Anthony Stark who lent his name, his wealth and the technological expertise of Stark Industries to the cause, S.H.I.E.L.D. was created to be America's last-ditch shield and bulwark against the Hydra menace.

In those early days, Strucker's role in the organization was a hidden one. Various persons played the subservient role of Imperial Hydra to Strucker's Supreme Hydra. Each time they were captured or killed, S.H.I.E.L.D. had believed the Hydra threat diminished, if not vanquished.

Each time, true to its inspiration, Hydra had returned. Its members, like its leaders, were unknown. They wore green hoods, even their eyes were concealed by green polarized lenses. Their emerald robes might have belonged to some secret society of long ago.

Over the decades, S.H.I.E.L.D. had broken the back of Hydra time and time again. In recent years, it would have seemed for the final time.

In truth, Hydra as a centralized organization had ceased to exist. Pockets of Hydra cells still survived on virtually every continent. A decision was made not to reform. Hydra now operated as separate heads, decentralized, accountable to no overriding authority. Which made it infinitely harder to track and combat in the field.

Today, Hydra operations were contained. Perhaps one day they would be strong enough to re-form, reintegrate, under a new Supreme Hydra, coordinating their tentacular arms into another unified push for global conquest. That was the day S.H.I.E.L.D. was dedicated to preventing.

"You people thinking what I'm thinking?" Nick Fury asked.

"If you're thinkin' that what happened here today signals that Hydra is gettin' ready to reorganize like the old days," Dum Dum grumbled, "I'd say that's about the size of it."

"We gotta find out for sure. Everyone get on this. I want answers by sundown. Now, move!"

The quartet deployed, each to pursue their individual missions.

Dum Dum sidled up to Fury, lowered his voice to a bearlike growl.

"You gotta be the sorriest undercover operative I ever did see."

Fury cocked a dubious eye at the big Irishman. "How's that?"

"That foghorn voice of yours. If it doesn't give you away, that ripe old cologne of yours will."

"What the hell's wrong with wearing Hai Karate?"

"For one thing," Dum Dum said through his grinning mustaches, "they stopped makin' the infernal stuff about twenty years ago."

"Come on, you old walrus. Let's see what Special Powers has turned up. I'm sick of looking at this hellacious mess."

NOBODY

KNEW

what to call that space where the clairvoyant mind went when it went operationally non-local.

In less technological times, they coined terms like the spirit world, the other side, or the astral plane. Even when the first quantum theorists discovered the sub-atomic underlying reality, with its photonic ghosts and particle-wave dualities and ever-shifting probabilties, it was decades until the parapsychologists saw in quantum physics the first glimmering underpinnings of human psy-chic function.

Some called it the Frequency Domain. Or the Void. Or the Matrix. Whatever it was, certain uncommon individu-als learned to access and roam it at will.

Not that it was easy. It was never easy.

For Starla Spacek, roaming the Frequency Domain was a mixture of terror and wonder. When she was down in her Zone, there was no place her mind could not go.

But there were limitations. The first remote explorers had trouble focusing on specific locations. The use of outbound journeys and human beacons to provide a focal point proved wildly successful. But scientifically, it was suspect.

Driven by funding needs, someone came up with the idea of using coordinates. Longitudes and latitudes. It worked perfectly. When it worked. When it didn't work, it worked badly or not at all. Just like any other psychic function. The human mind had its good days and bad. There was no getting around biorhythms, or headaches, or phases of the moon.

But longitudes and latitudes, too, could contain sub-concious keys. So some brave soul took it to another level. Attaching computer-generated ID numbers to target photographs, and feeding the number to a remote viewer should not have worked. But in the wild, weird world of RV, it did. Just as reliably as grid coordinates or human beacons.

The hardest RV tasking still remained the temporal search.

Starla Spacek was in temporal search mode, her supple body prone and relaxed as soft music was piped in through the waterbed couch sound system.

It had taken her longer than usual to cool down. Too much had happened too fast. By the time SPO Mark Youngblood had arrived on the Helicarrier, she was beyond being shocked by anything—including the solitary Re-Vue chamber that awaited her on Deck 12, just above the massive shielded electronics pod that jutted down from the bow keel of the ponderous ship.

Cool-down took a half hour. She lay on the couch listening to Bach in stereo on a dual-track hemi-synch audio tape. Once her body was relaxed, she reached down and flipped a console switch. The soft strains of Bach faded. In their place was a sound like a cross between white noise and a distant, almost subliminal surf.

It lulled her brain state into deep Alpha, taking it to that twilight realm called the Theta state. The threshold of sleep.

In the monitor booth, Mark consulted an EEG monitor tied in to Starla's pillow. "I'm reading Theta waves."

"I hear you." Her voice sounded eerily far away.

"First, I want you to go back to this morning. To exactly

0500 hours. Vinegaroon Flight 334 is coming in for a landing at Kennedy. What are your impressions?"

"I sense—nothing."

"Nothing at all?"

"The passengers. Their minds are . . . blank."

"Move forward. To the flight deck."

"There are two men. Their minds are on . . . death. Their deaths. They expect to die. The pilot is touching his throat microphone. He is trying to communicate with the Helicarrier. He has been cleared to land. Emergency landing."

"Is the aircraft in trouble?"

"It is doomed. But it is not in trouble."

"Starla, what do you mean by that?"

"They understand that they are to die. That is their mission. They are accepting of their fates. Now the copilot is tripping a switch. It sends an electrical impulse to a small device hidden in one of the wing turbines. It explodes. Now the turbine is smoking and spilling flames. Slipstream is beating the fire back.

"I don't need details, just facts. Follow the pilots in."

"They are lining up on the Helicarrier flight deck. They have a good approach. 'Wheels down,' the pilot is saying. I don't think he's speaking English."

"What language is he speaking?"

"I can't tell. A foreign language. It's very guttural."

"Keep going."

"The pilot is watching the deck rush up to meet him. He has his eye on the roll indicator. It is showing that his wings are almost level. Now he throws the control wheel hard. Hard left. He screams something. Two words."

Starla gasped.

"What's happening now, Starla?" Mark urged. "Tell me."

"They've crashed. The cockpit has crashed into a rotor. A ball of flame explodes. It's the right wing-fuel tank. Bodies everywhere. Fire. Everyone is screaming.

But they're already dead. They're dead, but they're screaming like a chorus. Or they were never alive in the first place."

"What else do you see?"

"A word."

"What does it say?"

"I can't tell. It's in green letters. Script. But the script is —it flows. I think it's in English but I can't read it. It's English. Now it's alien script. It keeps flashing back and forth, but I can't read it."

"Never mind. Break."

Starla had been straining up from her prone position. Now she relaxed. Beethoven came on the sound system.

In a soothing voice, Mark said, "Relax. We'll retarget in a minute. Just relax."

"I want to go to forward search mode now."

"Give yourself time . . . there's no rush."

"I think I'm getting something."

"What?"

"I see a Hydra."

"It's probably overlay."

"It's gone now. Maybe it *was* overlay."

"Hold on," Mark said. "I'm going to drop into Alpha myself."

A silence filled the room.

"Mark, are you here?"

"I'm scanning for Remote Vipers. Just a minute."

Starla shut her eyes.

A moment later, Mark said: "I thought I had a flash of something. A presence. I have the impression of the color green. Could have been a Remote Viper, but his energy signature is gone now."

"Try to stay in Alpha in case he comes back," Starla directed.

"Okay. Are you ready for forward search mode?"

"I'm in my Zone."

"Starla, using the incident today as a jump-off point, I want you to tell me what's coming up in the future."

Starla didn't answer. She was floating on the threshold of sleep, drifting in and out of Theta, hovering close to the deeper Delta state where the mind shuts down and sleep overtakes the brain. It was a tricky dance. The lower you went, the flatter your brainwaves became. Too flat, and the brain succumbed to sleep. The brain was programmed to shut down in Delta, but for the psychic who could stay awake in Delta, the rewards were tremendous.

Watching the monitor, Mark let her drift. If she found a comfortable zone, the information she perceived could be invaluable.

Minutes passed. Starla began murmuring. It was a subvocal susurration. Mark dialed up the volume so the tape would capture every soft syllable.

"I see . . . airliner. It's struggling to fly. Now it turns. One wing goes up. The other drops. Like a wounded seagull. It's in a death spiral. Above a city. It's about to crash. Now it is crashing. The plane hits the center of the city. I see a fireball rising into the sky. It looks like a mushroom cloud, but the colors are strange. Cool, not hot. It's boiling high in the sky."

"Can you make out the type of plane?"

"A 757. Or 767. Something like that."

"When does this take place?"

"Tomorrow, I think. Time is so hard to do. It's transparent. I can see right through it. But I think it's tomorrow."

"Did you see the plane livery, Starla?"

"Green. It was green. Very green. Emerald green. A Hydra green."

"Go back. Go back to the time before the plane augers in. Read the name on the hull."

"I . . . I can't. It's just letters. Script letters."

"Try. Focus on the first initial."

"It . . . it's like an S. Now an E."

"Is it an E or an S?"

"It's both."

"Second letter," Mark prompted.

"I can't read it."

"Go on. Find a letter or group you can read."

Starla was struggling now. "I . . . see . . . P Y R E."

"Pyre?"

"Yes. It's very clear. No, now it's gone. It's turning into script. It was so clear a minute ago. Now it's unreadable."

"But you're certain you saw P Y R E?"

"Yes. Positive. But only for a minute. It kept switching. Back and forth. Back and forth."

"Starla, did you have the feeling that the jet augering into that city was deliberately crashed?"

"Don't lead me."

"Sorry. Let me rephrase: What are your impressions of the accident's—There I go again. I mean, the event's cause?"

"Revenge."

"Revenge?"

"Yes. That's all I feel. Revenge."

"Were there people on board?"

"Yes."

"Can you identify the city? Do you recognize the skyline?"

"It's on fire now. There's smoke everywhere. It's very hard to make out. . . ."

"Go back to just before the crash. Can you do that?"

A full minute passed. Then Starla spoke: "The city has domes. Towers. No, minarets. I think it's a Middle Eastern city. But I don't recognize it."

"You're confident it's Middle Eastern?"

"Yes. Highly confident . . ."

"Okay. Good. My instruments indicate you're drifting downward, Starla."

"Tired . . . Very tired. . . ."

"Do what you feel you have to. Go deeper into Delta if you need to sleep."

"Sleep. . . ."

"Sleep . . ."

Nick Fury snapped off the audio tape. Swiveling in his chair in the conference room, he inserted a fresh cigar in his mouth and bit off the end with his teeth. A custom lighter ignited the end. He was himself once again. The only difference between now and the last time Starla had spoken to him was his unusually close shave.

After taking a few deep puffs, Fury said, "Sounds like you had an interesting little nap."

"I'm exhausted," Starla admitted. She looked drained. Even her eyes were paler than normal.

"But what we have here is a whole lot of chaff."

"What do you mean?"

"Number one, we're done processing all those bodies up there. Every one of them turns out to be a Life Model Decoy. No trace of any live pilot or copilot. Intel assures me that the pilots were incinerated with the rest, and they were LMDs."

"Did you compare the passenger and crew lists against the number of bodies recovered?" Starla countered.

"Good point. They're working on that now."

Starla frowned. "Shouldn't you have it by now?"

"I'll get to that part later. Number Two," Fury continued. "You've got the pilots speaking a foreign language. Both of 'em . Not likely with a domestic airline like Vinegaroon. They're a regional carrier operating out of Phoenix."

"It's not impossible," Starla said stubbornly.

"True. But it ain't likely, either."

"You should check the port outboard turbine for an explosive charge."

"It was the port bottle that came in flaming. I'll give you that," Fury admitted. "And another thing. You sensed

Hydra. We can be pretty sure that Hydra is behind this. They're the only outfit other than S.H.I.E.L.D. that possesses LMD technology."

"I think I was picking up a Remote Viper, Colonel."

"But you're not sure, are you?"

"It's difficult to tell what you've seen floating above the threshold of waking consciousness," Starla admitted.

Fury tapped the tape recorder. "Then there's that name you think you picked up: E or S P Y R E. Sounds like Empire, with some letters missing or scrambled."

Starla said, "I can't vouch for that. But the letters were a Hydra green."

"Empire's livery is kinda that color," Fury mused. "But you're not positive?"

"The human mind processes psychic information in highly individualistic ways. Just as no two singers sound alike, and painters have distinctive styles, psychic ability manifests itself in ways that might seem quirky. I get most of my information visually, but I still couldn't see the name clearly. Half the time it didn't seem to be English script. As for the letters P Y R E, I saw that clearly. I'm certain of that."

"You know, I read your book. Seems to me somewhere in it you wrote about how the mind can mix up pictures and words."

"It's true."

"You saw a jet dive-bomb a city. Then you saw the word *pyre,* as in funeral pyre. Think that might explain it?"

"I can't say that it doesn't," Starla admitted.

"So, all in all, we're not any further along than we were before you remote viewed the situation? Is that right?"

"We know that tomorrow an airliner is going to crash into a major Middle Eastern city."

Fury shook his grizzled head. "No. We won't know that until it happens. And our job is to see that it doesn't happen. But just in case, I'm putting field agents onto every

flight that originates or lands in a Middle Eastern City tomorrow. We'll see how clairvoyant you really are."

"I've been uncannily right in the past," Starla insisted.

"And way, way off," Fury said flatly.

"It's the nature of the work, Colonel. Like a meteorolo-
gist, I'm trying to read dynamic energies. You don't fire
the weatherman when his forecasts go awry."

"But if you get caught in a blizzard he didn't see coming, you're just as stuck," Fury growled. "Get back to
work. I want you to focus on Remote Viper Countermeasures. This belongs to Intel and Operations, now."

"Yes, sir." Starla rose to go. "Colonel?"

"Yeah?"

"I'd like to have some of my people on those flights."

"You got 'em. Let's hope we don't lose any of 'em."

"Was that a prediction, Colonel?"

"You tell me."

Starla closed her eyes. "You get hunches a lot."

"Sure."

"And you act on them."

"True."

"And your hunches are usually correct."

Fury shrugged. "So what?"

"What do you think a hunch really is?"

"A hunch. A gut feeling. A—" Fury groped for a better
way to express it. None came.

"What you call a hunch is an intuitive feeling, or flash
insight. Perhaps we should sit you down in the Re-Vue
chamber sometime to see how well you do?"

"Special Powers Director Spacek," Fury barked. "Dismissed."

Starla walked out wearing a thin smile. Nick Fury was
human, after all. . . .

NEED

"I **NEED** VOLUNTEERS,"
Starla Spacek was saying.

The scene was the Re-Vue deck area in the Helicarrier's bow keel. Before her stood assembled the core of S.H.I.E.L.D.'s new Special Powers unit. They wore standard S.H.I.E.L.D. midnight blue kevlar suits, gold eagles against purple insignia patches on their right shoulders. Their holsters and straps were an identical purple. Purple, the color of royalty, spirtuality and, Starla recalled ruefully—madness.

Hands began going up.

"I'll go."

"Count me in, too."

"Make that three."

"That's enough," Starla said. "The rest of you will remain here for scanning and countermeasure operations. The three volunteers will be paired with three anchor telepaths here. Pair up according to your ability to connect psychically. That way no one's out there without a net."

One of the volunteers asked, "We'll be beacons?"

Starla nodded. "You'll operate as human beacons only as far as staying linked to Special Powers. Otherwise, you are on your own. You will use any and all psi skills at your disposal to preserve your life and the lives of any threatened persons. Understood?"

"Understood," they sang in unison.

"But first, we're going hunting for Remote Vipers. I picked up a vibe earlier. High confidence Hydra impression. Let's see if he or she is still active."

On a tabletop monitor, Starla punched up a schematic of the Helicarrier interior. She tapped keys. The system started isolating sections and displaying them in exploded fashion.

"I've divided the ship into localized search areas," she explained. "We'll break into teams of two, sweeping psychically through the ship. If you pick up anything—anything, no matter how thin—I want to know about it instantly."

They paired off. Starla selected one of the volunteers, saying, "SPO Yost. You're with me."

A black-haired woman with delicate features said, "Yes, sir." She stood less than five feet, four inches tall, and couldn't have weighed more than 100 pounds. As delicate as she seemed, a quiet strength infused her pale face. It showed in her hauntingly pale blue eyes.

"We're going to sweep the flight deck. Grab a flight helmet and let's go."

They took a lift to the flight deck. Topside, a security officer challenged them, looking quizzically at their purple uniform accoutrements.

"Flight deck is off-limits to all but cleanup teams," he said coldly.

"Special Powers," Starla snapped. "Get used to our colors. We're sweeping the flight deck for Hydra extrasensors."

The security officer hesitated. Starla fixed him with her green-gray eyes. "Three nights ago you had a dream. In the dream, you were flying a kite. The kite was red. Lightning hit it and it caught fire. It fell onto your childhood house, setting the roof afire."

"How the hell did you know that?" the man blurted.

"You're an open book. Now kindly make way."

The security agent got out of the way. He was turning red, as if Starla had caught him in the shower.

"You picked up his dream?" SPO Yost breathed. "You're good!"

"If that security guy had any idea how to interpret his dreams, he might have warned us about the crash," Starla whispered. "That was a precognitive dream."

Activity on the flight deck had shifted since the morning. It was cold now. A bitter late December cold. But the high sun took the edge off the wind. The remaining operational rotors tended to redirect airflow away from the Helicarrier as well. The deck itself was heated, so it was tolerable.

A helicopter skycrane was lifting the main part of the airliner off the deck. Another hovered off the port, ready to come in to take another.

Machines like a cross between street sweepers and Zamboni ice smoothers were scurrying here and there, sucking up loose debris for later analysis.

Over on the damaged middle rotor, gray-suited Technos were busy at access ports, troubleshooting the electronics.

"We'll start at this end," Starla decided. "Just walk with me. Close your eyes if it's more comfortable. We'll take turns sweeping for impressions so we don't get tired. What's your first name and specialty?"

"Janine. Psychometry. Call me Jan."

"Feel free to help yourself to any loose debris, Jan. I'll take point."

Starla started down the deck. She dropped the sunvisor of her helmet. It gave her something to bounce off. That way she could keep her eyes open but block enough of the real world so that any mind's-eye images would be clearer.

She hadn't walked three feet when an image popped into her mind. A black scorpion. She threw it away. It felt like random Beta chatter.

"Getting anything?" Starla asked.

"He's alive!" Janine hissed.

"Who?" But the answer jumped into her head. "Quiet. Don't repeat it. Don't even say it out loud," Starla admonished.

"I'm sensing you-know-who on board," Janine undertoned. "If I picked him up, Hydra can, too. Someone should tell Intel there are no secrets anymore."

"They're still stuck in left-brain Beta thinking," Starla said off-handedly.

The second skycrane was settling over what was left of the downed Vinegaroon airliner. Huge straps were slung under the stabilizers and tail assembly, while dangling cable eyes were lowered, then riveted to the hull.

Janine's boot kicked at something. It went skittering along the deck. She found it with her eyes. A sheared bolt.

Retrieving it, she wrapped the fingers of her right hand around the bolt. She closed her eyes.

Starla waited.

Janine frowned. "Strange . . ."

"What?"

"I'm getting a scorpion."

"I got that, too! I thought it was junk."

"My scorpion is black. It's not moving. Like it's a drawing or emblem."

Starla puckered her brows together. "So was mine."

Opening her eyes, Janine said, "If we both got it, it means something."

They resumed walking. The skycrane, its rotors beating a clattery tattoo, began hoisting the last big section of jet airliner off the deck. Metal creaked audibly. One stabilizer let go, and the section began to twist.

The section swung wildly, then settled. The skycrane tentatively resumed lifting.

As she swept down the deck, moving toward open air, the tail section came into view. It read: VINEGAROON AIR.

Starla tracked it with her eyes. "I think I found our scorpion."

"Really?"

"Look. Vinegaroon Air. A vinegaroon is another name for a whipscorpion."

"Mystery solved, then." Janine's pale eyes narrowed. "Director Spacek, I'm getting something from the area where the plane came to rest."

"Follow your feeling," Starla directed.

The feeling took them to the very edge of the Helicarrier deck. They walked up to the lip and looked down. A thick nylon cable mesh fluttered in the wind to catch falling objects or personnel. It was a long way down to the churning cold Atlantic below.

Starla asked, "What are you feeling?"

"I think the flight crew went overboard."

"If they did, they should have landed in the net. I don't see anything."

Janine insisted, "That's what I'm sensing."

"Well, they're not there. Better not mention this in our report. Special Director Skindarian will jump on any unsupportable PSINTEL like a pit bull."

A jolt like an electric shock caused Starla's spine to stiffen erect. "I'm getting something. Something going on belowdeck."

Her belt com link chirped and she grabbed it up.

It was Mark Youngblood. *"We have a sensing on the observation deck."*

"On our way," Starla snapped. "They have something."

They took the nearest lift, grabbed a passing people mover. It whisked them through the stainless steel bowels of the Helicarrier and unloaded them in the observation lounge.

A vast bank of Plexiglas windows gave a bow's-eye view of the Atlantic Ocean. A clutch of SPOs stood looking out at the clouds. At their approach, one turned.

"We were sweeping this area when we spotted something weird," SPO Youngblood reported.

"What's that?"

"A pair of eyes. Just eyes. They were floating outside this window."

"Did you sense anything else?"

"That was the weirdest part. I saw the eyes. Literally saw them. They weren't a clairvoyant image. They closed, then disappeared. But I sensed no mind behind them."

"Let me get this straight. You didn't sense a presence. You just saw disembodied human eyes?"

Mark nodded. "They were dark brown. Almost black."

"That doesn't make sense. What you're saying doesn't conform to any verified psychic phenomena."

"Unless Hydra has figured out a way to shield their extrasensors from psychic detection."

Starla shook her tawny head stubbornly. "It doesn't fit."

Something touched the Plexiglas. It made a sound like a bony finger tapping. Once. Then again.

"What is that sound?" Starla wondered.

They gathered around the pane. The sound came again.

Mark said, "I saw something. There! A cord. See it?"

"Where?" Janine Yost blurted. "I don't see anything."

The tap came again and they perceived the thing peripherally.

It looked like a cord—but it was transparent, as if manufactured from clear mylar or spun glass.

Starla narrowed her clairvoyant eyes. "Hydra Remote Vipers don't need ropes. There was someone out there. Let's find out where that cord is anchored. Come on."

They raced for the nearest lift. Starla began chanting into her communicator.

"Dum Dum Dugan. Special Powers Director Spacek reporting. My people have detected a breech in external security. Meet us on the flight deck. Bow section."

"Acknowledged," came Dum Dum's gruff voice.

The cord was anchored by a folding grappling hook to the external bow nets, where it would go unnoticed except under close inspection.

Dum Dum clambered down onto the net, a feat that made some of the Special Powers recruits shudder visibly. The big Irishman sat down and gathered up the cord. It came easily.

Unhooking the grapnel, he tossed the rig upward. Starla caught it, handing it to Jan Yost.

"What are you getting?" she asked.

"Give me a minute to clear my mind."

Dum Dum clambered topside and saw Janine holding the rig with her eyes closed in expectant concentration. He cocked a curious eyebrow at SPD Spacek.

"Psychometry," Starla explained. "It's the ability to gain psychic impressions from physical artifacts. She's trying to visualize the person who touched it last."

"That was me," Dum Dum pointed out dryly.

"I *am* getting a big red mustache," Janine said unhappily.

"Can you push your perceptions past him to the previous person?" Starla asked.

"One sec." Janine's face frowned and relaxed by turns. "I just see the scorpion."

"What scorpion?" Dum Dum wanted to know.

"It's the symbol of Vinegaroon Air," Starla supplied. "We both picked it up before." She snapped her fingers. "I wonder. Could a saboteur have gotten off the jet alive?"

"There were only LMDs on board," Dum Dum reminded.

"That could explain why I'm getting a scorpion and not impressions of a human being," Janine admitted.

A jet-black Humvee raced down the length of the flight deck, braking to a stop nearby. The driver's door opened up and a redheaded field agent Starla did not recognize strode up to them.

"He's with me," Dum Dum said.

The agent nodded wordlessly. His name tag read SAVAGE.

Dum Dum conferred with him. "They found this grapple and stealth cord hanging down. No sign of who planted it there."

"My team spotted a pair of eyes outside the observation deck," Starla added. "But they received no useful impressions."

"Could be an LMD on the loose," Dum Dum told the other.

Field Agent Savage nodded wordlessly.

"A Life Model Decoy probably wouldn't read as a human being," Starla said. "Although I know of no research done in this area."

Savage leaned into Dum Dum's ear and whispered a few words. Then he got into his Hummer and drove back toward the tower island on the starboard side of the carrier.

"Who was he?" Starla asked. "I feel as if I've met him."

"Agent Savage. He's going to look into your idea. All of you—come with me."

They followed Dugan to the lift.

"Where are you taking us?" Starla wondered aloud.

"To the security processing area. In another minute, klaxons are going to sound off to beat the band. Everybody's going to have to go through what you people are about to go though."

"I don't like the sound of that," Janine told Starla.

"Welcome to S.H.I.E.L.D.," Starla said archly.

Then the klaxons went off. It sounded like the Helicarrier was going to combat-ready status.

It was not as bad as it threatened. They were walked through a battery of ID checks, from computerized fingerprint and retina scans, to a powerful High Resolution

Functional Magnetic Resonance Imagery chamber designed to display their internal organs on an oversized monitor.

"Congratulations," Dum Dum told Starla when she emerged on the other end of the MRI. "You pass the test."

"What test?"

"You're not an android."

"I see," Starla said. "Everyone on the ship is going to go through this. What happens if you don't uncover the LMD?"

"You're going to have to explain why your people couldn't detect the intruder's presence."

"Damn."

IT WAS # LATE EVENING
by the time the last critical maintainence people had
been processed through.

Starla Spacek was with her Special Powers team when
word reached her. Dum Dum Dugan conveyed it.

"All personnel accounted for. There's no LMD on board
that we can find. And believe me, if there was one, we
would have smoked it out."

"I see."

"But there's some interestin' news for you."

"Yes?"

"We found the missin' flight crew. And they're not LMDs.
They're alive. Or leastways they *were* alive."

"I knew it," Starla said.

"Better come down to the infirmary."

"Coming." Starla turned to her team. "We have a break.
The pilots turned up, and they weren't LMDs. I'm on my
way to check it out."

"We're getting ready to ship out on assignment," Janine
said.

"Good luck, people." Starla took Janine aside. "You and
I worked well together. I feel we have a connection. I'm
going to be your contact here."

"Thanks. I won't let you down."

"I know you won't."

But as Janine left, Starla felt a twinge of . . . something.
She shook off the vague feeling. It was probably nerves.

Understandable. This was the first time she had ordered people into the field.

Dum Dum was almost smiling when Starla turned up in the infirmary. Starla sensed that might be a bad omen. He was looking over a half-covered corpse with FA Savage.

"Take a look at this," Dum Dum invited.

Starla hesitated. Steeling herself, she obeyed.

The body on the autopsy table had been through a lot. But it was human.

Dum Dum explained, "We found this one and what we think is the copilot in the incinerator processing bay belowdecks."

"What were they doing down there?"

"That's where we were storin' the LMDs off the jetliner until we figured out what to do with them."

"How did two live people get through analysis?"

"They didn't," Agent Savage said. His voice was hoarse. A smoker's voice. "We figure they were dumped there by your invisible man."

Dum Dum added, "We figure it this way: the bodies landed in the safety nets just like you said. They musta rolled down out of sight. Nobody noticed them. The Hydra—or whoever he was—went up there to retrieve them. That's why you caught him danglin' outside the observation area. He was lookin' up at the netting. It was risky, but with all the activity topside, it was the best way to go about it."

"Why not dump them overboard?"

"Our sensors would have detected a fallin' body, if not the splash. Guess he couldn't risk it."

"How could he lug two dead men from the flight deck all the way to the lowest deck area without being seen?"

"That's the jackpot question," Savage muttered.

"Here's somethin' else you oughta know," Dum Dum offered. Lifting the dead man's right hand, he exposed the inner wrist. There, against the dark skin, was the splayed outline of a scorpion.

Starla frowned. "Tattoo?"

Savage nodded. "Looks like one. Not ordinary ink, but it's a tattoo."

"It's just like the image I saw in my mind's eye," Starla said, brightening.

"The copilot had one just like it," Savage said. "But you don't want to look at him."

A flash image intruded on Starla's mind. She shook it off.

Starla smiled broadly. "I guess this goes a long way to validating Special Powers' operational worthiness."

"Not exactly," growled Agent Savage. His voice took on a harsher, more gravelly tone.

Starla blinked. "I don't understand."

"How reliable a telepath can you be when you don't recognize your boss when he's standing right next to you?"

Starla blinked in disbelief. "Colonel Fury?"

"Savage" nodded curtly. "This is my walking-around disguise."

"I'm sure I would have recognized you if I wasn't so preoccupied with—"

"Stow it. I ain't issuing demerits. It's just my little way of testing you, that's all."

Starla eyed him narrowly. "I *did* feel there was something odd about you."

"Hindsight is 20-20," Fury muttered. "Now forget that. We gotta start adding up what we have here. I don't think that spy your people detected is an LMD."

"It *had* to have been."

"Call it a hunch."

"Logic says that my people would have sensed him before they spotted those . . . eyes."

"Logic ain't got nothing to do with it. And your people ain't perfect. You just told us so. My gut says we're looking for a living human being. One that's either infiltrated our crew or has found himself a nice little hideyhole that defeats our best detection systems."

"It's possible," Starla allowed.

"Possible nothing. It's all we have left. I want this intruder found. Put all your people on it. Consider this the acid test of Special Powers."

"My people were the first to ferret this person out."

"I'll give you that. That's why I'm putting it in your hands."

"What about these scorpion tattoos? This doesn't seem to point to Hydra, does it?"

"Hydra's all it could be," Dum Dum said. But he didn't sound as sure of himself as he should have.

"I'm on it," Starla said. She noticed Fury was looking at the dead pilot's face. A flash image of the man's dark mustache touched her mind. She saw it for only a brief second, but understood she was seeing it through Fury's perceptions.

"That mustache is familiar to you," Starla suggested.

Fury started. "Yeah. How'd you know that?"

Starla only smiled knowingly. She went on, going with her impressions. "You saw a mustache just like it this morning. The pilot of the Empire Airlines plane."

"Lots of people wear mustaches," Dum Dum said, giving his own a stubborn twist.

Starla pressed on. "Did the copilot have one, too?"

"Yeah," Fury admitted.

"What about this man?"

"Can't tell. His face is just raw bone."

"I think if you look, you'll discover the Empire pilots also wore scorpion tattoos on their wrists."

"Is that a hunch, a guess, or what?" Fury challenged.

"Maybe it's all three," said Starla. "Now watch me find your spy for you."

Fury nodded. "Go to it."

"There's one thing. A favor."

"Spit it out."

"I'd like one of my people to infiltrate Empire Airlines' corporate base."

"Anyone special you got in mind?"

Starla smiled. "All my people are special, Colonel."

"I think I know who you want to send," Fury said slowly. "And her initials are S.S. Find our spy and I'll consider it. Now get cracking."

Locating Mark Youngblood, Starla led him to the Re-Vue chamber.

"Up for an open search?"

"Are you? You pushed yourself pretty hard today."

"I know. That's why you're doing the searching."

Mark shook his head. "I'm not that good. I get gestalts. Outlines. Impressions. And a ton of analytical overlay."

"Then you need the practice. Jump on the platform and we'll see where you can go."

Starla took the console and rolled tape while she looked over the EEG as Mark lowered his waking mind into a steady rhythmic Alpha state.

"Tell me when you're in your Zone," she said over the loudspeaker.

Mark's voice dropped a full octave. "I think I'm there already."

"Go to open search. Sweep the Helicarrier. Find anything unusual, anything at all."

Mark started off speaking disjointedly. Starla frowned. She could see he needed a lot of RV practice.

"I'm picking up a man . . ."

"What color are his eyes?"

"Glassy."

Starla wanted to ask, "Like an LMD?" But that would be leading. Instead, she said: "Specify."

"They're brown. Very dark, almost black-brown. But I see glass in front of them."

"What else?"

"I think the eyes are closed."

"How can you see the color of his eyes when they're closed?"

"I just do. I think it's a secondary impression. The sense of glass reads as primary."

Starla nodded to herself. "All right. Go on."

"I have the further impression he's asleep. But he's wearing a helmet of some kind."

"What kind of helmet?"

"It's big. Huge. He has trouble lying comfortably it's so big."

"Describe this helmet in detail, please."

"I can't. It's too . . . complicated."

"How are your drawing skills in Alpha?"

"Rudimentary," Mark admitted.

"Try sketching what you see."

Every platform bed came equipped with a tablet of paper and a pencil. Many remote viewers preferred to sketch what they saw. It helped resolve the difficult images. Starla moved past that primitive form of RV long, long ago at CIA.

Mark was speaking. "It's oblong. There's an antenna array on top. It's very complicated. Reminds me of computer symbology. Could be overlay, though. I don't know if I can replicate it."

"Do your best," Starla encouraged.

A minute later, Mark said, "I think that's it."

"Okay. Now try to touch this man's mind."

"I . . . I can't."

"Why not?"

"I don't sense a mind. None at all. It's creepy. There's just nothing there."

"Is he an LMD?"

"I can't tell. I just perceive no mental processes, no emotions, no feeling. He's asleep, I think."

"Try to read his dreams."

"That's beyond me, Starla. I'm lucky to get surface impressions."

"Okay. Visualize for me his environment."

"He's in a narrow room. Typical S.H.I.E.L.D. personal quarters. There's a cot. A small desk and monitor. I see nothing unusual or distinguishing."

"Can you move outside the room? See where he's situated?"

"Yes—Oh, damnit!"

"What?"

"I'm outside the ship. I moved out over the ocean."

"Come back. Try to relocate."

"I . . . I can't. I'm fading."

On the EEG, stress-induced Beta waves overtook the Alpha rhythm, indicating Mark was coming out of his Alpha state.

"Okay. Break."

Starla shut off the tape, and rushed down to the platform.

She looked at the drawing. It was wilder than she expected. The helmet was larger, more cumbersome than an old-fashioned cast-iron diving helmet—almost like the head of a futuristic robot. There was an oblong face plate. Jutting from the top, twin intersecting metallic circles formed a dual antenna loop.

Mark came off the bed and looked at it. "That's pretty much what I visualized," he said.

Starla pointed to three sketchy symbols emblazoned on the helmet's forehead. "What are these?"

"Letters. I couldn't read them clearly, so I just roughed them in."

"Close your eyes. Try to recall them."

Mark obeyed. His dark brow corrugated.

"They're coming back to me," he said. "But they look like stickmen, not letters."

"Take them one at a time," Starla said. "I know how tough alphanumeric resolution can be."

"Okay. First letter . . . looks like an E or an F."

"Do better."

"E. Definitely an E."

Starla turned the first sketchy letter into an E. "Second letter."

"Z. Definitely Z."

"Great. You're doing great. Last letter."

Mark frowned. "B or P. I can't differentiate. Damn. This is like reading an eye chart without my contacts on."

"Okay. E Z B or P. Could this be a company logo, I wonder?"

"Search me. Maybe it's the initials of the group our bad guy belongs to."

"Hmmm. Well, if it's A.I.M., your clairvoyance needs a lot of work. But we can figure this out later. Now, how big was this guy's head in relation to the helmet?" Starla asked.

Taking the pencil, Mark sketched in the oval representing a face behind the face plate.

Starla made an unhappy face. "This helmet must weigh a *ton*. And how could he sleep with his head inside something this cumbersome?"

"He lay flat on his back. I don't think he can move without taking it off."

"I've never seen a helmet like this."

When the drawing was laid before Nick Fury, he said, "I know exactly what this is. What you've got here is an old-style S.H.I.E.L.D. anti-ESP scramble rig. In the early days of the old S.H.I.E.L.D. ESP Division, we used to wear them to protect against unauthorized mindreading." Fury tapped the sheet. "These letters here are wrong. They should read ESP."

Starla's face fell. "Did they work?"

"Yeah. Don't ask me how, though."

"Is there anyone on board who understands the theory?"

"Doubt it. But we might have a few of the old helmets in storage. Why?"

"Number one, I'm very interested in the operating principle. And two, maybe I can use one to locate our spy."

"Dum Dum, give the little lady what she wants."

"A pleasure."

The scramble helmet was lighter than Starla imagined it could be. Dum Dum placed the light-weight aluminum shell on her head and adjusted the straps.

"Just say when," Dum Dum said, "and I'll fire it up for you."

"Does this thing come with a manual?" Starla asked. Her voice echoed in the padded interior. A button mike picked up her words and piped them out. The helmet was completely insulated against external sounds.

"Right here," Fury said.

Starla tried flipping through it, but the bulky headgear kept interfering. She had no peripheral vision, and looking up and down was impossible. Her entire head felt like it was encased in a neck brace.

Dum Dum lifted the spiral-bound operating manual into her field of vision and began turning the pages for her convenience.

"According to this," Starla said, "the helmet shell is a Faraday cage—copper mesh and other EM shielding. There's no way this could block psi energy. It's impossible."

"Keep reading," Fury suggested.

Dum Dum found the appropriate page. "Here."

Starla read. "My God. Turn this on for me."

Dum Dum snapped the switch.

White noise filled Starla's ears. It shifted from ear to ear, modulating and remodulating constantly. After a minute, she felt herself splitting in two.

It happened too fast. There was no time to react. Starla was aware of herself standing in one place, her head encased in the absurdly huge but claustrophobic helmet.

At the same time, her perceptions shifted to another place entirely.

Dimly, as if it were coming from far, far away, the helmet pickup mike relayed Nick Fury's gravelly voice saying, "Grab her, you old walrus. Can't you see she's out on her feet?"

STARLA

"I BILOCATED," Spacek was saying.

"Say that again?" Fury growled.

She closed her unusually green eyes. "It happened to me once before. When I first broke through psychically."

"Better spell it out for us, lady," Fury suggested.

Starla took a deep breath, then a sip of offered water. She was lying on a couch in the Infirmary. She sat up.

"I think you all know what an Out of Body Experience is."

"Sure. Dr. Strange is supposed to do it. Calls it astral projecting, or something like that."

"That's the old-fashioned term for it. An OBE is understood to be a purely Theta function. The spirit, or consciousness, or whatever you like to call it, leaves the physical shell of the body and roams the material world at will. It's very different from remote viewing. During an OBE, the body is dormant and unaware of itself and its surroundings. The consciousness resides in the—um—spiritual vehicle."

Fury and Dum Dum looked dubious.

"In remote viewing," Starla continued, "the spirit remains in the body. Only the perceptions travel. At the same time, the viewer maintains self-awareness, awareness of surroundings, as well as speech and some motor function. This enables us to speak and relay our clairvoyant impressions when we go non-local."

"We're with you so far," Fury said.

"At least *one* of us is," Dum Dum echoed.

"Bilocation is a rare phenomenon that's not quite astral travel, and not exactly remote viewing. What I experienced a moment ago when the scramble helmet kicked in, threw me into a rare, almost unexplored brainwave state—Gamma. It stimulated my brain hemispheres in such a way that I bilocated. I was aware of standing there with you, but I was simultaneously cognizant of being someplace else."

"That's a little hard to swallow," Fury said, doubtfully.

"Bear with me. I understand why the scramble helmets worked back then. And why they had to be abandoned."

"Go on."

"The Faraday shielding was useless. A layer of protection built in because the old S.H.I.E.L.D. Technos wrongly assumed that ESP was a signal phenomenon that could be blocked. But the helmet also generated two separate frequencies, one designed to stimulate the right hemisphere of the brain, the other the left. That threw the brain off balance, kept the mind from focusing on one thought for too long. That's what made it effective against mind reading and other psychic eavesdropping. The problem was the white noise signals had a destabilizing effect on the right and left hemispheres, essentially throwing them in and out of synchronization."

"I think I follow," Fury admitted.

"By accident, S.H.I.E.L.D. had stumbled across a primitive form of hemisphere synchronization, a technique used to induce altered states of consciousness. One of the best uses of hemi-sych is to facilitate remote viewing or OBEs with people whose psychic development is so low artificial techniques are needed get their minds operating on that level."

"With you so far," Fury said.

Dum Dum looked puzzled. He cocked his trademark

Bowler hat forward at a comical angle, then shifted it back.

Starla continued, "In this case, the competing signals created a kind of hemispheric desynchronization. The effect it had on me—purely by accident—was to throw me into an extreme disassociative state. Since it was induced, I couldn't handle it and blacked out."

"So where were you?" Fury asked.

"In the Re-Vue chamber. And I had an overwhelming feeling of dread."

"Dread of what?"

"I felt as if something terrible was going to happen."

"You're talkin' about a premonition, ain't ya?" Dum Dum muttered.

Starla's face twisted. "I don't know. But the feeling was overpowering. I've felt such things before." Her voice went quiet. "They usually come true."

Fury turned to Dugan. "Dum Dum, put a security detail to watching the Re-Vue chamber round the clock. It's the only one we have on board. The way this is shaping up, we can't afford to lose it now."

"And for another reason," Starla said, getting to her feet.

"What's that?" Fury asked.

"I now understand why that infiltrator was lying in bed wearing that helmet."

"Yeah? Why's that?"

"He wasn't sleeping. He was using the scramble helmet to remote view us, while blocking our ability to read his mind—and identity."

Fury's single brown eye went sharp. "Are you saying there's a remote viewer on board?"

"Definitely. We never suspected it, because logically Hydra wouldn't need to place a Remote Viper physically on board the Helicarrier. There's no operational advantage. Remote perceptions are not bound by the known laws of the physical universe. Why risk planting an agent who could be physically captured?"

"Maybe I can explain that one," Dum Dum muttered.

They all looked at him.

"I ain't a big one on all this gee-whiz spook stuff, but I do know that Hydra Remote Vipers use coordinates to get their fixes. Right?"

"Correct," said Starla.

"And the Helicarrier is mobile."

Starla's eyes widened. "I hadn't thought of that. To remote view the Helicarrier consistently, it would have to be tracked in real time and space and her coordinates fed to the viewer."

"But if the viewer was on board," Fury growled, "there'd be no need for any of that."

"And it would be almost perfect cover," Starla added. "Who would think of looking for a Remote Viper locally, among the crew?"

Fury lifted a heavy-knuckled fist. "Well, this Hydra's number is up. We know he spent the last few hours in his bunk. All we gotta do is find him, and flush him out."

"I'll get on it right away," Starla promised.

"You do that," Fury said. "Meanwhile Security will do its part. Between us maybe we'll have this guy's green hide by midnight."

The minute Starla Spacek lay down in the Re-Vue couch, her blood ran cold.

A chilly trickle of sweat ran down the gully of her spine. Her heart started pounding.

"What's going on?" SPO Mark Youngblood asked from the booth.

"I feel like I'm suffocating."

"My instruments are going wild. Heartbeat. Respiration. Galvanic skin response. Everything. Try to calm down. You're in Beta, and the peaks are pretty ragged."

"Give me a second."

Starla centered herself within herself. It was always easier to go into Beta from Alpha, but not the reverse. She was picking up her premonition of danger. It had returned. Very strong now. Almost imminent. But there was no way to verify that. It was all she could do to fight off the rising waves of fear that seemed like a living thing.

"I'm still reading you in the Beta range, Starla."

"I can't find my Zone. Damn. I can't find my Zone."

"Take your time."

"You don't understand. They're depending on me. I have to find this Remote Viper before Beta Security does. This is the acid test."

"You're only putting pressure on yourself. Making it harder."

Starla tried again. The ceiling above was a soft azure. It reminded her of the perfect summer sky. She had insisted upon this precise shade of blue because color theorists had determined it was the perfect hue to induce an Alpha state. If she could only get to Alpha. If she could only fight down this growing fear, this overwhelming sense of danger . . .

"I don't suppose you have any Saint-John's-Wort on you," Starla muttered.

"No—why?"

"It helps me flatten my brainwaves into Alpha rhythms."

Mark grunted. "From the look of these waves, you'll need a sledge hammer."

Starla shifted to tantric breathing. In, out. In, out. Relax. Relax, she told herself. There's no rush. You'll get there. . . .

"Try to visualize a waterfall," Mark urged. "A waterfall spilling down a cliffside, giving off soothing negative ions."

Starla tried. The waterfall filled her thoughts. It was cool and free flowing. It was the most beautiful waterfall she had ever seen.

Until it exploded into a fireball of red-orange hell.

"Noooo!"

Coming off the platform, Starla caught her breath.

"What's wrong?" Mark demanded.

"I got fire. Horrible fire. I could feel the heat on my skin. I can almost smell the burning . . ."

Mark looked surprised. "You can *feel* remote events psychically . . . ?"

"Believe me, this is one time I wish I couldn't," Starla said thickly. Something caused her head to jerk erect. Her eyes tracked the room. The door was designed to fit flush with the curved inner chamber walls. There was a single port, but it was made of one-way glass, so that an observer could look inside without destroying the blue serenity of the experience.

Starla's eyes went to the bluish mirrored surface. She sensed eyes in the other side. Malevolent eyes.

"Mark . . ."

Without warning, the door opened. Just a crack.

Shiny and cold, something rolled in along the blue carpeting. It made faint sounds, like a serpent slithering through wet grass.

"Evacuate!" Starla screamed. "Now!"

Then the pure blue interior exploded into a paroxysm of reddish-orange hell and Starla experienced a flash of déjà vu instantly obliterated by the rush and roar of the rolling inferno sweeping inexorably toward her.

Over the decades, the Strategic Hazard, Intelligence, Espionage, and Logistics Directorate had sprawled across the globe, establishing regional headquarters in many friendly capitals. And in a few cases, unfriendly ones.

It had not been planned that way. When set up, S.H.I.E.L.D. was envisioned as a paramilitary extention of the United Nations. A cooperative venture, its Manhattan headquarters, combined with its mobile Helicarrier base to project power and influence, was judged sufficient. Concerns over encroaching upon normal UN global authority were a major consideration.

But as Hydra waxed powerful, waned and re-formed, continually shifting like some fluid, shapeshifting octopus, S.H.I.E.L.D. found itself taxed to stay on top of the monster. Regional headquarters were established where needed. And when the need abated, they had remained.

Most were fronts. A barbershop in New York City. An apothecary in London. A cheese shop in Amsterdam. Whenever compromised by direct attack or intelligence leaks, they were instantly closed and reconstituted at new locations.

Owing to local sensitivities, the S.H.I.E.L.D. Regional Headquarters in Riyadh, Saudi Arabia was classified as an "information mission." Open to the public, it dispensed public information and accepted recruitment applications. Saudi nationals were welcome to bring matters they felt beyond the reach of the Saudi government to the attention of S.H.I.E.L.D. simply by walking in. It occupied the top two floors of a downtown office building. Standard S.H.I.E.L.D. uniforms were forbidden, and female agents were sequestered when they were on station. It was not the most popular posting.

So it was that Janine Yost arrived in mufti shortly after midnight Saudi local time.

The necessary S.H.I.E.L.D. van took her to headquarters, where she was officially tasked, handed tickets to an Air Carcassone flight leaving within the hour. There was just enough time to make her flight. The entire procedure put her back in the air so rapidly that she could have testified she had never visited Saudi Arabia and have hardly shaved the truth.

The flight was a short hop. Riyadh to Persopolis, capital city of the Islamic Republic of Niran. There, she was scheduled to grab an Empire Airlines flight to Cairo.

Saudi customs passed her with only a systematic luggage check. No other hassles. She hoped it would be just as easy on the other legs. Her tasking called for frequent plane changes until something happened, or the 24-hour event window had closed.

Once in the air, Janine relaxed. She felt tension on the ground. They had warned her that as a woman she would feel that way anywhere she went in the Middle East. Relaxation techniques lowered her blood pressure and brought her to a smooth, stable Alpha state.

The tension didn't go away completely, but it was sufficient to begin working the cabin.

Unbuckling her seat belt, Janine worked her way along the aisle to the rear lavatory. She took her time, scanning every face in every seat. They were a mixed bag of Middle Eastern businessmen and tourists, garbed in everything from business coats to native abayas and chadors.

Every glance she gave was met and returned with a fierce assertive glare typical of Middle Eastern body language. That made it easier to lock and scan for negative vibrations. She sensed none. Not that she expected anything. The event window had yet to open.

Back in her seat, Janine turned her attention to the cabin. The door was closed. No known locked door could shield against the psychic mind, of course.

But there were other blocks. The pilot was blocked to the point that all she received on the bounceback was a deep negative vibe. She tried to get around it. No dice. Switching to the copilot, she got the same thing: a cloudy negative darkness.

Frowning deeply, she checked her own gut. The tension she had felt before take off was still there. It wasn't that.

Janine had worked as a professional psychic reader before being recruited by S.H.I.E.L.D. Blocked people were common. Depression could block a reading. So could any number of drugs or alcohol if it lingered in the system.

On the point of deciding that—given the Muslim flight crew—alcohol was an unlikely explanation, Janine noticed a flight attendant pulling small bottles of a popular liquor from a beverage serving tray. Wrapping them in a white linen cloth, she smuggled them into the control cabin.

So much for that theory, Janine thought ruefully.

Settling back, she closed her eyes and attempted to make contact with Special Powers Director Starla Spacek.

Visualizing the agreed-upon call sign—a soaring sea-gull—she mentally "sent" it to the Helicarrier. If success-ful, she would receive a counterpicture of a glass rose in return. Years and years of psychic experimentation had determined that trying to transmit words or letters or num-bers was a crapshoot. Pictures, images and emotions moved with great clarity, however.

Distance did not matter much. If Starla was in a recep-tive state, there should be no problem.

The trouble was, Janine herself was having trouble staying focused. It was the tension. It was still there. And it seemed to be growing thicker. The persistent drone of the airliner's four great turbines wasn't conducive to quiet concentration, either.

Staring at the inside of her own eyelids, Janine waited for the correct image to come. All she discerned was a swirling visual phenomenon that made her think of holo-graphic interference patterns. Were they real? Or a trick of the human retina when shut off from direct light stimu-lation? Janine had always wondered. There were new theories of the universe that claimed everything humans experienced were frequency patterns the mind uncoded into what was understood to be physical reality.

A stewardess tapped her on the shoulder, jolting her from her reverie. Janine's heart leapfrogged.

"Something to drink, miss?" the flight attendant asked in her thick accent.

"No. Nothing, thank you." Closing her eyes, Janine went back into Alpha.

Instantly, she got something. But it was no glass rose. The impression was quick, abrupt, shocking. A ball of fire. Reddish-orange, it was as vivid as if it were heading straight for her.

The sudden violence snapped her eyes open. She half expected to see a voracious fireball tumbling down the aisle in her direction.

But no. The cabin was calm.

Refocusing, Janine tried to recapture the image. Was it a premonition. Or had she reached Starla in distress?

When no bounceback image came, Janine dug her hands into the padded seat rest.

A sick feeling of fear settled in her psychically-sensitive solar plexus.

"Starla . . ." she moaned. "Let it be a mistake. Oh please, let it have been just a bad dream . . . ."

Starla Spacek's S.H.I.E.L.D. training overrode her shock, surprise and most importantly the sheer, paralyzing fear of facing a roaring fireball.

Her S.H.I.E.L.D. uniform was a sandwich of Kevlar and polyurethane, with a fireproof Nomex middle layer. It was designed to buy precious time in the event of incendiary situations.

Whipping out Nomex gloves, she pulled them on. That was the first thing they taught you: protect your hands. That done, Starla yanked the coverall hood from a pouch, pulling it over her head.

The fireball hit in that instant. But it was an instant too late. There was a reserve bubble of oxygen in the shielded mouth area. Just enough for three strenuous minutes.

The waterbed mattress began melting. Starla slashed it with her boot knife, plunging into the cool, spilling water. It remained cool for mere seconds. But that was enough. The hot core of the fireball had passed, leaving a swatch of blazing carpet in its wake.

Jumping up, Starla raced through the fire, eyes open

behind the polarized eyeshields. The heat was tremendous. But she had to take it. For no more than a minute if she found the hatch in time.

Overhead, concealed sprinklers and fire-suppressing jets of white chemical foam kicked in. A red light winked on just ahead. That would be the door latch beacon.

She found it, yanked. It released. Rolling through, Starla shut it, containing the hungry flames.

Off came the hood. She looked around. Section control doors were rolling shut in either direction. Fire alarms were jangling nervously. The corridor was completely deserted.

Then she remembered.

"Mark!"

The monitor entry door stood sealed. She grabbed the handle. Hot. And growing hotter. She kicked, screaming, "Mark! Mark! This way! Out this way!"

The door refused to open. Evil grayish-black smoke was dribbling up from the lower edge. Only then did she realize the entry keypad was slowly turning to taffy . . . and with it any hope that Special Powers Officer Mark Youngblood was coming out of there alive.

The first Security Officer on the scene found Starla Spacek sobbing uncontrollably.

"Blast that door!" she screamed through hot tears. "Hurry!"

The SO hesitated, thrown by her unfamiliar purple insignia.

Reaching out, Starla took his plasma blaster from him and turned it on the stubborn door. She lazed the latch into slag, dug at the frame with her Nomex-protected hands.

The door rolled open. Out came a horrid coil of intense choking smoke. Oblivious, Starla started in.

The SO grabbed her by the waist and pulled her kicking, screaming and biting, back from the suffocating stuff.

He got her through a section control door and buttoned it down.

"You couldn't have done anything," he told Starla as she crumpled into a sobbing heap.

"He's still alive! I can feel his mind. He's still alive and he's burning! Don't you understand? He's alive and he's burning. . . ."

Starla buried her face in her gloved hands. It didn't help. She could see a partial image of something like charred meat sliding off human bone. . . .

Nick Fury took charge of the situation with his unmistakable voice.

"Were you the SO on duty?" he demanded.

The SO said, "No, sir. I was not."

"Then who the hell was? And where the hell is he?"

Dum Dum Dugan barked, "I'm on it."

Fury pulled Starla to her feet. Her knees shook. She could barely stand unsupported, so Fury propped her against the wall, holding her up with one heavy hand and the sheer force of his personality.

"What happened?" he asked, the gruffness in his voice muted by concern.

"Someone threw a firebomb into the Re-Vue chamber," Starla choked out. "Mark's gone. He . . . he couldn't get out."

"It's tough, kid. But this is S.H.I.E.L.D. We lose people sometimes."

Her eyes squeezing out hot tears, Starla said, "I saw the killer's arm. He was wearing a S.H.I.E.L.D. security officer's uniform."

"And the SO on duty is nowhere to be seen," Fury growled. "Want to bet he's our Remote Viper?"

Dum Dum returned, blue eyes blazing, fiery mustaches bristling. "The missin' SO is Feroze Dagius. Security says he volunteered for the duty."

"Find him. I want his traitorous face smeared on every video screen on the ship. Got me?"

"On it," said Dugan. He lumbered off.

"We'll get him," Fury promised Starla. His voice was brittle.

Starla folded shivering arms and shut her pain-dulled eyes. "Special Powers isn't a day old, and we've already lost an agent."

She looked at her watch. "Janine! She's due to check in on the hour."

"Don't sweat it. The main event ain't set to start until tomorrow."

Starla leaned her back into the wall. She shut her eyes. Tears had coursed down through the soot on her cheeks, making clear rills. She wiped them. Her face assumed that placid yet focused expression that indicated she was operating.

Moments crawled past.

"I'm getting a soaring seagull," she reported.

"What's that mean?"

"It's the all-is-well sign."

"How do you know it ain't just your imagination?" Fury wondered.

"The image is fixed, like a slide. My imagination would show me a seagull in motion."

"If you say so," Fury said dubiously.

"Please be quiet. I need to send the countersign."

Fury watched thoughtfully as Starla's face knit in a kind of open concentration.

"Oh, my God! I'm seeing fire. I—it's—oh dear Lord—"

"Spit it out."

Starla's eyes flew open. They seemed to be staring into eternity.

"Fire! It's the fireball I saw before. A jet has crashed! Somewhere in the Middle East. A city is burning. I can see it."

"Are you sure it's happening now? Right now? In real time?"

Starla's eyes lost focus, refocused, then sought Nick

Fury's searching gaze. They were sick. They were the eyes of a person slipping in and out of denial. . . .

"Colonel," she said thickly. "Not only is it happening now, but I think—" Her voice sank further into despair. "No, I'm sure."

Her voice twisted. The words came out of her with difficulty.

"Janine Yost was on that plane."

"WHAT THE # HELL'S # THE matter with everybody?" Nicholas Fury was raging.

Security officers surrounded him, blunt-nosed blasters drawn. Their faces were stiff and hostile.

The director of S.H.I.E.L.D. had gone directly to the cavernous bridge, where he could direct shipwide search and capture operations. No sooner had he stepped off the elevator, than his own SOs challenged him.

"For one thing," Dum Dum muttered, "they're wonderin' who the heck you are."

Fury peered into a radar scope. He saw a vaguely familiar face staring back at him: Agent "Savage."

"Can't anybody recognize the voice of their executive director when they hear it bellowing at 'em?" Fury howled.

That did it. Crisp salutes were thrown his way.

"Who's got a console that can punch up CNN?" he asked.

The Sky Boss jumped out of his swivel chair, offering it to Fury.

"Here, sir."

"Thanks." Fury dropped into the seat.

The CNN bulletin was datelined Persopolis, Nira.

"A 747 jumbo jet carrying an estimated 500 passengers and crew plunged into the heart of Persopolis, Nira at 1:45 Tuesday morning, igniting a conflagration that still rages out of—"

Fury's face twisted in anger. "Tuesday? It's still Monday."

"Not in the Middle East," Val pointed out. "They're one day ahead of us."

Fury grimaced. "Damn. Starla was dead-on, but we all forgot to factor in the international dateline."

The newsreader went on.

"At this hour, there is no word on why the Air Carcassone jetliner lost control while flying over the Niran capital."

"Air Carcassone? What happened to Empire?"

"An estimated twenty square blocks of Persopolis are fully involved. Early reports suggest the stricken jet may have struck an oil storage depot or some other highly combustible site. The damage far exceeds what aviation experts say would be expected of a 747 crashing into a populated area, horrific as the consequences have been."

Executive Officer Valentina Allegro de Fontaine strode over. "Colonel, we have confirmation that SPO Janine Yost was on board that flight."

"That's confirmation I didn't need," Fury growled. "Now put a lid on it until I have the whole story."

But there wasn't much more. The fire was less than an hour old. Early reports were still coming in. But from the aerial shots, it looked as if Persopolis had been hit with a small tactical nuke. The flames were a weird pinkish hue.

Dum Dum lumbered up. "Who's gonna break this to poor SPD Spacek?"

Fury stood up. "I am. Right now."

At the Infirmary, Starla Spacek had refused a traditional tranquilizer, but had agreed to take a shot of ketamine. Mothers in childbirth took it to promote twilight sleep as an alternative to undergoing the pain of childbirth.

Starla was somewhere in that twilight now. On the edge of Theta. And she was dreaming.

In the dream, she was looking down a long arched corridor. It was lit in a sickly Nile green from hidden spotlights.

At the farthest end of the corridor, a man stepped out of the shadows. He was robed in emerald. Starla could hear herself asking, "Who are you?"

The man said nothing. He took a step forward. Another. Advancing, his lizard green robes switched angrily with every forward step. The sound of his heavy boots were like drumbeats of doom.

When he stopped advancing, he unfolded his arms to reveal a large yellow H formed by his sash of a belt and two vertical stripes that went from the shoulders to the trailing skirt of his tunic.

Raising his arms out to his sides in a two-fisted salute, he shouted, "Hail Hydra! Immortal Hydra! Cut off one limb and two more will take its place! We serve the Supreme Hydra, as the world shall soon serve us."

Then eerily, a second set of arms lifted into view, to make fists at oblique angles to the body, followed by a third that stopped at the 20- and 40-minute positions on a clock dial. The six-armed Hydra held his defiant post like a multiarmed sentry standing at the gates of the Underworld.

Starla muttered in sleep, "Who are you? I can't see your face."

For the face was shrouded. The visored hood of a Hydra agent was absent. Instead, there was a white thing like a shroud, or a monk's hood. The face within was concealed by deep shadow.

"Who are you?" Starla demanded again.

The face zoomed into view. But all she saw were skull-like hollows for eyes and a cruel slash of a mouth half concealed by a military-style brush mustache.

Floating out from that shadowy visage was a symbol she had come to hate.

A splayed black scorpion.

"You were right," a harsh voice was saying.

Starla Spacek felt the needle retract from her arm. She was coming out of it.

She tried sitting up. Her head spun. It was too soon. "What do you mean?"

Nick Fury said, "Your Special Powers agent went down with her flight. It crashed into the heart of Persopolis. But it wasn't an Empire flight. It was Air Carcassone."

"Does it matter now?" Starla murmured weakly.

"You're damn right it matters. I have to rely on your intelligence. So far you're batting about .500. Good enough for government work, but not for S.H.I.E.L.D."

"How can you be so cruel, so heartless? Two of my agents are dead and you—"

"If we're not on our game, we lose the whole ball of wax," Fury growled. "But we've fouled up on our side, too. We didn't factor in the international dateline. It's already Tuesday over there. So you called that one right. All except the airline."

"What does this mean?"

"It means we're going to have Skindarian climbing our trees until we raise your batting average some more."

Starla slipped off the bed. "I'm ready. For whatever comes."

"Glad to hear it. Now listen up. We've got Security combing this overgrown tub with every sensor and electronic sniffer at our disposal. But so far they're coming up with goose eggs."

"How are my people doing?"

"No better. Figure the spy's wearing his scramble helmet?"

"Probably."

"That would make him kinda conspicuous, don't you think?"

"Of course."

"So how come we can't pinpoint him?"

Starla shut her eyes. "I see a chameleon. Its colors are shifting, green to blue to brown."

"Meaning what?"

"Meaning he's wearing some kind of exotic camou-flage."

"I'll buy that. Now, let's hunt this lizard down."

Starla accepted the .30 caliber machine pistol and 5mm plasma beam blaster. She was not comfortable with offensive weapons, but they went with the job.

"Don't sweat the armament," Fury told her. "That's my department. You're going to be my psychic bloodhound."

"I don't know where to start."

Fury punched up a Helicarrier schematic on a tabletop monitor.

"We can rule out cramped corridors. He ain't brushing past Security wearing that oversized Fry-o-lator on his head."

Starla peered into the screen.

"As long as he's wearing an operating helmet, I can't find his mind. But the other side of that is he can't continue wearing it for very long. It's only a matter of time before the alternating frequencies trigger Gamma brain-waves, and a disabling disassociative state."

Fury checked his bulky ELBOW. "I ain't planning on waiting until then."

"Hush. I'm picking up images."

"Of what?"

Starla looked surprised. "Of fruit."

Feroze Dagius was frightened. His physical presence on the Helicarrier was known now. But there had been no avoiding it. It became absolutely necessary to destroy the remote-viewing chamber, now that S.H.I.E.L.D. had reactivated its psychic countermeasures program.

A S.H.I.E.L.D. Security Officer for three years, Dagius had insinuated himself into Helicarrier operations only the previous year. No one suspected his loyalties belonged to another, higher calling.

His ongoing mission had been simple: collect intelligence and relay it to his masters through extrasensory means.

When the Vinegaroon Air 737 had crashed itself onto the Helicarrier, he intuited the true meaning of the incident. This made him realize how expendable he really was. But he understood this. Accepted it. It was only a mild shock to his ego. Ultimately, he expected to die for the cause. It was only a matter of when.

In the aftermath of the crash, Dagius had remotely viewed the scene, discovering by this means the two dead pilots who had fortuitously gone into the safety netting where they had been overlooked.

Dagius understood that they had once been living men, and as such, it was critical to dispose of their bodies, the better to confound S.H.I.E.L.D.

This had been done. Opening a cargo hatch low on the hull of the great airborne weapons platform, Dagius had lowered the bodies one by one via a line. Then, rappelling down himself, he had secreted the dead amid the piles of charred LMDs where they would never be discovered. He hoped.

But the very fact of accomplishing this great, important thing had exposed his presence on the Helicarrier. It was only a matter of time before they discovered him and his unauthorized ESP countermeasures helmet.

His course thereafter was clear: He must destroy the ESP agents. Volunteering for the Re-Vue security detail, it had been simple. Too simple. One thermite grenade was all that was necessary to accomplish this.

But now the enemy knew his identity. Once the unsuspected serpent in their bowels, Feroze Dagius was now the prey, being hunted through the commodious innards of the vast vessel, from which, he knew, there was no escape. Except death.

The problem with being the prey was that after so much running, one became tired and hungry.

Most of all, Feroze Dagius was hungry.

There were a thousand corridors and access tunnels throughout the Helicarrier. Moving along them, unseen, his mind shielded by the scramble helmet, he carefully worked his way to the kitchen galley area of the ship.

Down where only cooks and serving people toiled. Down where there was food, and perhaps rest.

It proved easy to do. He could reconnoter with only minimal difficulties, even with the cumbersome scramble helmet, thanks to technology that even S.H.I.E.L.D. did not possess.

After all, he was visible only as a pair of disembodied eyes—and not even that if he kept them shut as much as possible. . . .

"The problem we have," Starla was explaining to Nick Fury as they drove through the main keel corridor, "is that I can't get a fix on his mind. But he can't sense us, either."

"What you're saying is that you're both psychically blind. Is that right?"

"Partially. As long as he's wearing that helmet, our minds are walled off from one another. But that doesn't mean I can't locate his personal energy signature and perceive impressions *around* him."

"And you're getting fruit?"

Starla closed her eyes again. "Apples. Bananas. I still see them."

Fury braked at a descending open lift. Dum Dum stepped off, and climbed aboard.

"Accordin' to his meal records," Dugan reported, "Dagius last chowed down at 0100—almost twelve hours ago. Time enough to have worked up a powerful appetite."

Fury drove on. "That can only mean one thing," he muttered.

The corridor began narrowing. A sign appeared ahead of them:

COMMISSARY AREA
VEHICLES NOT PERMITTED PAST THIS POINT

They dismounted. Fury addressed them.

"Okay, I figure this for a cat-and-mouse operation. The fewer operatives the better. That way we're not stumbling over one another. We go in, fan out and flush this joker out."

"He shouldn't be hard to spot if he's wearin' a scramble helmet," Dum Dum pointed out.

"It may not be that simple. Special Powers first spotted him as a pair of eyes in the middle of a distortion area. Figure the helmet for the distortion area. The rest of him is camouflaged somehow. You're looking for distortions, funny shadows and any other optical anomalies."

"Don't look for a man," Starla suggested. "Look for the *impression* of a man."

That understood, they went in.

It was after food service hours, so there wasn't even a skeleton staff present. The commissary area was vast. Shrouded in the gloom of lights off, it looked even more so.

An imposing shape like a bristle-skinned monster stood in one corner. A heavily-decorated Christmas tree. It was the only sign of the coming holiday permitted on the vessel.

Starla took point. She didn't even realize she was doing it. Her steps quickened. Her head tilted left, then right, then left in alternation. It was as if she were looking about, but her eyes were closed. She was accessing her temporal lobes, going clairvoyant and clairaudient by turns.

"Anything?" Fury undertoned.

She shook her head. "Bananas. That's all."

Fury grabbed her shoulder, guiding her toward the refrigeration section.

It takes a lot of foodstuff to feed a crew as large as the Helicarrier's usual complement. There wasn't a single meat locker. There were six. Vegetables were stored in their own walk-in cooler. Fruit in another.

Fury led the way to the fruit locker, ELBOW in hand.

Dum Dum wielded a laser pointer. It beamed just enough light ahead of them to pinpoint obstacles without betraying their approach.

It bounced off the vegetable locker, came to rest on a plate that read FRUIT.

The stainless steel door was closed. They took up positions on either side of the huge portal, Fury on the left and Dugan on the right.

Eyes open, Starla stepped up to the door. Taking off one glove, she touched the chill surface with her bare fingers.

After a moment, she shook her head in the negative.

Fury motioned for her to take the door latch and pull, indicating that Starla jump back so they could go in.

The moment her hand touched the latch, she froze.

A jumble of images jumped into her brain. She felt first a low sense of fear. Under that a persistent hunger. Eyes, disembodied and alien, floated in her mind's eye. They were very, very dark. Almost black.

"He's inside," she whispered.

Fury indicated she proceed.

Steeling herself, Starla pulled on the latch. The door unlocked with all the subtlety of an exploding firecracker. She jumped back, pulling the huge stab of steel with her.

Cold white light spilled out, along with a sudden puff of chilly air.

Fury stormed in like his namesake, Dum Dum hard on his heels.

Starla followed, blaster poised.

The sight that greeted her was so weird, so bizarre that the weapon fell from her fingers.

Inside, fruits of all varieties stood on shelf after shelf, still in their producer's wooden shipping crates. This was all backdrop, registering at the periphery of awareness.

A single crate stood in the center of the floor, open and overflowing with bananas. About a foot above the floor, a solitary banana floated. Its peel hung down in three sections, like a droopy flower. The top of the banana was gone.

There was a man's head there, too. It floated at the same level as the banana, mouth poised to take another bite. It swiveled around. A pair of very dark eyes widened in fear and surprise.

That strange sight held her for just a split second.

Then the head began levitating. It floated off the floor to the height of an average man. Except there was absolutely no sign of a supporting body.

"Freeze, mister," Fury ordered.

"I am your prisoner," the floating head said in a sad, resigned voice.

"Keep your hands where we can see them," Dum Dum barked. The absurdity of his command barely had time to register when the floating head yawned wide. Too wide. Every lower filling was displayed.

Starla was never certain she heard an audible click. A screaming sixth sense cried "Danger." The rest was a frantic mix of precognition and autonomic reflex.

Lunging forward, she threw Fury and Dugan to the floor.

A voice cried, *"Allahu Akbar!"*

Then a flash turned the inside of Starla Spacek's closed eyelids a pinkish-red. She saw tiny veins. The concussion struck her eardrums with sound-deadening force that promised—no, threatened—the extinguishing of all life, all hope.

After what seemed like forever, sound and hearing returned. Starla looked up.

Where the Hydra extrasensor had stood, there was nothing. It was as if he had been obliterated from the world.

There was blood everywhere. Blood, and other discolored matter Starla did not want to look at.

Everything stood still as if waiting. Then it happened. There was a sensation of falling. A puff of chill air. A thud.

And Starla turned away from the raw stump that fell into view—a stump that only moments before supported the human head whose remains were splashed over the cooler's interior.

Fury and Dum Dum came off their feet, surrounded the body. They absorbed the situation in an instant.

"Musta had a detonator concealed in a filling," Dum Dum muttered. "Rigged to arm when he yawned real wide, then go off when he bit down again."

"Yeah," Fury said. "Designed to turn his head into an anti-personnel fragmentation grenade, with his skull bones supplyin' the shrapnel."

Fury felt along the body, found plasticky cloth. He gave it a hard yank. With a mushy tear, something came away, exposing the body in its S.H.I.E.L.D. suit with red Security strapping.

"Looks like some kind of fiberoptic light-bending cloak, with a hood attachment," Fury decided. "That's why we only saw his eyes."

"Are you all right?" Starla asked weakly.

Dum Dum said, "Yeah. Ain't it obvious?"

"There's blood all over you both."

Fury said, "Look in the mirror, kid. You're covered in it, too. We all are."

Fury stood up, still clutching the swatch of cloth that was slowly resolving into normal substance.

"If you hadn't pushed us down like that, we might have taken skull fragments to the head, and that would have been all she wrote."

"What Fury's tryin' to say," Dum Dum added, "is that you done good."

They found the scramble helmet in a corner. It wasn't as transparent to the eye as the fiberoptic cloak had been. Starla perceived it peripherally as a shifting, unstable distortion.

She scooped it up. It wavered.

"I don't know what to make of this . . ."

Taking the helmet, Dum Dum felt around its rounded cranium with reddish fingers that looked strong enough to crush a coconut husk into raw pulp.

"A switch where it's not supposed to be," he said. He pressed down. Something went click.

Chameleon-like, the helmet changed hues, going through a short metallic spectrum before settling down to the burnished aluminum its designer had intended.

"What'd he do to it?" Fury wanted to know.

"Some kind of liquid crystal mirror surfacing maybe," Dum Dum decided. "Powered by what looks like a small nickel-cadmium battery pack. The lab boys'll be able to tell us."

"Now we know how he was able to tramp through the ship without settin' off alarms," Fury grumbled. "Anybody catch what he yelled before he blew himself to kingdom come?"

"I was too busy praying," Starla admitted.

"'Allahu Akbar!'" Fury supplied. "It means 'God is great.'"

Dum Dum muttered, "That don't sound like Hydra to me."

"He did look vaguely Middle Eastern. . . ." Starla said.

"With a name like Feroze Dagius, what would you expect?" Fury growled.

Dum Dum thought to check the man's wrists. He found a long scar that exactly corresponded to the size of the scorpion tattoo that had been found on others.

Starla knelt down and laid two fingers against the scar. She closed her eyes.

"I perceive a scorpion," she reported.

"That's good enough for me," Fury said. "Now for the sixty-four-thousand-dollar question: Is he a Hydra?"

Starla went deeper. The image of the Hydra in the dream recurred. It came too fast, too easily. She threw it away. The scorpion tattoo came up again. She pushed past it. There was nothing there.

"I think I'm pulling overlay," she admitted, opening her eyes.

"What does that mean?" Fury demanded. "Is he or isn't he?"

"It's not that simple," said Starla, standing up. "Maybe I'm drained from all that's happened, I don't know. But I'm receiving both Hydra impressions and the scorpion symbol. I think the Hydra may be my imagination. If you try too hard, you sometimes pull on preexisting information."

"This ain't exactly adding up," Fury pointed out.

They stared at one another in baffled silence for a long time, the blood of the dead extrasensor running down their uniforms like slow, remorseful red tears.

Intelligence Director Art Skindarian was working late in his office at S.H.I.E.L.D. Central in Manhattan when his desk phone trilled.

He finished typing his thought before answering:

"As a consequence of the reorganization certain to follow the appointment of a new executive director, I recommend dismantling the Special Powers unit, or in the alternative subsuming it under the direct operational control of Level 2 Security."

Skindarian picked up the phone.

"Bad news, Skindarian," a voice said. "We just rooted out a mole in the Helicarrier crew."

"Mole?" Skindarian said. "Impossible." Then he asked: "Who is this?"

"Fury. Who did you think it was?"

"You're alive?"

"Be here in fifteen minutes. Emergency briefing."

"Yes, Colonel."

"And you can trash that memo you're writing. It was the psychics who found the mole that got past your people."

"Yes, sir."

Skindarian hung up the phone. After saving the file, he hit the delete key. He had a feeling this was not going to be a very pleasant meeting. . . .

When he arrived at the conference room on Deck 4, Security Director Art Skindarian began to get an inkling of how serious.

At either side of the door stood two Security Officers, standing with feet apart, arms akimbo, hands clasped behind their backs. They looked smart, and alert. A credit to S.H.I.E.L.D.

Inside, it was a different matter.

The section chiefs were seated around a circular steel table. Nick Fury sat at the far end, the inevitable cigar in his mouth. He did not look happy. Then again, it was rare to see the director of S.H.I.E.L.D. looking like anything other than like a man chewing nails.

Skindarin said, "Good to see you again, Colonel."

"Sit down," said Fury gruffly.

"And you, Miss Spacek," he added, taking the empty seat beside Starla Spacek.

"SPD Spacek, please," Starla corrected.

Then he saw the two agents positioned on either side

of the door. He had not noticed them on entering. They wore standard S.H.I.E.L.D. combat suits, but their belts and insignia were purple. The odd thing about them was while they stood at attention, their eyes were shut tight. Headphones covered both ears.

"What are *they* doing here?"

"Alpha security," Fury told him. "They're scanning the room for extrasensory eavesdroppers."

"Security officers at a Level 2 meeting? This is unacceptable."

"They're wearing white-noise earphones," Fury explained. "Can't hear a word."

"The earphones enable them to maintain the Alpha state needed to continually sweep the room," Starla added.

Skindarian sized up the mood in the room. It was neither the time nor place for an argument. He nodded silent assent.

"First things first," Fury began. "I ain't dead. Secondly, we found a mole in security. Feroze Dagius. Middle Eastern extraction. He's our Remote Viper. Somehow, he got through all our security procedures. This will not happen again. Do you all read me?"

"I assume that was directed at no one in particular," Skindarian said stiffly.

Ignoring him, Fury went on: "Up 'til now we've been operating on the assumption that what we've been dealing with here is a Hydra threat. That theory ain't out the window yet. But there are some holes growing in it. Dagius is Egyptian and maybe not even Hydra. I smell a rat."

Skindarin said, "Recent intel out of the Middle East indicates low-level Hydra activity in that region. But it appears unfocused."

"You telling us a Hydra Middle East is forming?" Fury asked.

Skindarian shook his head. "Improbable. When they backed the wrong side in the Gulf War, Hydra apparently abandoned all serious activity in that area. But recent reports indicate they are conducting operations of some sort. Hydra aircraft have been spotted in the Quoraki no-fly zones, although there have been no reported incidents."

"How far back do these reports go?" asked Starla.

Skindarian searched his memory. "Three months. No more. All routine."

Fury asked, "Any chance Hydra is trying to cozy up to Nadir al-Bazinda, Skindarian?"

"The dictator of Quorak? If they are, it's to conduct smuggling operations. I see no threat of an alliance there. The U.S. has been in what amounts to a state of low-intensity warfare with Quorak since the Gulf War ended, with the result that al-Bazinda and his inner circle have been increasingly marginalized. The Arab world has virtually turned against Quorak. There's not much incentive for Hydra there. Quorak has nothing to offer but crude oil. Oil is cheaper than bottled water these days. Hydra might as well buy it on the open market like everyone else."

"Or steal it," Dum Dum suggested.

Fury turned to Starla. "What's your read, Spacek?"

Skindarian glowered. "I object. This woman's operational purview does not include intelligence matters."

Fury waved off the objection. "We're making some changes. From now on, she's in charge of Alpha Intelligence."

"Alpha—"

"And your bailiwick will be what we're calling Practical Intel," Fury added.

Skindarian brought his facial cast under control. "That sounds almost reasonble, I suppose. Provided we rigidly maintain the distinction."

"Under the circumstances, it's a better deal than you deserve. From here on, Alpha and Practical Intel will share intelligence. Alpha's job is to feed reliable PSIN-

TEL to Practical. Practical's job is to verify PSINTEL. That way we have backup, crosscheck, and we don't stub our toes in areas where we're functionally blind."

Fury nodded to Starla to continue.

"My read is that we're dealing with a hybrid threat," she said. "Hydra with a Middle Eastern connection. Last night I had a dream—"

Skindarian snorted. "I trust we're not trading in dreams now."

"—a dream in which I saw a Hydra operative wearing what looked like a shroud. Or burnoose, I suppose. I couldn't see the face, but I did see what appeared to be a mustache. A very distinctive mustache. The same mustache Feroze Dagius wore." Starla's green-gray eyes went from face to face. "The style of military mustache men in Nadir al-Bazinda's inner circle traditionally wear."

Skindarian made a distasteful face. "Sounds thin . . ."

"There's more. I happen to know that Nadir al-Bazinda was born on Halloween. That makes him a Scorpio. It could explain the significance of the scorpion tattoos we've been finding on these terrorists."

Skindarian sniffed. "That's a reach—astrology and tattoos?"

"That's enough," Fury said. "We've got a lot of pieces, but no puzzle. That says to me we don't have enough pieces. I want more. ASAP. And no excuses. Dismissed."

Fury left the room trailing cigar smoke.

Skindarian stood up.

Starla put out her hand. "I want you to know I hold no grudge. We're on the same team."

Skindarian hesitated.

Dum Dum Dugan put in, "I'd take it if I were you, Art. Right now her stock is high, and yours is mighty low."

A pained expression on his long face, Art Skindarian reluctantly shook hands.

"I need everything you have on Nadir al-Bazinda," Starla told him.

"Done. And I need to verify your . . . perceptions."

"That's the way it's supposed to work."

"Then that's the way it will work," Skindarian said stiffly.

An hour later, Starla was viewing files on a S.H.I.E.L.D. monitor screen. The text files were massive—much too much information to digest. It was late. She was growing sleepy. But she kept at it. Past experience told her the more tired she got, the more psychic she was. If she could just keep her eyes open. . . .

Somewhere past the midnight hour, Starla was scanning captured file footage of Nadir al-Bazinda when something caused her finger to stab the Pause button.

And there it was. Almost too small to make out. A tiny black configuration at the right temple. Starla squinted. It literally popped. The phenomenon was one she knew well.

Blowing up the image, she brought the blotch into higher contrast. The grain was too rough, so she enhanced it.

And there, as if crawling out from under the dictator of Quorak's hairline, was a spidery black scorpion. The same image she had picked up clairvoyantly. The identical symbol tattooed to the inner wrists of all captured terrorists.

Eagerly, Starla called up more footage. This time she focused on al-Bazinda's inner circle. Everywhere their inner wrists showed, she expanded up the image.

In picture after picture, identical black scorpions were revealed.

Nick Fury arrived five minutes later. Silently, he went through the files.

"Looks like you hit the jackpot, lady."

"I still don't understand the connection to Hydra," Starla said slowly.

"There're more pieces to this puzzle yet to be found,"

Fury growled. "But you just handed us a great big arrow pointing to the Middle East."

"It will be interesting to see what Practical Intel digs up on Empire Airlines."

At that moment, half a world away, a S.H.I.E.L.D. F-16 Fighting Falcon was shadowing an Empire Airlines flight en route to Bahrain.

There was weather over the Gulf. The Empire Airbus 320 was cruising along at 20,000 feet, Flying above it, the S.H.I.E.L.D. jet, operating at 25,000 feet, hung back, tracking it from high vantage.

It had been a routine surveillance.

S.H.I.E.L.D. pilot Captain Wim "Dutch" Schipper had picked up the Empire flight outside Cairo, Egypt. The skies had been clear then. When the weather front rolled in, the Empire jet had climbed to ride over the masses of anvil-shaped cumulonimbus clouds.

Inevitably, the Airbus began to approach its descent to Bahrain.

That's when things got very strange indeed.

The Empire aircraft slid into a particularly dark mass of cloud. As the Airbus vanished from view, forked lightning played in adjoining thunderclouds.

From the vantage point of Angels 25, it looked to Schipper as if a dark pulsating monster had swallowed the Empire flight.

Holding his altitude, he continued to monitor radio traffic emanating from the Empire cockpit. It sounded routine—handoffs and weather updates from various regional air traffic control centers.

Then Empire went silent. A frequency jam-up preceded the silence. Came a burst of static. After that, silence.

The S.H.I.E.L.D. pilot frowned. He checked his instruments. There was no Ident bounceback. Radar showed only weather ghosts.

"Empire 045, do you copy?" Schipper asked.

Silence.

"Empire 045, do you read me? Over."

Static hiss rewarded his efforts.

Schipper rolled right, sending his tiny white-and-gold-trimmed warplane diving into the cottony mountain range of dangerous cloud formations. He zoomed through the storm cell, fought turbulence, then found clear air. Rain drummed on his glarescreen and cockpit.

There was no indication that the Empire flight had gone down. In fact, there were no sign of it anywhere.

Regaining altitude, Schipper picked up the descent flight path of the Empire jet. Still no sign of it, visual or instrument.

Then out of the clouds came a lumbering Airbus. Schipper started to breathe a sigh of relief. It was the Empire flight. It had come through okay.

Then he got a close look at the livery.

Instead of Empire green, it was a silver-and-scarlet fusion. Dropping level, Schipper lined up with the airliner. Rain was beating down on it, rushing back from the nose and control surfaces. But the airliner name was readable.

Or it would have been if it hadn't been in Arabic script.

Schipper couldn't read it. His command of Arabic began and ended with *salaam*.

Buttoning his throat mike, he asked, "Unidentified passenger aircraft, request Ident. Please ID."

A garble of what sounded like guttural Arabic came back at him.

"Do you speak English?" asked Schipper.

"English . . . No. No English," the pilot replied.

Which was strange in itself. English was the international language of pilots worldwide, even when flying in their native airspaces.

"Have you seen an Empire Airlines flight?" Schipper asked. "Yes or no?"

"No. No Empire Airline," the captain reported back.

"Have you visually sighted any other passenger jets in the last fifteen minutes? Over."

The pilot's voice came back curtly, almost annoyed. *"No. I have seen nothing."*

"Thanks. Out."

"Good-bye."

Turning back, Schipper swept the front for over an hour. No Empire jet turned up. There was nothing in the rain-troubled waters of the Gulf to show one had crashed along its flight path. And was nothing anywhere to prove that any such flight had ever existed.

Buttoning his mike, Schipper muttered, "I don't know what they're going to make of this back at S.H.I.E.L.D. Central."

FURY

NICK DIDN'T KNOW what to make of it.

Four hours had passed since S.H.I.E.L.D. had received the report out of the Persian Gulf of an Empire Airlines flight that had flown into a thunderhead and not come out again.

The report had been duly passed on to Empire Airlines corporate headquarters in Phoenix, Arizona. The response out of Empire was a polite, "Thank you."

"What else did they say?" Fury asked Gabe Jones.

"Thank you. We'll look into it," Jones replied dryly.

Fury eyed Jones skeptically. "That don't sound very concerned to me."

"I thought it was strange myself," admitted Jones, one of the senior Special Field Officers in S.H.I.E.L.D., currently on Helicarrier duty. "I gave them the flight number, destination city, but they didn't ask for its last known position or any other data you'd think they'd want to know."

"We got a missing Empire jet that the airline doesn't want to know about," Fury said slowly, "and a Vinegaroon 737 that splashed itself all over our flight deck that Vinegaroon claims wasn't theirs."

"Except that Vinegaroon was plenty worried when I brought that crash to their attention," returned Gabe. "They asked for every detail, called me back three times, and finally said all their planes had been accounted for, and was I sure that I had one of their birds?"

"What did they say, exactly?" asked Art Skindarian.

"I told them I had a Boeing 737 with the Vinegaroon corporate logo on it. They told me their fleet doesn't include 737s. They fly Fokker 100s and Canadair regional jets exclusively. That was when they lost interest."

In the conference room, Fury smoked furiously for several minutes in silence.

"Up 'til now," he said, "we've been looking at the possibility of planted pilots on different carriers. We had that Empire jet where I almost bought it, the Vinegaroon jet, and now another Empire jet goes missing."

"Don't forget the Air Carcassone jumbo jet that crashed into Persopolis," Gabe added.

"I ain't forgot it. Just applying Occam's little razor. Empire has come up twice now. Skindarian, what have we got on them?"

Art Skindarian consulted a laptop computer.

"Empire Airlines. Created out of a merger between two failed regional carriers in the southwest in 1997. They've been growing at an unprecedented rate, in part because of an unorthodox approach to commercial flying."

Fury eyed him. "Unorthodox?"

"Well, for one thing most airlines fly a fleet of matched planes. These people will fly anything. Most of their jets are used or refurbished aircraft. But the flying public doesn't care. They just want to get to their destinations on time. Empire's been flying internationally only for the last six months."

"Who owns them?"

"A parent corporation, Phoenix Ltd. I don't have much on them. But they seem to be legitimate."

A buzzer sounded in the meeting room.

"Go ahead," Fury said.

It was Val. *"Colonel, Technical reports that the disabled rotor has been replaced."*

"Thank Technical for me. That was good work, and the turnaround time couldn't have been better."

"I will. Val, out."

Fury leaned back in his chair and blew a smoke ring toward the ceiling. It grew, expanded, somehow holding its perfectly circular shape. Fury sent a thin stream of focused smoke right up its exact center. Stream and ring collapsed against the ceiling, and soon dissipated.

"I think we should put a man inside Empire's corporate headquaters," he said at last.

Skindarian started to rise. "I'll assemble a Tactical Tiger Team."

"I said *a* man," Fury reminded.

"Colonel, this sounds like a three-man mission to me."

Fury took his eyes off the ceiling and swiveled around in his chair.

"Which is why I'm going to be the man to execute it," he said. "Follow up on Empire. I want everything you know before I attempt the penetration."

"Yes, Colonel."

Skindarian started to leave. Fury called after him.

"You'll notice I left SPD Spacek out of this little briefing, Skindarian."

"I did notice."

"That's just to let you know Practical Intel ain't being pushed aside for exotic methods and measures."

"I appreciate that, Colonel."

"But exotic methods and measures are going to be critical to our operational future. Keep that mind."

Skindarian frowned. "I will, Colonel."

Fury watched him depart. This was the part of the job he didn't like: the politics. Keeping the different departments and divisions of S.H.I.E.L.D. synchronized and performing at peak. Inter-directorate rivalry kept people on their toes, gave them an edge. Too often, however, it degenerated into narrow-minded mission compartmentalization and intelligence hoarding. Sometimes being director of S.H.I.E.L.D. was like refereeing a welterweight boxing match.

Which was why, when the opportunities presented themselves, Nick Fury liked to go into the field himself.

Starla Spacek was running her people against various targets.

She was working them in shifts. No more than an hour per RV session. That was so they didn't get too fatigued, or worse, spacey. In the days of the Stargate program, agents too long in Alpha started behaving in strange ways. Flushing their car keys down the john. Or taking the TV remote controls into work with them instead of their wallets. It was the kind of erratic behavior that helped the political and budgetary enemies of Stargate bury the program.

Starla was determined no such thing would happen at S.H.I.E.L.D. Especially now that two Special Powers Officers had given their lives in the performance of their duty.

Right now, Starla had an SPO named Sippo in the Re-Vue chamber. It had been completely gutted by the fire. All the carpeting had been removed. The Plexiglas window had melted into so much transparent taffy, so she had ordered it removed.

Technical had cleaned it up as best they could. It was not perfect, but her people could work. That was all that mattered.

"Empire Flight 67, out of Dallas," Starla was saying. "Can you locate it?"

On the bed pulled out of an empty room, Sippo lay quietly.

"I keep hearing crosstalk. But I can't differentiate the words. It sounds like radio traffic."

"Try visualizing," Starla urged.

"No go. The audio is overpowering everything."

"You're primarily clairaudient, Sippo?"

"Today I am. It goes in cycles."

"Okay. Stand down."

Footsteps coming up the control room stairs caused Starla to turn.

Nick Fury was suddenly in the room with her. His presence seemed to fill the narrow cubicle. It was like being in the presense of a tiger. There was a feeling of danger, of imminent threat, hovering about the big director of S.H.I.E.L.D. The angel of death, Starla thought to herself, must give off a similar psychic aura.

"Colonel?"

"Got an assignment for you, Spacek."

"My people are ready."

"I don't need them. I want you. I'm going to nose around Empire Airlines corporate HQ in Phoenix. I'm going in alone. Tonight. I want you to keep a psychic eye on me."

"What do you mean?"

"When you used to do your remote tasking back at Stargate, you used human beacons, didn't you?"

"Yes. Early on. A human beacon would be sent to a target site, blind. The remote viewer tasked to visualize the site was not told what it would be, only to tune into the beacon at a designated hour. But that was during the exploratory phase of RV. It didn't have a lot of practical use, operationally."

"I'm going to be your human beacon. You tune in on me. I'll communicate back by com link, as needed."

"Be happy to. I'm pleased you've decided to look at Empire, but may I ask why you need me?"

"Let's just call it another test of your batting average. One of our jets was tracking an Empire flight over the Gulf. It disappeared. No trace. Something's fishy about that."

"I can run my people against that target, if you'd like."

"Infiltration's more important. I want you with me when I go in."

The disappointment on Starla's face caused Fury to relent. "Go ahead. Zone out," he said. "See what you get."

Taking a deep breath, Starla went into clairvoyant mode. She made faces as she talked. Her eyes were closed.

"I'm seeing a patch of shiny aluminum, like a portion of airliner hull." Her eyebrows knit together in perplexity. "Oh, damn. It's not a plane at all. It's a scramble helmet. Now why would I be getting *that?*"

"Nice try," Fury said. "But let it go. Infiltration's more important."

"It may mean something, Colonel. Give me another minute."

"You had your shot, Spacek," Fury growled. "I got places to go and things to do. First, I gotta brief you. . . ."

Over the years, S.H.I.E.L.D. had been both the recipient and repository of assorted exotic technology that had never been implemented by the U.S. government. Sometimes, the agency was gifted with experimental aircraft that needed quiet field testing without the political problems that went with possible public failure.

Fury stood on the flight deck as green-strapped Maintenance Officers scurried about in preparation for launch. He was dressed in the uniform of a Special Field Agent, midnight blue with red strapping that after dark tended to read as black. It was the perfect infiltration uniform. Especially with all insignia "sterilized" with strip-off black velcro patches.

A deck-edge lift was hoisting one of S.H.I.E.L.D.'s most recent acquisitions topside. The Dyna-Soar. A delta-winged variable-geometry jet, it was capable of vertical takeoffs and landings, suborbital hops, as well as long-range unpowered gliding.

The Dyna-Soar could be launched vertically like a rocket, or conventionally, making it for tactical purposes a multirole reconnaissance/interceptor, as well as a single-stage-to-orbit spaceplane.

Fury had ordered a conventional launch configuration.

Resembling a cross between a manta ray and a flattened shark, the Dyna-Soar trundled off the lift in jet mode. Its smooth hull—unbroken except for the underslung maw of its big intake and a dorsal fin that belonged on a tiger shark—was composed of space-age alloys and heat-resistant ceramic tiles.

The tow brought her to the angled flight deck, the most perilous of launch areas because the end of the runway ran between and under the arcs of two of the great Heli-carrier rotors. But that was the way Nick Fury liked to do things.

From his platform on the portside of the vessel, the gold-strapped landing signal officer signaled when they'd finished locking the nose landing gear bridle to a heavy cable attached to the C13 Mod 1 steam catapult concealed under the flight deck. Below, a gigantic steam-driven piston lay coiled, ready to be unleashed on command. Already, hot clouds of vapor were boiling up through the reinforced groove in the flight deck along which the cable would race, dragging the aircraft with it.

"All yours, sir," the LSO called out as Fury buckled on his white and gold S.H.I.E.L.D. flight helmet.

Fury gave his cigar a toss. He climbed aboard, dropped the canopy and fired up the Dyna-Soar. An exhaust deflector plate popped up from the deck to catch the dangerous afterburner product.

From the tower, the Air Boss cleared Fury for launch. The LSO popped a salute. Fury unlocked the brakes.

And the steam catapult uncorked.

It was and always would be the wildest ride a pilot could experience: zero to 120 MPH in three compressed seconds.

Yanked by its nose gear, the Dyna-Soar went scream-ing along the centerline. The end of the runway came rushing up.

Fury could see the glittering arcs of the swirling rotors.

He had plenty of space between them to make his escape.

Unless, of course, something went wrong.

In the middle of the run to the edge, something went *very* wrong.

The Dyna-Soar suddenly lost forward momentum. One second, it was thundering along, the next Fury felt the aircraft's hurtling impetus lose force. It happened in a fraction of time, but some instinct communicated the danger to the S.H.I.E.L.D. director.

"Damn! Cold cat shot!" Fury snapped.

It was the worst nightmare of carrier launching. A catapult misfire! It meant he might not have the momentum to get off the deck.

Fury jammed the throttles forward. The afterburners kicked in, but their thrust seemed weak compared to the catapult's powerful kick.

The Dyna-Soar leaped off the deck hesitantly, now-useless cat cable dropping free. It slewed left, toward the newly-replaced rotor's glittering, whispering arc. And certain death.

Fury squeezed the sensitive fly-by-wire stick. The Dyna-Soar responded. It rolled, evading the rotor by a margin that could only be called safe because any less of a margin would have been catastrophic.

Fury broke away from the Helicarrier's sphere of operations like an unleashed meteor.

He sent the white spaceplane out over the Atlantic, waited until he was satisfied with the exotic bird's handling. Pulling back, he turned her on her thundering tail.

The Dyna-Soar went straight up like a skyrocket. Fury rode her on his back, G-forces pushing his spine into the padded seatback until he could almost count the springs.

A voice cracked in his ear. *"Hel-1 to Saint Nick. How's the ride?"*

Fury buttoned his throat mike. "Saint Nick to Hel-1. The ride so far is fine. Somebody better get that blasted cat fixed before I get back. This bird is a loaner, and we almost lost her."

"Roger, Saint Nick. Godspeed."

"Right. Godspeed, and let's see if this bird will live up to advance notices while we're at it."

Staring up into a clear sky, Nick Fury lost all conception and contact with Mother Earth. The altimeter read off the miles too fast for the digital letters to register. The blue of heaven shaded to cobalt, then midnight blue and on into the jet black of outer space.

At the edge of space, Fury punched in new targeting coordinates. Once the on-board nav system confirmed his reentry trajectory, Fury chopped power.

All at once, the silence of space overtook the aircraft. It was eerie, wonderful. The spaceplane kept climbing. Gravity took hold. She rolled, dropped and went into a shallow noiseless downward glide not much different than a shuttle reentry.

Fury settled back to enjoy the ride. According to his system, ETA over Phoenix would be exactly 12 minutes from launch. That was including the cat mishap.

"Not bad for a one-man bird," he told himself.

Fury set down at Luke Air Force Base in just under 12 minutes. He was cleared to land with the same alacrity that greeted him wherever he went.

The Dyna-Soar was hangared for him as he picked up an official car. A trenchcoat—about the only thing that would conceal his S.H.I.E.L.D. uniform and all its equipment—encased his big body.

Fury took Route 60 into Phoenix, and kept going. The drive took three times as long as the flight. Such were the quirks of transportation technology, Fury mused.

Empire Airlines corporate headquarters occupied an industrial park west of Mesa, within sight of the Superstition Mountains. Fury had been told to expect a sprawl of two- and three-story drab concrete slab buildings clustered around a horseshoe-shaped parking lot. It was even less impressive than he imagined. A dreary wind-swept cluster of buildings in the middle of nowhere, it looked more like a plastics factory than the corporate headquarters of a growing airline. Even the company logo—the letters EA entwined in green surmounted by a silver crown—had a makeshift look.

There had been no time to secure ground intel, so Fury reconned it himself. Driving past the area, he found a desolate stretch of cholla and saguaro cactus, ditched his car and peeled off his trenchcoat.

He stood strapped in red, a S.H.I.E.L.D.-issue plasma blaster on his hip, a .45-caliber Colt automatic snug in its shoulder holster. Between the Colt's sheer stopping power and the plasma blaster's raw destructive energy, he was ready for anything.

As he waited for darkness to finish falling, Fury smoked slowly, with deep enjoyment. There was some-thing about the nicotine that helped him focus. So he took his time, smoking the cigar down to a fingertip of rolled tobacco leaf.

Lifting his belt com link mike to his mouth, he said, "Saint Nick to North Pole. Over."

"North Pole to Saint Nick. Password of the day."

"Psi War," said Fury.

"Password confirmed."

"Patch through Special Powers."

"Patching."

After a hiss, Starla's voice came on. *"Space Shot here. Go ahead, Saint Nick."*

"Anything to report?"

"Yes," Starla said dryly. *"I don't appreciate my code name."*

"Tough break. Now listen up: I'm going in. Are you with me?"

"We'll know for sure once you go in."

"That don't exactly sound reassuring," said Fury.

"I have high confidence in this mission, Saint Nick," Starla said.

"That's good. Because it'll be your butt if you foul up and lose your executive director. Saint Nick out."

Fury signed off and reholstered his com mike. From a canvas travel bag, he took out an ELBOW. He checked its various systems. All beeped green. He clipped the lanyard to his belt and slung the ELBOW over his hard shoulder, so that it hung down his back. A breakaway clip secured it to the back of his belt so that by flipping the lanyard, the weapon would jump into his hands when needed.

A multipack of assorted rounds fitted snugly to the other side of his belt.

Fury started off for the Empire building, corking his face black as he went along. He expected an easy penetration. The area around the complex was flat on three sides. A low range of cactus-dotted hills backed the area. Fury picked that as the best approach. There was no fencing or other obstruction. The target was exactly what it appeared to be: a corporate complex with no obvious security issues.

Still, as Fury approached, a feeling of unease overtook him.

"Spacek, I hope you're with me," he murmured under his breath.

For a moment, Fury paused in the spindly shelter of a palo verde tree, as if to listen.

But he heard nothing. Not in his head. Not in his alert ears. He went on.

Nick Fury's strategy was simple: Go in while the building was still open to staff, find a secure place to hide and emerge after hours. That way he would have the run of the place with a minimum of interference from security.

But this was too easy. As he approached, Fury spotted a green-painted steel door at the rear. It faced a pair of industrial-size Dumpsters. Various spoiled food odors—

predominately rancid meat—wafted his way. The door led to the commissary area, he figured.

Fury lay down behind a clump of octillo and watched the door for the better part of twenty minutes. No one came in or went out.

Moving in, he made for the door on a direct line. He reached it, apparently unseen.

Kneeling before the door, he found the lock latches visually. The plasma blaster came off his hip. Fury trained the needle-like beam on the crack where the door fitted into its frame. The beam flickered for an instant. Metal hissed and ran, smoking.

Whipping the ELBOW up and around by its lanyard, Fury tugged the door open a crack. Placing the muzzle into the still-smoking crack, he angled it around, watching what the side-mounted monitor screen showed itside.

It showed an empty pale-green corridor. Heavy gray PVC piping snaked along the walls, branching off like questing tentacles. Nothing else.

Carefully, Fury eased in. He pushed the door shut behind him with the heel of one boot. It closed with a minimum of noise. Overhead, EXIT glowed in red letters.

So far, so good, he thought.

Fury reconnoitered carefully. At each door, he dropped to one knee and let the ELBOW see into the room for him.

The back of the building was exactly what it appeared to be. A kitchen and commissary area. The last place to be occupied after hours. Long tables were cleared and spotless. Stainless steel pots and pans hung on their hooks in the kitchen beyond.

Yet the atmosphere seemed wrong. At first, Fury thought there was something out of place—missing. He stepped into the dining area.

"Something ain't right," he muttered under his breath.

His mind flashed back to the Helicarrier's commissary.

They were similiar in layout, although the Empire food service wing was much, much smaller.

It hit him then.

"Where the hell are the Christmas decorations?"

There were none. At any other time of year, nothing would have seemed odd. But here it was only days away from Christmas, and there was no tree, no decoration, no tinsel—nothing.

With growing confidence, Fury swept the wing of the building. Not even a mouse. Although his foot, inching forward, did encounter a mousetrap. It was coiled to spring at a touch. He went around it gingerly.

Satisfied that the area was devoid of active security, Fury took up a position close to the double doors leading to the rest of the complex. Here, he intended to wait until the building had been emptied for the night.

The hours passed. Except for the need to refrain from smoking, Fury found it tolerable.

It was also very dark. Fury used the night scope of his ELBOW to sweep his surroundings periodically. But it wasn't practical to keep on doing it. All weapons systems ran off the batteries. They drained mighty quick.

Boredom overtook him. Fury considered contacting HQ by radio, but decided not to chance it. If this was a Hydra front, no telling what kind of electronic eavesdropping equipment might be operating.

He wondered if Starla was monitoring him. He sensed nothing. He didn't know what he should feel, if anything.

On a hunch, Fury closed his eyes and tried to send her a mental question.

Is there danger?

He received nothing in return. Then, remembering that pictures transmitted better than words, he tried to come up with a picture that symbolized the question. It was harder than he thought.

For some reason, he kept envisioning a mousetrap. Identical to the one he had come across. Fury shook his head. Stubbornly, the mousetrap image kept coming back. He couldn't shake it.

Backtracking, Fury found the trap. It looked like an ordinary mousetrap, except it was big enough to snap a rat's neck. There were no wires leading from it, no sign of unusual construction. The brand name was one he knew.

Fury decided it was just an ordinary mousetrap. He returned to his position, and back to trying to establish a link to SPD Spacek.

Finally, out of sheer frustration, Nick Fury thought of a simple red question mark. He kept it in his mind's eye for as long as he could.

Then he waited.

In his mind's eye, he saw only an unrelieved blackness. He wasn't sure what he should see, or how he should see it. Should the image be clear, or vague? He remembered that it should be fixed, like a slide.

After what must have been a dozen minutes, he saw something.

A skull. It was like an optical afterimage. But it was clear. The skull was stark white, bony, its edges etched against a black background.

Nick Fury had an imagination. He knew what imaginary images looked like to his mind's eye. This was different. It wasn't that it was clear, but it was distinct.

He opened his eyes and it was gone. He closed them again.

This time, the image was different. One eye socket seemed less like the other. Deeper, blacker. Like a cave, more than an eye socket. Then he saw why. The outline had changed. It was rounded, more regular, without that rough quality of bony ridge.

Fury stood wondering why it would look that way when he noticed the black line that swept down from the top of the skull to cross the socket and disappear at an angle behind the hollow cheek.

An eye patch! The skull wore an eye patch!

"Damn!"

Then, like a firecracker going off, the skull was replaced by a fire-red image that made the hair stand up on the back of his neck.

A red EXIT sign.

Fury began moving, moving fast. Maybe it was only his imagination. But it didn't feel like his imagination.

Gotta get to the exit, he thought.

Fury moved through the main corridor like chain lightning. He whipped around the corner, then another, using the ELBOW sight to find his way back.

Then came a terrific grinding and growling. Like the early stages of an earthquake. The floor trembled and shook. As if something was building up toward a thunderous explosion.

Fear overtook Nick Fury's mind. Something was wrong, really wrong. And in the pitch darkness, it was impossible to tell what it was.

Staggering around a last corner, Fury found the red EXIT sign over the back door. Feet pounding, he raced toward it.

But he couldn't keep his feet. The floor was shaking too much. The whole joint felt like it was shaking itself apart.

Fury stumbled. He fell. He picked himself up. His senses told him something was happening to the building—something he couldn't process or understand. He only knew he had to get to that exit door. So he picked himself up and ran. And fell again.

When he finally reached the door, it refused to open. It was shuddering and shaking as if bullets were slamming into the other side. But there was no accompanying sound of firearms.

Stepping back, Fury extracted the clip of steel-jacketed rounds and rammed home a short clip of explosive BLAMS.

Stepping back as far as he could, around a corner, Fury dropped to one knee, sighted and opened up.

The BLAMS hit the door like a procession of hand grenades. Hot shrapnel flew backward. Fury withdrew the ELBOW ahead of the storm of flying steel.

When he came around the corner, Fury could see dim outer light through the now blasted-open door.

The door was almost completely gone. But chunks of it hung off the surviving hinges.

Those chunks were being chewed and ground up like they had caught in the blunt teeth of a car crusher.

Fury popped a flashlight at it.

Then he saw clearly—knew why the building was shaking so violently.

For the open door no longer looked out on the Dumpsters in back. They were rising out of his line of sight. Still where he last saw them. At ground level. Ground level—now several feet higher than when Nick Fury had entered the building.

For the building itself was steadily, remorselessly burrowing into the cold earth.

FURY

NICK COVERED THE dozen or so yards between his position and the shrinking space under the illuminated EXIT sign.

He made it in record time. Where there had been a doorway, Fury saw a rising plate of chilled steel. Like a guillotine in reverse, it marked the rising layers of hard Arizona earth into which he was steadily sinking.

Fury grabbed at the top. He could feel hard-packed dirt over the upper lip of the steel containment plate. He started to lever himself up. Only seconds now.

The noise was excruciating. The brick face of the building was scraping steel. He tried to block out the noise. It made him think of bones breaking. His own.

Fury pulled himself off the ground. His booted feet found the plate steel. It offered little traction. Fury dug his fingers into the dirt and gave a Herculean pull.

Maybe he would have made it. Maybe he wouldn't. Nick Fury would never know.

A stuttering of percussive weapons-fire sounded at his back. He recognized the hideously distinctive chattering: Hydra AutoCobras!

To his right, a wavering line of vicious puncture holes ate into the cinderblock wall. To his left, another chipped and splintered its way toward him. Two bullet tracks trying to make an X with his body as the target.

Letting go, Fury dropped and rolled as the converging bullet tracks crossed harmlessly overhead. One hand went for his blaster, the other for the shoulder-holstered Colt.

When he landed on his chest, Fury opened up, two-handed. He took no time to aim. Aiming was not important. He had to nail his foes before they could redirect their fire.

A stream of purling blue energy swept left to right, crossing the track of his Colt's blaze of bullets.

He saw two green-masked Hydras go down. The Colt ran empty. Using the blaster for cover, Fury reclaimed his ELBOW. Leaving the blaster aside, he began unloading explosive rounds.

That did it. The Hydras retreated in a cacophony of ineffectual return fire. Fury jumped up and pursued them.

This was a perfect ELBOW situation. Fury came to every corner, stopped, looked around it in safety and shot at any moving form.

Return fire came back sporadic—and useless. All he exposed was the hard bulletproof ELBOW casing. And it didn't seem to occur to the retreating Hydras to shoot at the weapon. They fired at the spot where his head should be.

This way, Nick Fury shot his way deeper and deeper into the building.

He counted five dead Hydras along the way, their vicious spike-barreled AutoCobra machine pistols lying smoking and useless on the floor. They wore standard Hydra field uniforms—metallic green combat suits marked by two vertical black bands intersecting black leather belts to form an ebony H.

And all the time, the building had continued its remorseless descent into the earth. At last, it settled. In the aftermath, the silence was deafening.

Nick Fury knew one thing. He was in a tomb. If there was a way out, it was going to take work to find it. But first he had to hunt down the last Hydra.

The last Hydra proved wily.

Fury worked from room to room. Along the way, he removed various items from his combat belt. Things that rattled and slapped when he moved. He removed his boots, going in his stocking feet. Anything to give him the edge.

Finally, Fury cornered his elusive foe.

Carefully, he slipped the ELBOW around the corner.

The side monitor showed a shadowy figure in formfitting green. The infrared light picked up the blotches of the polarized lenses.

Fury centered the luminous crosshairs on the spot between the Hydra's artificial eyes. Carefully, he squeezed the trigger.

He never got off the shot. Something—he never knew what—caused him to recoil, the ELBOW unfired. He let it go.

The ELBOW erupted in a blue crackle of electric fire. One minute it was poised in mid-air, waiting for gravity to cast it onto the floor, the next it was a splash of molten metal and plastic that hit the floor as stinking slag.

Fury rolled away from the hot splatter of materials. He kept rolling.

Running footsteps pounded his way. At his back, Fury slapped his utility belt, searching for help. He found a TrikStik, armed it.

The Hydra came around the corner with the blundering confidence of an armed predator stalking unarmed prey.

Fury uncorked from the floor like a striking snake.

Giving the Hydra a disabling kick in the kneecap, he jammed the TrikStik into the silvery-blue maw of the weapon.

Fury rolled clear.

Reflexively, the Hydra's trigger finger came down on the trigger.

The weapon began discharging. The TrikStik went off. Coruscating bolts of electricity ripped up and down the length of the high-tech weapon. The Hydra screamed. He fell. He was still jerking and jolting when the TrikStik charge gave out.

Fury walked over and knocked the weapon from his dead hands.

He hefted it. It was unfamiliar. A new Hydra energy weapon. Something for the lab boys to look over when he got back.

If he got back.

Fury reconned the building. Every window looked out onto plate steel. The doors did the same. When he could get them open.

Exhausting all the obvious exits, Fury collected his equipment and tried to reconnect with Starla Spacek.

He gave a mental thumbs-up.

Back came a clear image. A smile. Disembodied, but genuine. Fury grunted. This ESP stuff was getting easy.

Fury waited for more. He wasn't disappointed.

He got a compass. It showed north-northwest. Fury found his north-northwest and began walking. He kept his eyes closed as much as possible. The clairvoyant images were clearer that way.

The compass changed direction twice. Fury followed it each time.

Finally, he got a stop sign. It was replaced by a clock face, its hands pointing straight up at high noon.

Fury looked up. He saw blank ceiling.

Lifting the energy weapon, he opened up on it.

The beam began peeling back ceiling matter. Plaster and insulation material fell, showered. Fury stepped away.

Taking up another position, he resumed firing.

When he had a hole large enough to exit from, Nick Fury threw the weapon up first and climbed out.

Starlight greeted him. He was standing on an asphalt roof. A roof that sat flush to the surrounding ground.

The rest of the Empire complex had done exactly the

same thing. Where a cluster of buildings had stood, there were only patches of black roof asphalt. And no signs of guards, or human habitation.

Fury dug out his communicator. Nothing lost by using it now.

"Saint Nick to North Pole. Over."

"Password, Saint Nick."

"Psi War."

"Go ahead, Saint Nick. You are verified."

"Send a mop-up team to Empire. We got ourselves a Hydra nest out here."

"Did you say Hydra?"

"Yeah. And it looks like we're back to square one on this operation," growled Fury.

Fury was smoking patiently when the mop-up team arrived from S.H.I.E.L.D. LA.

They dropped down in long-range Orca class helicopters. As soon as their wheels touched ground, red-strapped field agents jumped off, weapons at the ready.

"Don't bother getting excited," Fury told them, grinding his exhausted cigar into the dirt. "The site is deserted. All buildings are now two stories under their foundations."

"Shall we sweep the location, Colonel?"

"Yeah. I want all records, all computers confiscated."

"At once, sir."

"But I'm betting you don't find any," Fury added glumly.

Nick Fury proved to be correct. Every file was empty. Every terminal removed or trashed. There was nothing left but the furniture and the telephones. Even they were disconnected, effectively erasing the redial memories.

The mop-up team leader finished reporting the disappointing news.

"What do we do now, sir?"

Fury told him, "You get to go home. I got me a mountain of headaches to sort through back at the North Pole. And I need a lift to Luke Air Force Base."

Within a half hour, Fury was suborbital once more.

He dropped down and lined up with the Helicarrier. It was night now. The big vessel was lit up like a Christmas tree. The flight deck was illuminated by hooded flood-lamps.

Fury found the groove and ran down the centerline. The gear touched, bounced slightly, then the tailhook caught the number two arrestor cable. It brought the hurtling ship up short, throwing Fury back in his seat so fast that if it hadn't been for the padded headrest, his neck would have been snapped in two.

Dum Dum met him on the flight deck.

"Intel on Empire is like a nest of Chinese boxes. Every time you open one, you find another one, and so on. It's starting to look like it's a front. Probably for Hydra. Want the details?"

"No," snapped Fury. "I want the FAA notified that we have good reason to believe Empire is a front for a foreign agent, and all her flights should be grounded, pronto."

"They're going to want proof."

"Tell them to take a good hard look at Empire HQ."

"That won't cut it, Nick. You know that. We gotta have more than missing planes and dark suspicions."

Fury frowned. "Did Empire file a missing flight report on that Cairo flight?"

"No. So we looked into it. The plane landed on time, at the scheduled airport. Whatever happened, it was as if it never happened."

Absently, Fury tore the cellophane wrapper off a fresh cigar. He dropped in into his belt igniter. It came out smouldering. Taking it in his mouth, he blew a steady breath down the tube of tobacco, producing an angry red tip.

"Ever ID that aircraft that flew out of the clouds instead of the Empire jet?" he asked.

"We still don't know. A Middle Eastern carrier."

"Have the gun camera footage squirted to us. I want to know the carrier's name."

Fury smoked thoughtfully as the lift lowered them deeper and deeper into the Helicarrier's cavernous innards.

"Want to be dropped off any place in particular?" Dum Dum asked.

"Take me to Re-Vue. I'm betting Starla's burning the midnight oil."

She was. They found her monitoring an RV session. She called for a break when Fury motioned for her to come down.

"Nice job of transmitting," he told her.

"It's a two-way street, Colonel. You received as well as anyone I've worked with."

"Was that mousetrap a message from you?"

"It was. I couldn't understand why you didn't evacuate. I thought you'd understand a mousetrap meant a trap."

"Simple. I ran across a real mousetrap. I kept seeing that one."

Starla frowned. "Overlay. Your brain presented you with a picture of a real mousetrap instead of the one I tried sending. It confused you."

"We gotta lot of bugs to work out on Special Powers, lady."

Starla nodded soberly. "Hydra was expecting you, Colonel. No doubt the location was guarded by extrasensors."

"Tell me about it." Fury nodded toward the Re-Vue chamber. "I hope this is follow-up."

"It is. But my people are tired. We're getting a lot of sensory leakage and white noise."

"Stands to reason. I got me a headache from trying to hold onto those images you were transmitting my way."

Starla made a face. "Clairvoyant fatigue. Occupational hazard. It passes soon enough."

Fury said, "I'll get to the point: You were right about

Empire, half right about Hydra, and the jury's still out on Nadir al-Bazinda, but I'm leaning that way myself. Add them all up and what have you got?"

"An alliance. But to what end?"

"Try scanning al-Bazinda. See what you get."

"Gladly. I'll take this one myself. Do you want to monitor?"

"Why not? My night's pretty well shot."

Starla was in Alpha ten minutes later. Fury watched her from the blackened control booth, Dum Dum looming over him.

"Okay," Fury began. "Ready when you are."

"Ready," Starla said, voice distant but clear.

"The target for tonight is Nadir al-Bazinda. What's he up to?"

Starla closed her eyes. She was silent a long time.

"I'm not getting anything."

"What's that mean?"

"I'm blocked. Something is blocking me."

"I thought you said RV can't be blocked."

"I'm not remote viewing. I'm trying to link with his mind, but I'm blocked. That could mean any number of things. He has drugs or alcohol in his system. Or maybe he's so far into Beta I can't read his brainwaves. Alpha can't read Beta any more than an AM radio can receive FM signals."

"Switch to RV mode," Fury ordered.

Starla settled down on the couch. Her body seemed to loosen and relax even more.

"I can see him," she reported. "He's meeting with his Military Command Council. He's pounding his fists on the desk. He doesn't look happy at all. I'd say he's in Beta, all right."

"Get anything of what he's saying?"

"If I were a better clairaudient, I might be able to repeat a few words in Arabic. But I'm not, so I can't."

"Give me something, anything," Fury insisted. "I got a

bad feeling there's a clock ticking and I don't know what's going to happen at zero."

Starla went deeper. "I'm getting scattered images. Like a kaleidosope. This is strange."

"Out with it."

"I see a Hydra symbol—a skull with the coiled tentacles of an octopus, but the skull is wearing a burnoose. It's definitely a burnoose. This is the second time I've received this image, Colonel. I would take it seriously."

"That means a Hydra Middle Eastern is forming."

Starla frowned. "Don't steer me. I didn't say that. Wait a minute. There's something imprinted on the skull's brow. I can barely see it. There! A scorpion. There's a tattoo of a scorpion on the skull's brow."

"I got me a feeling I know what that means," Fury growled. "Keep going."

"Now I'm seeing a Christmas tree. It must be overlay. Christmas is two days away."

"Maybe not. Keep going."

"It's just a Christmas tree. But I feel something sinister about it. It looks like an ordinary tree, but I have a feeling of impending negativity around it. The green is wrong. There's something about the ornaments, as well. They're too red—almost a blood red. The colors are sick. They clash."

"Anything else?"

"Colonel, I don't like the energy I feel around Nadir al-Bazinda. It's malignant, almost palpably evil."

"Okay, break off." Fury killed the video and audio.

Starla rolled off the couch. She sat for a long minute, looking pale and dazed and holding her stomach.

Fury was at her side, asking, "You okay, Spacek?"

"Nausea. When I connect with some people, I merge with them. I get a kind of contact psychic sickness. This is an extremely evil man, Colonel."

"Tell us about it," Dum Dum said.

Nick Fury helped Starla to her feet. Her knees wobbled. She sat down again.

Fury said, "I want you to get some rest. I'm going to really need you tomorrow."

"Tomorrow?"

"On what you've given me, I'm ordering the Helicarrier to the Persian Gulf. Whatever's about to go down, it keeps pointing back to Nadir al-Bazinda and Hydra. They're in cahoots. We're taking the investigation to the head scorpion himself."

Starla Spacek snapped awake to the sound of Nick Fury's menacing growl coming through her bedside intership com.

"You rested enough?"

"I slept," Starla admitted, her words mushy.

"Suit up. We're on station. You got ten minutes to meet me at your end of the main keel corridor."

"Ten minutes doesn't give me time to shower."

"Fair enough. You got eleven." The speaker clicked dead.

Starla stood at the appointed place in exactly ten minutes, 28 seconds.

Fury rolled up in a massive Humvee, painted a stealth black. He popped the door open. Starla slid in and Fury wheeled the vehicle around in a tight circle and floored it.

"Aren't we exceeding intership speed limits?"

"Gotta get where we're going," Fury growled as the small people movers and S.H.I.E.L.D. operatives lunged left and right to fling themselves out of his way.

"You could run somebody over . . ."

"If I can do it, Hydra can have them for breakfast any old day of the week. I like to keep my people on their toes. Besides we got a great medical package." He flourished his ever-present cigar. "I wouldn't still be smoking these cheap cheroots if we didn't."

Something like a smile crossed his face after his teeth reclaimed the cigar.

Starla shuddered.

Coming up to a deck-edge lift, Fury turned in and parked. The SO ran the lift up to the deck. Starla watched the man-sized deck numbers descend and sink away, reminding her once again of the prodigious immensity of the vessel that was now her home and base of professional operations. It was a long, long way from the windowless building at Fort Meade that concealed the CIA Stargate program.

When they broke daylight, there wasn't much of it. The stars were still out. Venus hung in the east. Up here in the high latitudes, the rising sun had not yet poked.

The lift came level and Fury put the Hummer into gear. Its diesel motor grew like the threatening roar of a mature lion.

It came off the lift. Fury executed a J turn, and laid it straight down the centerline of the main deck. His booted foot floored the gas.

The Hummer went from a respectable 40 MPH to an unnerving 90, compressing them back into their seats with almost g-force.

"Wave good-bye to the nice people on the Bridge," Fury suggested as the lighted island tower windows zipped by.

Starla sat frozen. Up until now, she had assumed Fury was personally ferrying her to a conference, or pre-mission briefing.

But as the end of the runway came looming up 500 yards away, then 300, then too fast for processing, she began to think differently.

Fury was saying, "The deck edge up ahead is flared just a little. They have this little ski jump feature on a lot of naval carriers to give takeoff an extra upward kick. Reason is once you fly off the end, you immediately sink. Even under power, sink too much and you're in the drink.

There ain't any drink within miles of the ship at this altitude, but for certain VTOL jobs, we like to give the short-takeoff boys an extra kick in the pants."

The edge came rushing up. Fury's voice was as calm as a rasp on metal. Starla felt like the metal.

"I hope this vehicle is—"

The Hummer jolted upward, then vaulted high.

The immensity of the dark world that opened up below was frightening. It was as if a vortex yawned wide. Reaching the apex of its vault, the Hummer paused for a momentary eternity, and began a sickening, stomach-churning drop.

Starla closed her eyes. This was too much like a roller coaster she had once gotten sick on.

"The manual says you should only perform this little maneuver in dire emergencies," Fury said, uncapping a fire-engine-red button. He thumbed it.

Like a jack-in-the-box springing, the Hummer's wheel assemblies flipped downward, hubcaps splitting as the wheel-rim turbines started their climb to serviceable RPMS.

"One of the downsides is that it takes a minute or so for the turbines to get up to speed," Fury continued. "Sometimes while fighting the downdraft, they kinda seize up."

When they caught, Starla knew it because the Hummer lifted, bobbing like a cork, and settled at an even keel. Only then did she allow her eyes to open. Her fingers were clutching her safety harness. She let go.

"But if you don't test the procedure out every once in a while," Fury added, grinning, "how are you gonna know it'll work when you really need it to?"

Fury had the wheel in yoke mode. He goosed the pop-up throttles, which Starla was pleased to see had popped up on cue.

The Hummer rocketed ahead, leaving the silvery star-lit hull of the Helicarrier behind.

Down below, the Persian Gulf twinkled. Lights were few. Gulf shipping traffic was thin. A solitary oil platform stood out as its gas pipe vented a steady blue flame.

"Where are we going?" Starla asked after awhile.

"Downtown Gullahbad."

Starla swallowed silently. "What's our mission?"

"Recon."

"You don't make it sound that dangerous."

"Lady, you ain't never been on a recon with me. Now listen up: a Hydra Seadragon chopper was spotted penetrating the southern No-Fly zone, bound for Gullahbad—or the City of Ghouls, as it's called in English. We're going to hunt it down, and see where it goes."

The dark coastline of Quorak came into sight. Soon, they were over an endless undulating plain of desert sand.

Fury remarked, "Nice thing about Quorak. It's mostly sand. We can pretty much go where we want, and the worst thing we'll catch is the spit off an occasional camel."

Fury brought the Hummer down close to the desert floor. The exhaust from the wheel-mounted turbines sent fine loose particles spraying out on either side of them.

Starla looked back. Even in the weak early morning light, she could make out the sandy wake they were leaving.

"Don't sweat it," Fury said. "Wind'll blow it back."

"I didn't say anything."

"You didn't have to."

Starla settled back in her seat. "You could have brought a more experienced field agent in this mission."

"Could have. Wanted you."

"Why?"

"I'm startin' to like your style. You're direct, Spacek. Stubborn, too. You don't play politics. You got guts. I appreciate those qualities. Mostly because I got 'em myself."

"Thanks."

"And you're psychic as hell."

"I hope you realize if we get into trouble, if shooting starts, the noise and confusion of combat will pop me into a Beta state. I'm going to be useless psychically."

"Don't sweat it. This is just a little recon." Fury was thoughtful a minute. "By the way, if we do run into trouble, your job will be to blast it apart."

"If I have to, I have to. I just hope I don't have to. That was one reason I was attracted to S.H.I.E.L.D.: so-called wet affairs are avoided whenever possible."

"Underscore 'whenever possible,'" Fury returned gruffly. "Hydra, A.I.M. and any number of other outlaw organizations we've gone up against won't let us play by S.H.I.E.L.D. rules all the time. Remember that."

"Understood." Starla eyed Fury speculatively.

"Except for the gray in your temples, you appear to be a relatively young man."

"I keep in shape."

"They say you were a commando during World War II. You fought in Korea. And again in Viet Nam. In between, you were attached to CIA."

Fury puffed thoughtfully. "A good cigar will do wonders for a man's constitution."

"You don't even *want* to be serious, do you?"

"I had a bellyful of serious over a lifetime of fighting and struggle. These days, I let the past stay in the past. I don't spend a lot of my time thinking about time, or birthdays, or calendars, or growing old."

"That's because you don't. Grow old, that is."

Fury said nothing. There was something new in his manner. In his tone of voice. A pensiveness.

Starla asked, "Why do I see needles around you?"

Fury looked concerned. "Needles. What kind of needles?"

"Medical syringes. Hypodermics. I see you injecting yourself with something. A fluid. It's pale yellow."

Fury was silent for a very long time. The sun crawled up on the eastern horizon. It touched the sharp edges of the surrounding sand dunes into thin fire, while transforming the hollows in between dunes into inky pools.

"I don't appreciate you reading my private thoughts," he said at last.

"Sorry. Things come to me. I forget to censor myself. Besides, I wasn't actually reading your mind. You were throwing off information. I captured it. When you're as receptive as I am, it gets to be like inhaling."

"Okay, I'll buy that." Fury chewed his cigar thoughtfully. "You know," he said, "I read your book, and nowhere in it does it say how you got so psychic."

Starla looked out the passenger side window. Her voice grew thin.

"You have to understand that it's easy for a psychic to be misunderstood," she said. "People can be incredibly skeptical. I see my mission in life as advancing the understanding of emerging human abilities. What the CIA used to call Enhanced Human Potential. It was a neat and tidy way to make psychics sound politically and scientifically acceptable. I wrote *Psi Spy* to teach people. I left a lot of things out." Her eyes grew reflective. "Some things are better left unsaid."

Fury ran his window down a crack. "Our background search says you're an orphan. You have no idea who your folks were. That have anything to do with it?"

"Everything, and nothing."

"You also went blind when you were eleven."

Starla's head snapped around. "How did you find out about that?"

"You were in a hospital for a month. The doctors couldn't explain why you lost your sight. Hospitals keep records. Our background check accessed those records."

"Did you turn up anything else?"

"Not about that." Fury knocked cigar ash out his window. "Wanna tell your story to a sympathetic ear?"

"Do you?" Starla countered.

Fury considered. "Sure. You go first."

Starla looked out her own window, as if into the past.

"I was an orphan, just as you said. Otherwise, there was nothing unusual or remarkable about my life. Until I turned eleven. I was in school. It was an ordinary day. I was sitting at my desk waiting for class to end when something drew my eyes to the ceiling. I saw—or thought I saw—a face. I caught only a glimpse. Then I blacked out. When I woke up in the hospital, I was blind. The doctors could do nothing. My adoptive parents were frantic. I was frightened. I kept trying to open my eyelids wider with my fingers, thinking if I got more light I would be able to see again."

"Must've been tough," Fury said.

"The doctors X-rayed my head for tumors, ophthamologists examined my eyes for foreign objects and optical nerve damage. They found nothing. They told my parents there was no hope. I overheard them. I cried for days. Everyone felt helpless."

A glimmer of sunlight crept over the undulating horizon.

Starla continued in the same strangely unemotional tone with which she was speaking.

"One night, I woke up out of a deep sleep. I wasn't in the hospital bed anymore. I had bilocated. I could see, but I didn't know where I was except that it was very, very dark. A bright light filled the darkness. The light had a voice. It said, 'Don't you know you are part of something greater?' Before I could respond, a man appeared to me. He wore the same face I'd glimpsed before I blacked out. This time, I saw him clearly. He was a Native American. He told me that his blood ran through my veins, that I was half Cheyenne. That I should be proud of my ancestry, for spirits that had lived before lived in me. Even though I didn't recognize his face, he looked familiar, strangely, hauntingly familiar. Then he told me to wake up and go home."

Starla looked at Nick Fury's chiseled profile, wreathed in tobacco smoke. "I woke up at that exact moment, and I could see perfectly. The doctors couldn't explain it any more than they could my blindness. I was discharged that afternoon. Ever since then, I've been operationally psychic."

Fury grunted. "That's it?"

"That's how it started for me. Over the years, I grew more psychic. I got a reputation for helping the police with unsolved murders. That's how I came to the attention of the CIA. The rest you know. Except for one thing."

"What's that?" Fury asked.

"Years later, I was driving through a blinding snow-storm when the face of the Cheyenne brave appeared in my windshield. It shook me up so much I pulled over to the side of the road—just in time to miss being demolished by a skidding oil tanker truck. But I knew—knew to a perfect certainty—who that man was."

Starla had been staring out into space. Now she faced Fury. Her voice grew clear and distinct.

"He was me. I was him in a previous life. I can't prove it. But I don't have to. I lived before as a Cheyenne brave. Somehow, the person that I was reached forward in time to save the person I am now."

Fury let out a slow breath. There was no smoke in it. He had stopped inhaling. "I can see why you'd leave that out of your biography. Instead of giving you a contract, the CIA might have found you a nice rubber room."

"Other people's doubts don't bother me," Starla said thinly. "When you know the truth, you know it. It's enough."

"I've seen a lot of strange things in my life," Nick Fury allowed. "And I've learned one thing: it's a lot easier to be a skeptic than it is to wrestle with the truth. I'll take your story the way you dish it out: without salt."

"Thank you," Starla said simply. "So what's your story, Colonel Fury?"

"Call me Nick. But only when we're in the field."

"Done."

"Back in the Big One," Fury said slowly, "my outfit was the First Attack Squad. Better known as the Howling Commandos. Finest pack of Joes that ever fought in any war. I got separated from them one day in France. Year was '42, '43. In around there. Stepped on a Ratzi land mine. I don't even remember the mission that brought us there. Should have bought the old farm. But I was lucky. I took a lot of shrapnel, but not enough to plant me six feet under."

Starla pushed away a wave of unwanted images. They were private. She didn't wish to see them.

"French partisans found me, dragged me off to see this doctor. Berman, his name was. He patched me up pretty good. But there was more to him than being a saw-bones caught in a war. He had been working on something he called the Infinity Formula. It keeps human cells from degenerating over time. Kinda like the fountain of youth in a syringe. He gave me a shot, said it would retard the aging process for a year. After a year, another dose would buy me another 365 days. I didn't believe him at first. It was war. A lot of people go crazy in war. Shell shock. Grief. Things like that.

"Anyway, while I was recuperating, the Nazis bombed the hell out of the area. The house went up. I got out alive. With enough of the Infinity Formula serum to keep me going for a while."

"You didn't believe him, but you still took the serum with you?" Starla asked.

"Guess I had me a hunch."

"So for all practical purposes, you don't age. Amazing."

"My body don't age. My insides sure feel like they got

old. In my heart, I sometimes feel like I've been walking this war-torn earth for a thousand years. Maybe that's the trade-off. I'm kinda an old soul in a young man's body. I seen all manner of war in my time. I can hardly remember seeing any peace."

"It sounds to me like you were chosen to follow this destiny," Starla allowed.

"That's one way of looking at it," Fury admitted. "But if there's anything to reincarnation, I hope this time around buys me a long, long furlough. I figure I earned my eternal rest."

Fury's cigar went out. He paused to light it, had second thoughts and muttered, "The hell with it. Maybe I'll live a couple of days longer."

They flew on in silence for a long time after that, lost in their private thoughts.

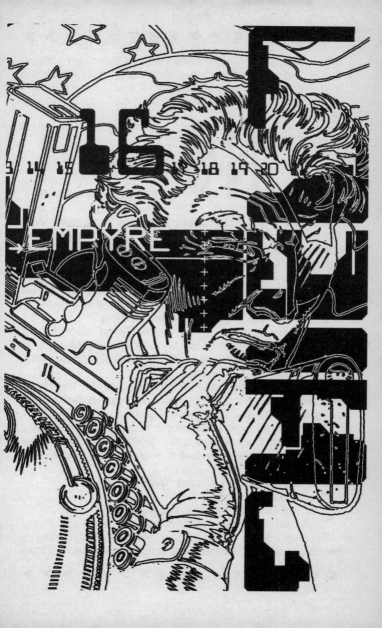

NO

THERE WAS **NO** MISTAKING GULLAHBAD from the air.

It was a forest of alabaster domes and minarets burnished copper by the rising rays of the sun. It might have been any ancient-yet-modern Middle Eastern city. But for the ruins. Over a long decade, Gullahbad had been pounded by U.N. Coalition warplanes, cruise missiles, and smart bombs. Rebuilding had for a time overtaken bomb damage, but in the most recent cycle of airstrikes, new areas of the skyline had been eroded.

Nick Fury frowned as he looked for a place to set down. The multimode Hummer was virtually invisible to ground radar, but getting on the ground undetected was going to take a bit of finesse.

Chopping throttle, he went into hover mode. The Hummer slowed to a drift. Fury goosed the forward retros, bringing the massive machine to a stop.

The road below was one of the main highways leading to Gullahbad. Fury settled to the ground. The clank of the deployed undercarriage feet brought Starla Spacek out of a sound sleep.

She sat up, looked around. "Where are we?"

"Gullahbad. Suburbs."

"Oh, my God. Why didn't you wake me?"

"I just did. Besides, you needed some shut-eye."

Starla made an unhappy face. "Alpha drift. An occupational hazard. Sometimes I zone out and fall into a Theta state. Another reason why psi agents don't belong in high-intensity combat situations."

Fury punched up the navigational computer.

"Word from the carrier is that the Hydra Seadragon set down about three miles due south, about where one of al-Bazinda's infamous palaces sits," he explained. "Probably a meeting going on."

The nav screen showed them a tactical overhead of their position relative to the destination zone. The main route flashed green. Alternate routes were steady white.

Once the wheel-rim turbines finished spiraling down to a cold stop, Fury tucked the wheels back into roadable position. The Hummer dropped back on its huge tires. He keyed the ignition. The diesel engine coughed into life.

"We're sort of conspicuous, don't you think?" Starla pointed out nervously.

"Al-Bazinda's inner circle bought themselves a fleet of Hummers after the Gulf War," he said. "This baby has Royal Quoraki license plates. But thanks for reminding me."

Out of the backseat area—a crowded nest of electronics and extendable offensive weapons systems—Fury brought two flat piles of white linen.

"Put them on. They're thobes—Arab national costumes."

They pulled them on with difficulty. Fury adjusted a burnoose over his head as if he'd worn one before. Starla needed help with hers.

"This won't pass muster on close inspection," she said doubtfully.

"Nobody inspects a Quoraki government Hummer," Fury said, throwing the vehicle into gear.

The Hummer ate miles like a stealthy tiger. The sun continued its climb into the sky. Somewhere in the city, the Muslim call to prayer came—a soulful masculine wailing.

Vehicles on the road were few. Camels and ox-drawn

carts were frequently met. A Quoraki Military Police checkpoint loomed ahead. Starla caught her breath. Fury accelerated.

They were waved through without having to stop.

"This is too easy," Starla said, looking back at the checkpoint.

"I told you: this is only a recon."

"You say that like you'd say this is only going over Niagara Falls in a teacup."

Fury said nothing. He was slipping into combat mode, his focus tightening like a steel mainspring winding to the breaking point. Starla sensed his mind walling itself off from extraneous distractions. The man's focus was absolutely ferocious.

Nadir al-Bazinda watched the Hydra Seadragon helicopter settle on the landing pad in the quadrangle that was surrounded on all four sides by what he called the Palace of Mysteries.

It was his favorite retreat. When the U.N. inspection teams struggled to gain access to the many personal palaces that were scattered throughout Quorak, seeking weapons of mass destruction, this is the one he protected to the very last. It was an insult, an abomination that his mortal enemies had gained entry into his sanctum sanctorum.

But those days were in the past. The U.N. inspection teams had been ejected. No more would they harry and harass his sovereign territory. It was true that there was a heavy price being paid. Almost daily bombings by the hated enemy air force. But this was a temporary condition.

These concerns faded from his mind as the Hydra envoys approached.

Al-Bazinda drew erect, as befitted the most powerful man in the Middle East. The Scourge of All Infidels. The Aladdin of the Arab world.

The Hydra came masked. It was their way. Nadir al-Bazinda accepted this. Masks meant fear. He knew no fear. Let them wear their ridiculous masks. All the world knew the face of Nadir al-Bazinda—and all the world feared that resolute visage.

They stopped, their serpentine-green thobes marked with the black H of Hydra rustling as they touched their hands to their concealed foreheads and intoned, *"Salaam Aleikim."*

"You sent word there is more trouble," al-Bazinda said after the formalities were concluded.

Their leader, who called himself Imperial Hydra, spoke in the Arabic of cosmopolitan Cairo.

"Yesterday, our mutual foes penetrated Empire Phoenix," he said. "This was foreseen by our extrasensors. All critical records and other documents were evacuated, and a snare set."

"It failed?"

"Yes. How did you know that?"

Nadir al-Bazinda curled his mustached lips in contempt.

"My warplanes have reported sighting S.H.I.E.L.D. Helicarrier over the Gulf."

The Imperial Hydra started. "Here?"

"Here. I am preparing to launch a sortie against them within the hour."

"That would be foolhardy, O Fist of Allah."

The honorific almost took the sting out of the implied insult. Al-Bazinda stayed the hands of his personal guard, arrayed on either side. They were lowering their AK-47 automatic rifles.

"Have a care. While you stand on Quoraki soil, you are under my rule, my laws—and my protection."

"Your warplanes have failed to challenge U.S. overflights," the envoy from Hydra said. "How can they hope to sting the S.H.I.E.L.D. Helicarrier? It is the most potent weapons platform ever constructed."

"You did not understand Quoraki thinking. Not to strike would be to admit weakness. To invite attack. If I lose a few planes and pilots, I lose a few planes and pilots. But I retain my honor and prestige among my countrymen."

The Hydra said nothing.

"Is it your belief that S.H.I.E.L.D. has penetrated the mysteries of our combined operation to come?" al-Bazinda asked.

"No. But it is clear they have connected Empire Airlines to the attempts on their two most prestigious symbols, Nicholas Fury and their fearsome Helicarrier."

"Attempts that would have succeeded had you allowed me to undertake them in my own way."

"They had to look like accidents. If either jet had been rigged like the jumbo jet that incinerated downtown Persopolis, Empire would have been shut down that day. And where would we be?"

Al-Bazinda said nothing to this. He was growing impatient. "And where are we on this new morning?"

"Despite the events of yesterday, no word has come from the U.S. FAA to suspend Empire's passenger carrier license."

"It may yet come."

"Until it does, we will proceed on schedule. I have brought an updated list of cities for targeting."

Nadir al-Bazinda took the list. He eyed it in silence for some moments. His face darkened like a thundercloud. The black scorpion birthmark on his forehead lost intensity.

"This list has been cut by two-thirds."

"We have discussed this among ourselves. Your original list was too sweeping, too comprehensive. Some of the target sights involve the interests of other Hydra cells. We have brethren in—"

"This is my campaign, and I and I alone will decide what targets are legitimate and which are to be spared," al-Bazinda barked.

"To destroy Washington, D.C., would be to bring the full wrath of the United States and S.H.I.E.L.D. down upon our heads," the Imperial Hydra retorted hotly. "Hydra Middle East is not interested in all-out global war. Our chief objective is to demonstrate our power, by this means attracting other Hydra cells to join with us as the nucleus of a new Hydra International—with Quoraki as our base of operations, of course."

Dark fire flashed in Nadir al-Bazinda's deep eyes.

"I do not like the way you put that . . ." he said in a low, menacing tone. It was a dog's growl coming from a human throat.

"We will be partners, of course," Imperial Hydra said hastily. "Equal partners."

"I have no equal on Quoraki soil," said Nadir al-Bazinda.

"This has already been explained to you. Once Hydra has been made whole, all of her resources, all of her technology, will be at your disposal. Gullahbad will be the capital city of Hydra Middle East. From here, we will spread out our tentacles to other Middle Eastern nations, bringing them under our yoke. This, Fist of Allah, is why the target list has been reduced to key Gulf-state sights and a few European capitals."

Al-Bazinda slapped the sheet in his hands. "There are no American cities on this list. I have consecrated my life to demolishing Americans, not my fellow Arabs."

"That will be Phase Two, O Future Emir of the Gulf."

"Phase Two?" al-Bazinda thundered, his growling voice erupting into full cry. "Empire has been compromised. There can be no Phase Two. There is barely time to implement Phase One—the destruction of major United States cities."

"Precisely why we must move Phase One up. We cannot risk Empire planes being grounded prematurely. We are two days from Zero Hour. We must strike the target list today—tomorrow at the latest. S.H.I.E.L.D. may not have the proof or the jurisdiction to stop Empire from fly-ing, but they are resourceful and dedicated. They will re-move the moon from the sky to find it."

Nadir al-Bazinda stood rooted. His dusky face was darkening with suffusing blood. It was as if he was a human thermometer and his rising blood pressure showed in his features.

The tiny scorpion on his brow seemed to fade with each successive darkening of his skin, until it was no longer visible. His eyes retreated into their hollows.

The Hydra felt a strange unaccustomed chill. The face framed in the burnoose now had less the cast of a human visage than a hybrid skull. For the first time, he had an understanding of the malignant enormity of the monster he had allied himself with.

"I am prepared to compromise," Nadir al-Bazinda said, snapping his fingers.

From niches all around the quadrangle, Quorakis in flowing white robes bearing heavy scimitars emerged.

The Hydras shrank into a pocket.

"State your compromise," Imperial Hydra said.

"If we are to be allied to the death, I must see your true faces."

"Our faces would mean nothing to you."

Al-Bazinda glowered. His voice darkened. "Your naked faces will press themselves into the dirt at your feet in ac-knowlegment of my supremacy over Hydra, or your heads will fall at your self-same feet, masked as they are. And that is how I will bury them."

The headsmen formed a circle. Their broad blades shimmered in the thin morning light.

The S.H.I.E.L.D. Hummer ghosted past the summer palace of Nadir al-Bazinda just as the iridescent green Hydra Seadragon helicopter settled out of sight behind its walls.

"Looks like Practical Intel was dead on the money," Fury said.

The main entrance was as big as that of an old English castle, but without the drawbridge and moat. The way was wide open. Two sentries in Quoraki camel-colored uniforms stood at their posts.

"What do we do now?" Starla asked.

"Continue the recon," Fury said casually. Jamming the gas pedal to the floorboard, he veered off the road and raced toward the opening, blowing his horn furiously.

"Are you crazy!" Starla exploded.

"Quiet. This will either work perfectly, or blow up in our faces."

It turned out to work perfectly. The sentries froze for an instant, took in the sight of the black Humvee charging at them like a metallic rhinocerous, and no doubt saw the green official license plate in the front.

They got out of the way in a hurry. The Hummer shot past them.

Fury pulled left, sending the Hummer along a narrow vehicular way. Coming to a set of slots where various black Mercedes limousines and other official vehicles were parked, he slid into an empty space.

Starla looked at him, her mouth open in shock.

"Let's reconnoiter some more," Fury said, grabbing an ELBOW from a backseat rack.

They got out. Starla found her knees were watery.

"Suck it up, Spacek," Fury told her. "This ain't a CIA psychic picnic. You're in the big league now."

The place was a maze of indoor and outdoor court-yards. It had more the look and feel of a Spanish-style hacienda than a Moorish castle.

Security was surprisingly light. Fury took point, using his ELBOW to see safely around corners. They pro-gressed several stages undetected.

Coming to an open cul-de-sac, Fury spotted a pa-trolling Quoraki.

He motioned for Starla to join him. She knelt. Fury indicated the side-mounted ELBOW screen, the Quoraki framed within.

"Needle gun on my hip," he undertoned. "Fires anesthetic needles. This one's yours."

Reaching in through a slash in Fury's thobe, she found the butt of the weapon.

"Thanks," said Starla.

"Aim for muscle," Fury suggested.

Creeping around him, Starla took aim and fired. The Needle gun hissed, sending a slim projectile into the man's side. He went down with 3ccs of Ketamine coursing through his veins.

They worked forward, section upon section, this way. Fury spotted the enemy. Starla took them out. All was accomplished without taking return fire.

At last they came to a niche that overlooked the central courtyard.

Hiding in the shadows, they watched in pent-up silence.

The Seadragon sat in the center of a red-ringed helipad like a resting dragonfly, its serrated rotors drooping slightly.

Off to one side, surrounded by personal guards wearing almost identical mustaches, stood the dictator of Quorak, Nadir al-Bazinda. He was dressed in an olive-drab ribbed military jersey and fatigue pants, a sidearm in a belt holster. Incongruously, a green burnoose sat on his head.

And clustered in a nervous knot before him, were five Hydra soldiers, each wearing green thobes marked with the Hydra initial, but otherwise indistinguishable by rank and uniform.

Nadir al-Bazinda was shouting. His voice was like a dark thunder. It was an ugly voice.

One of the Hydras—obviously the spokesman—returned speech in the same language, his voice twisted in a mixture of fear and anger. His lizard green robes fluttered as he gestured.

And advancing on the Hydras were a shrinking circle of men wielding uplifted and very deadly-looking scimitars.

"Can you get what they're saying?" Fury hissed to Starla.

Starla listened. She shut her eyes. "It's not going well."

Fury grunted, "I can tell that much by their voices."

"I read fear off the Hydra agents. They're unarmed. They're regretting it now. From al-Bazinda, I get only a malignancy."

Nadir al-Bazinda repeated something in Arabic. It was sharp, cutting. Obviously a command.

The Hydras looked to one another, their empty hands fluttering in a kind of resigned helplessness. The way their visored eyes exchanged glances made Fury think of locusts silently communicating with one another. There was no impression of human thought or feeling. They were like bugs. Trapped bugs.

The spokesman nodded to the others. Taking a deep breath, he reached up and whipped off his mask. The face that stood revealed was shiny with sweat. The man was Middle Eastern. That much was clear. He had the look of an Egyptian.

One by one, the others followed suit. Their masks came off in their hands. They held them, looking nervous for a minute. Then the spokesman dropped onto his hands and knees at Nadir al-Bazinda's booted feet. His forehead touched the ground.

Al-Bazinda looked down at the prostrate Hydra, a slow smile curling the corners of his half-hidden mouth.

He gestured for the other Hydra agents to follow the example of their leader. As one, they did.

And in unison, the headsmen fell upon them.

The blades flashed up. The headsmen moved in. It was perfectly timed, excellently coordinated. A single downward chop of each blade, and four human heads rolled clear of their collapsing bodies.

All except one.

The lead Hydra, sensing what was to come, twisted clear. A dagger came out of his sleeve, to impale the kneecap of his would-be executioner. The man screamed. His blade fell. It happened to fall onto his right foot, bisecting it.

That made him scream even more so.

Nadir al-Bazinda whipped a .45 automatic from his hip holster and calmly shot the headsman dead. That dispensed with all screaming.

The surviving Hydra made a lunge for the Seadragon. A stream of bullets took apart the Plexiglas cockpit, discouraging him from that mode of escape. He reversed direction, zigzagging like a frightened rabbit, and cut straight for the niche where Nick Fury knelt watching.

Fury leaped out, the big boxy ELBOW in his hands. He opened up. A withering stream of BLAMs vomited forth.

They came out in a single-file stream, but once in open air, the internal guidance system kicked in. They deployed every which way, each one a heat-seeking round.

The heat they sought first were the hot muzzles of the Quoraki Kalashnikovs. Changing direction in mid-flight, they struck, blowing them apart. Weapons fell from shrapnel-lacerated hands. Men howled. Nadir al-Bazinda had the presence of mind to drop his .45 before one found him.

Unerringly, a skimming BLAM dipped toward the fallen weapon, taking it apart.

"This way!" Fury called to the stumbling Hydra.

The Hydra halted, hesitating. And Fury lunged for him. Grabbing him up in one big paw, the director of S.H.I.E.L.D. dragged him to cover.

To Starla, he barked, "Discourage 'em."

Starla rolled out from behind a pillar and emptied the needle gun. All 300 rounds. The withering stream of .15-

caliber anesthetic needles peppered the walls and took down everyone still standing. They dropped, landing like porcupines with quills erected in fear.

Fury said, "Good work. Follow me."

He yanked the Hydra after him. Starla took up the rear.

"Who are you people?" the Hydra demanded.

"Shut up. You're being rescued. Act grateful."

The Hydra said nothing. He pulled himself together and began running under his own power.

The burst of fire was drawing sentries. They came pounding toward them.

Fury met each group with a burst from the ELBOW, cutting them down before they could react defensively. Soon, they reached the waiting Hummer.

"Pile in," Fury ordered, pushing the Hydra into the front seat, and jamming in after him. Starla grabbed the passenger side, pinning the green-uniformed prisoner between them.

Fury kick-started the Hummer's diesel engine, backed it up. Quoraki soldiers came rushing up. Fury gave them a blast of his horn as a warning. They opened up with their rifles.

Bullets spanked harmlessly off the rear window and body.

"One side," Fury growled, "or consider yourself roadkill."

The Quorakis tried to get out of the way. One succeeded. Two more took the brunt of the reversing Hummer. The cruel crunch of bone made Starla cover her ears.

Reaching the arched exit, Fury got the Hummer turned around and onto the road. Then he floored it.

The Hummer leapt forward like an ebony lion. It picked up speed.

"Once we're clear," Fury told Starla, "we'll switch over and fly our prisoner back to base."

Starla shucked off her native thobe, saying, "We don't need these things anymore."

Fury followed her example. But he simply grabbed a fistful of cloth and tore it from his body, revealing his combat uniform.

"You are S.H.I.E.L.D.," the Hydra said, his voice dull of emotion.

"Them's the breaks," Nick Fury told him. "Look at it this way: at least you still got your head, which is more than I can say for the jokers you brought to the party with you."

Jammed in between them, Nick Fury and Starla Spacek could feel the Hydra shudder violently as the memory of his near-fate came flooding back.

They took a dusty corner hard.

And coming up the road, three abreast, were a trio of desert-camoflage Quoraki military Land Rovers, soldiers hanging off back-seat-mounted .50-caliber machine guns.

"Slow down," Starla urged. "Maybe we can bluff them."

"Bluff them, hell," Fury said fiercely. "Let's show 'em what we're made of."

And to Starla Spacek's utter horror, the director of S.H.I.E.L.D. pressed the gas to the floor and sent the Hummer roaring at the traveling roadblock like a man possessed.

NICK FURY WAS NOT AS

reckless and foolhardy as he sometimes seemed.

Over a long military career, he had encountered many unique situations. After a while, they started repeating themselves.

Fury's mind flashed back to a time in Italy where he was nursing an ailing Jeep through enemy territory and encountered a group of German military motorcycles with machine gunners in the sidecars.

That situation had looked impossible at the time. And since it was death to go forward as well as back, Fury had rushed into the teeth of death bellowing out the cry of the Howlers, "Wah Hoo!"

It had worked then. It stood to work again.

"On the count of three, I want you two to yell 'Wah Hoo,'" Fury told his passengers.

The Hydra looked blank. "What?"

"Who?" asked Starla.

"Wah Hoo," Fury explained dryly. "It's a battle cry. On the count of three, give out with both lungs."

Fury aimed the blunt nose of the Hummer directly at the middle Land Rover. The man riding the flexible Fifty was cocking it. Not a reassuring sign.

Fury began the countdown.

"One."

He gave the Hummer more gas.

"Two."

Fury dropped the windows. Dry dust blew inside. "Three!"

All three voices lifted in unison. "WAH HOOOOOO!"

That froze the enemy for a split second in time. A split second in which Nick Fury blasted the Hummer directly at the middle Land Rover. The one with the cocked Fifty.

The Land Rover was heavy. The Hummer, loaded down with avionics and munitions and encased in a bullet-proof titanium-ceramic body, was heavier still.

It struck the Land Rover dead in the grille, and jolted it backward in a sudden cloud of smoking rubber.

Clashing, the opposing engines roared as wheels and tires fought for traction.

It was no contest. The Hummer pushed the Land Rover back, ruining the drivetrain, knocking it aside and onto the sandy shoulder of the road.

When they got their hearing working again, Fury and Starla looked back.

The surviving Land Rovers were coming around in hasty, sweeping circles that nearly threw their gunners off. They lined up, roaring in pursuit.

"They're gaining," Starla reported.

"Let 'em gain. I got me a plan."

"What kind of plan could you pursue here?" the Hydra said bitterly. "You are only two in an enemy nation."

Fury lifted a meaty paw and gave the Hydra a casual slap that rattled the latter's teeth.

"You're supercargo this trip. Remember that," Fury admonished.

He came to a fork in the road. Fury took the left.

"This isn't the main highway," Starla pointed out.

"I know that."

"Do you know where you're going?"

Fury shrugged. "We'll see when we get there."

Starla bit her lower lip. Sometimes the man could be so infuriating, she thought. She concentrated on holding on as the Hummer careened along.

The Land Rovers were steadily gaining. They were lighter, more nimble, and the drivers probably had an excellent idea of the reward for their capture of the fleeing Humvee—not to mention the dire punishment that awaited them if they failed.

Fury took each winding turn on two wheels. The wide wheelbase Hummer was almost impossible to overturn in motion. Yet Fury managed to nearly accomplish that feat a couple of times.

"If only we could stop long enough to convert," Starla said anxiously.

"We'll get our chance," Fury said tighty. "Now clam up. I gotta stay focused."

The first sporadic shots from one of the pursuing Fiftys began breaking asphalt rocks behind them.

"Can this armor turn a .50-caliber round?" the Hydra wanted to know.

"Never read the specs that far," Fury told him.

Then, coming out of a particularly hairy turn, they spotted the bridge.

It had once been a stone bridge. On this side of the muddy Taurus River, a short section lifted. Its mirror image rose hopefully on the opposite side. But there was no middle span. It lay in the water, a scummy pile of rubble. And it was a very, very wide river. Starla stole a glance in the side mirror. "If we stop now, we might have time to convert. It would be cutting it close, but—"

"Too close," said Fury, wrestling the steering wheel. He lined up on the bridge.

"We can't make it," the Hydra warned.

"I think he's right," Starla said.

"Shut up, the both of you. Let me drive, can't ya?"

They fell silent. Starla was holding on to her web harness. Her eyes were as wide as they had ever been in her life.

Out of nowhere a helicopter gunship rattled into view.

It came in low, lined up on the stone bridge remnant, and a rocket ran off its rail in a spurt of hissing fire.

The rocket struck. The opposite side of the bridge went up in a shower of broken stone and dusty mortar.

"That was our last hope," Starla groaned.

"Think again," said Fury, locking down the wheel.

On dead reckoning, the Hummer raced unerringly for the incline. The steady hum of asphalt under their tires became the rattle of rough cobbles.

Starla focused on her navigational screens. The Hydra buried his face in his shaking hands.

And Nick Fury calmly pulled a cigar from his belt and said, "Bars."

The Hummer leapt into the air when the last foot of bridge ran out. All time seemed to cease. The world became a different place. There was no sound, other than the suddenly muted roar of the mighty diesel engine.

The nose struck something hard, bounced. And the wheels gnawed at rock and rubble. The Hummer started to slew sideways, but its forward momentum was greater.

The rear deck pitched up. The three-quarter ton vehicle went into a slow, sickening somersault. At least, it felt slow to those inside. It was happening at high speed, but the human mind, faced with inescapable death, often processes time at a slower-than-normal rate. This was agonizingly slow.

To Starla Spacek, it was the beginning of a roller-coaster ride that could only end with her head being bashed open against the heavy bulletproof windshield.

To the Hydra, it signaled the climax of a very bad morning.

To Nicholas Fury, director of S.H.I.E.L.D., it gave him time to unwrap a fresh cigar.

The Hummer struck at an awkward angle, rolled and kept on rolling.

Inside, popping sounds signaled the deployment of

numerous airbaglike devices. But these were not airbags. Individual charges released a beige substance like a cross between Jell-O and Silly Putty. It surrounded them, protecting their bodies from being slammed against the hard angular interior of the hurtling vehicle.

Four times the Hummer rolled over. It started into a fifth somersault, but gravity reasserted itself. At the top of the roll, the Hummer lurched back, landing roughly on all four tires.

Fury let the vehicle settle on its jostling springs.

Then he hit a switch at his elbow. The taffy-like stuff withdrew. Fury looked around. Dust obscured his view through the windows. Otherwise, everything seemed okay.

"No bones broken?" Fury growled.

Starla looked at her arms dazedly. "Not here."

Hunching over in his seat, the Hydra began retching. Apparently he had a nervous stomach.

Fury spoke up. "Rollbars retract."

A green dashlight turned red and a mechanical clanking brought their attention fore and aft.

Over the wide hood, a segmented girder-like rollbar split in two, to fold into the sides of the vehicle. Another was withdrawing at the rear.

"Retractable rollbars?" Starla sputtered.

"New accessory to this year's model," Fury said, lighting his cigar. "If you hadn't been so scared, you would have noticed them deploying."

Starla Spacek let out a long, grateful sigh of relief.

It lasted long enough for the helicopter gunship to come hunting them.

It was a Russian-made Mi-24 Hind-D, stub wing-mounted pods heavy with Swatter air-to-ground anti-tank missiles. It began unleashing them. They swooshed into life.

Fury got the Hummer back into drive. He sent the black vehicle careening around in a long skittery circle.

Three Swatters arrowed toward the road—and all three detonated harmlessly 500 yards to their rear.

"So much for Quoraki shooting," Fury grunted. "Okay, Spacek. It's time to show them what we've got."

Starla opened the glove compartmemt. Out popped a standard alphanumeric lapboard. She began inputting commands.

From the crowded back seat area unfolded a .30-caliber autocannon on a swiveling mount. She activated the gun camera, and started tracking the gunship through a radar screen.

The Hind came sweeping in low, cool and confident.

The .30 caliber began chattering. Superheated smoking cartridges dribbled and rained down like corn kernels being stripped off a cob.

Gold tracers marked the stream of death, showing clearly that the Hind was still out of range.

Realizing it was riding into the teeth of a metallic storm, the Hind gunship abruptly vectored way.

"Good work, Spacek," Fury said. "You just bought us the time we needed."

Fury began conversion procedure. In less than a minute, the Hummer was in Air Mode.

Still tracking the orbiting Hind, Starla poured out more rounds. The range remained insufficient, but hits were not what she was seeking. It was precious seconds while the wheel-rim turbines wound themselves up to flying RPMs.

Fury took the Hummer off the ground.

"Liftoff," he called. "Now we're back in the game."

Fury sent the Hummer in a tight turn. Starla rattled keys. A 20mm electric cannon dropped down from under the front bumper. It switched back and forth as she tested its tracking system.

They went hunting the Hind.

It was no contest. The Hind was the bigger target, and with a top speed of 200 miles per hour versus their 700, it was slow and clumsy compared to the airborne Hummer.

They swept in from the side, sickling the gunship's tail off with a concentrated stream of rounds. The Hind buckled, began twisting itself in two as the tail rotor forces pushed one way, while the main rotor torque twisted the body another.

The crash was anticlimactic. The two sections hit, main rotor pounding itself to pieces when it struck solid ground. After that, it just lay there. No fuel explosion marked the big chopper's demise.

"Nice shooting," Fury growled. "For a mind reader."

Starla said nothing. She was pale.

"I know what you're thinking," Fury said. "Are they dead? Wrong question to ask. Tell yourself it was them or us. Us won. And we're the good guys."

Starla nodded wordlessly.

Fury took the Hummer up to a more defensible altitude.

"Next stop," he announced, "the Helicarrier."

"Not a minute too soon," Starla breathed.

Abruptly, a tire blew. It was the rear left. The turbine began laboring, then screaming.

"What the hell?" Fury muttered, checking the engine profile screens. The rear left turbine was going into the Red Zone. The awful whine climbed into a squealing cry of distress.

Fury killed the turbine.

The Hummer began to yaw. He gave the throttle a nudge. Afterburners kicked in, slamming the vehicle forward.

The Hummer recovered slightly, but the absence of one quadrant of lift showed in her wobbly handling.

"A stray round musta knocked tire tread into the fans," Fury said. "I thought we were a little too lucky back there."

"Can we limp back?" Starla asked.

"Can do," Fury replied. "That's not the question."

"What is?"

Fury blew out a gusty cloud of smoke. "Will do, or won't do?" He vectored the Hummer toward the high desert. Out there, flying low over empty, featureless terrain was an advantage. Here, over populated areas, they were vulnerable to being spotted and targeted.

Fury expected to be challenged from the air. It was probably only a matter of time.

The Quoraki Air Force did not disappoint him. A camel-colored Hind gunship lifted up from behind a rise. It oriented itself toward them, then moved in on a dead heading.

"Get ready to splash that bird," Fury told Starla.

Starla began jockeying the nose-mounted 20mm around experimentally with her trackball. But the Hind prudently declined to come within range.

"I'm getting a radar tone," Starla warned. "They're locking on with their rockets. I can hit them with a Sidewinder."

"We only got two. Hold on. I have me a hunch he ain't gonna fire."

Fury's hunch proved correct. The Hind orbited them at a respectful distance. It showed no indication that it was about to close in for the kill.

Before long, they understood why. Another Hind clattered up from the south. A third materialized on a westerly heading. The fourth was not far behind it. The first gunship broke off, and the four big helos raced parallel to their course, then as if controlled by one mind, pulled ahead.

Gathering in their path, they pirouetted until all four ships hung in the air directly ahead, chin-mounted quad-barrel Gatling guns and pylon-mounted rockets pointing directly at them.

Starla swallowed. "Permission to fire, Colonel."

"Are you mad!" the Hydra snarled. "We are outflanked and outgunned."

"Nick?"

"He's right," Fury growled. "We're dead meat if we engage."

"What's our alternative?"

"Surrender." His voice was subdued, almost bitter.

"Surrender is certain death," the Hydra pointed out.

Fury said, "Maybe for you. Maybe not for us."

"What do you mean by that?"

"It means they'll be sure to finish beheading you. But they might have something better in mind for us."

The Hydra's hands went to his throat. It turned a pale but appropriate shade of green.

Reluctantly, Nick Fury bled off power to the turbines. The Hummer began to settle on the ground. They landed on a winding road near a bombed-out power plant.

The Hinds stood off, as if fearing a trap.

"What are they waiting for?" Starla wondered anxiously.

Fury glanced into the rearview mirror. He saw a trail of dust. It grew in size.

"Ground units," he said.

The clattery rumble of tank tracks reached their ears, growing like the approach of death. Soon, they emerged from the sandy dust clouds that rolled before them. Dome-turreted T-62 battle tanks, Fury saw. Old by modern standards, their 115mm smoothbore cannon could still pulverize the disabled Hummer with a single well-placed shot.

"We could make a run for that old plant," Starla suggested.

"What's the difference?" Fury countered. "They can pound us into so much chuck meat here the same as over there."

"Shall I arm the self-destruct?" Starla asked thickly.

Fury reached under his seat. "Don't bother. I'm disabling all systems. This thing might as well be up on blocks now."

Starla reached for the dash mike.

"Space Shot to North Pole. We are down, and surrounded." She activated the Hummer's Global Positioning beacon. "Request immediate rescue."

Dum Dum's voice came through the speaker. *"Now why would you go and get yourself captured on a simple little recon?"*

Fury grabbed the mike. "Take your time, Dum Dum. Situation under control." Fury signed off.

Starla looked at him, aghast. She tried to speak. Found she was speechless.

Taking a last long puff of his cigar, Fury said, "Let's show the nice Quorakis that we'll be surrendering all peaceable like."

He stepped out and dropped his sidearms to the ground.

Whispering a short prayer, Starla did the same. They raised their hands in surrender, and waited for their captors to take charge of them.

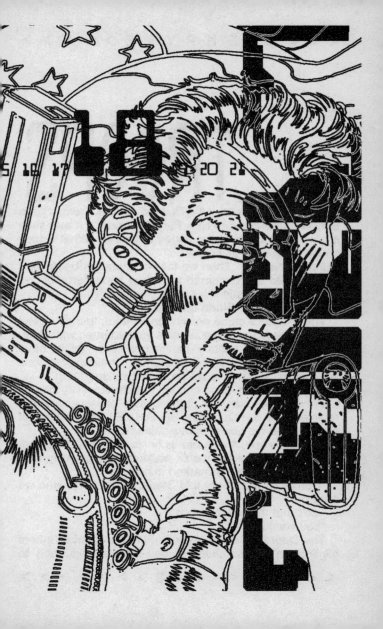

TROOPS

AS THE QUORAKI approached on foot, AK-47s held before them, Starla Spacek undertoned to Nick Fury, "I wonder if it was such a good idea to drop our native costumes. What if they shoot us on sight as spies?"

Fury shrugged. "Then we fall down and probably die." He sounded as concerned as if they had been stopped for a running violation.

A moment later Starla saw why.

The Quorakis came on with grim intent. In their desert camouflage fatigues, each one's face adorned with Nadir al-Bazinda–style military mustaches, they might have been a platoon of identical clones. Their expressions were identical. Their looks promised instant death.

Until they came close enough to see Nick Fury clearly.

Fury's sheer size, his unmistakable one-eyed visage, registered on the Quorakis. His S.H.I.E.L.D. combat suit accentuated his powerful musculature.

Almost as one, the Quorakis hesitated. Two conferred. They resumed the approach, walking more gingerly, as if stepping into a poorly-marked minefield.

"Don't sweat it," Fury told Starla. "They know who we are now."

"Isn't that more dangerous?"

"You watch."

The Quoraki platoon leader—Fury saw captain's bars glinting on his shoulderboards—signaled his men to sweep out and form a horseshoe with the open ends fanning out to surround the disabled Hummer.

They found themselves in a circle of foes. A circle that seemed reluctant to tighten any more than absolutely necessary.

"Anybody speak English?" Fury called out.

The captain yelled back, "I speak English. Identify yourselves to my satisfaction. At once!"

"Nick Fury, S.H.I.E.L.D. As if you didn't know."

The Quoraki captain looked unhappy. "You are prisoners."

"Tell me one I don't know," Fury retorted.

"Lay down on the ground. Hands behind backs."

Fury dropped. Starla lay down beside him.

Three Quoraki soldiers fell on them. Cold AK-47 muzzles pressed into the backs of their necks. The Hydra was hauled bodily out of the Hummer and slammed onto the ground beside them.

The captain came up. He surveyed the situation.

"Take the two men," he ordered. "Kill the woman."

Fury lifted his face. "You kill my operative and I will make you kill me. You got that? Leave her alone and I'll go quietly. Do it the other way and I'll fight you every step of the way. And you know I'm more valuable alive than dead."

The captain made thinking faces. They were almost comical.

"Your choice, pal," Fury reminded.

"We will defer her execution," the captain said stiffly.

"You made the smart move," Fury told him.

They were lifted to their feet. The Hydra's loose green robes were taken from him. He wore an ordinary white shirt and gray jogging pants under it.

A battered Armored Personnel Carrier roared up to collect them and they were shoved into the hot, darkened back, their hands bound by plastic wrist cuffs.

Fury undertoned to Starla, "Don't sweat any of this. These guys are rank amateurs."

"Their bullets are not," the Hydra spat.

"You stay out of this," Fury said.

"You are no longer in control of this situation."

"Don't count on that, either."

The APC took off, followed by a convoy of other vehicles. The four Hinds flew low cover. They were visible through slits in the vehicle's side.

"See?" Fury said. "We're practically getting the VIP treatment."

"Now I know why you go into the field wearing your own face," Starla whispered. "If you were just another S.H.I.E.L.D. field agent, we'd probably be dead now."

"We will be dead soon enough," the Hydra muttered darkly.

Fury gave him a hard kick. The Hydra subsided.

They were not surprised to find themselves being driven into the gaping maw that marked the entrance to Nadir al-Bazinda's Palace of Mysteries. They expected it. But expecting didn't make the reality any more welcome.

Nadir al-Bazinda stood in a pool of drying blood in the center of the courtyard. The bodies of the beheaded Hydras still lay where they had fallen.

Al-Bazinda was idly rolling one head along the pavestones with a booted toe when they were escorted before him at gunpoint. He looked up. His face was dark and troubled. It brightened. He flashed a smile so white it was almost reassuring.

Except for the unmistakable fact that the smile sat on the face of Nadir al-Bazinda, self-styled Scourge of the West.

"You are Nicholas Fury," he said in a thick voice. His English was acceptable.

"Congratulations," Fury returned, unafraid. "You win the blue ribbon."

"And you are without fear. I like that. Fear is for followers, not leaders like us. We are both men of action."

"Appreciate your not mentioning my name in the same breath as yours," Fury returned coolly. "No particular offense meant."

Al-Bazinda flinched. He reached out toward one of his hovering headsmen. A scimitar was surrendered, hilt-first. Al-Bazinda took it. He began swinging it idly, like a golf club. With each stroke, a lock of hair flew off the head at his feet. He seemed very intent on the precision work of chopping hair without cutting flesh.

When he spoke again, his tone was subdued.

"I am at the end of my life, it is said."

Fury said nothing.

"Of course, they have been saying that for almost ten years now. The Gulf War was my Waterloo. I would surely be assassinated by political rivals. Before that, it was predicted I would fall during my long war with Nira. That did not happen, either."

Fury said, "Just a matter of time. Your country's broke. Your neighbors would be happy to read your obit, and your own people hate your guts."

"My followers are also weary of me, and my adventures." Al-Bazinda's dark eyes flashed to his circle of bodyguards. They pretended to look at their feet, their expressions uneasy.

"Once, I was admired and respected in the Arab World. Nadir al-Bazinda, Vanquisher of the Persians. No more. Once my people revered me. Now they only mouth the words. In the last year alone, I have executed three generals for disloyalty and foiled five separate assassination attempts. My inner circle has the look of condemned men. If they side with me to the end, they will die, and they know this. If they conspire against me, they know I will ferret out their perfidy and make of their heads a plaything for my idle moments."

"If what you're leading up to is that you got nowhere to go and nothing to lose," Fury said, "we get the message."

"On my last birthday, I have had my horoscope cast. Did you know that the ancient art of astrology was invented in this land? No? No matter. My horoscope has been cast, and my end foretold to me. It will be glorious. A warrior's death. But it will be death nevertheless. The end of Nadir al-Bazinda."

Taking another swing, Nadir al-Bazinda accidentally sent an ear flying. Glowering, he looked up. His meaty face was doleful as he met Nick Fury's one-eyed gaze.

"I will not die without avenging the insults the world has visited upon me," he said, voice rising. "If the Fist of Allah will not survive, then neither will my mortal enemies."

"You're talking about half the world," Fury pointed out.

"Not half. All. For those who have not come to my aid are complicit in my downfall, and will be branded as my oppressors."

"You can't beat the whole world. You don't have the standing army, the technology or the weapons."

"Incorrect. On a certain day, at a certain hour, world capitals will fall before my multistealth missile strike."

"Stealth missiles?" Fury snorted. "They ain't no such thing."

"Intercontinental stealth missiles," Nadir al-Bazinda insisted. "Launched from Quorak."

"Who are you kiddin'? You don't have ICBMs. You hardly got any SCUDs left."

Starla nudged Fury.

"Nick, I think I'm getting an image of what he means . . ."

"Quiet. Let him talk. He's giving us good Intel. He just don't realize it. Or care."

Starla subsided.

"I have missiles such as the world has never seen," Nadir al-Bazinda boasted. "Armed with an explosive unknown to modern warfare. An unquenchable fire will rage across the globe, punishing the aggressors and their allies alike. After that, I will die fulfilled."

"Not as long as S.H.I.E.L.D. is still operating," Fury countered. "And we're on your case. You know that now."

"I know this. Which is why you will be held as human shields against further attack." He nodded to his personal guard. "Take them away."

They were seized and dragged off.

Nadir al-Bazinda watched them go past. To the lone surviving Hydra, he said, "You, I will behead when I have the time. For this hour, I must coordinate the attack on the S.H.I.E.L.D. Helicarrier that has dared penetrate my Gulf."

"Good luck with that," Nick Fury growled.

"I do not need your luck," al-Bazinda sneered. "For I have been assured that my destiny is to sweep the face of the globe with my punishing, purifying fire."

They were taken inside.

"Search them for weapons and devices," the Quoraki captain ordered.

"Anyone who lays hands on either of us," Nick Fury promised, "is going to get to listen to the sound of his scrawny neckbones snapping."

The Quorakis digested this earnest threat, and decided it was serious. Fury towered over the tallest of them and outweighed the heaviest by twenty hard pounds. His battle-scarred fists looked hard enough to break brick.

They were taken to another room—a bare stone chamber—and locked in. There were no windows at all.

"Looks like this is where we stay for the duration," Fury said. A little too loudly, Starla thought.

She looked at the S.H.I.E.L.D. director. There was absolutely no fear in him. None. His confidence in himself was almost serene. She imagined a man who had lived this long and overcome as many dire situations as Nick Fury had would naturally feel invulnerable.

There was a single grate in the center of the room. The stone floor sloped toward it on all sides. A drainage grate.

They paid it no particular attention until a pinkish mist began rising up from between the rusted grillwork.

Starla noticed it first. "Nick!"

Fury wheeled from his position at the door. One eye focused in the exhalation rising into the chamber.

"Relax," he said.

"Relax? It might be poison gas."

"Poison gas ain't normally pink. And I don't smell any of the usual warning signs of death gas. Not fruit, not almonds. Nothing like that."

Starla shrank into a corner. "But what is it?"

The answer came when the Hydra captive abruptly keeled over. He fell on his face, breaking a front tooth in the process.

Holding his breath, Fury went to him. He popped open his lids. The eyes jerked. The man's body seemed untroubled.

"Sleep gas," Fury said. "Looks like they're serious about searching us for gadgets."

"What do we do?"

Fury thought about this a moment, then asked, "You got a blaster on you?"

"No. Do you?"

"Not that I remember." Fury shrugged and said, "Might as well make it easy on ourselves." He lay down and folded his hands over his muscular chest.

Starla stared at him in disbelief. After a moment, she did the same.

"What's that I smell?" Starla asked anxiously. "It's not the gas."

"Must be my aftershave."

"Is it new?"

"The boys in the lab mix it up special for me," Nick Fury said as he drifted off to sleep.

When they awoke, they were in a different chamber. This one had a single barred window. Starla woke up to discover Nick Fury looking out. The window was set very high in the wall. Fury was standing on the still-sleeping Hydra's back in order to get a good view.

"Where are we?" she asked, climbing to her feet.

"Looks like the dungeon."

Starla joined him. The window was tall and narrow. Three iron bars were sunk into the frame. There was no glass.

Outside, they could see a worm's eye view of the courtyard with the fallen Hydra agents still sprawled in ignominious death. A few flies buzzed around. They looked as big as walnuts.

Starla looked around. "I have the strangest feeling . . ."

Fury eyed her. "Yeah?"

"I don't know what it is. Something is wrong here."

"Sort it out for me."

Before she could, the Hydra stirred.

"Guess we should climb off him," Fury muttered. "Seein' as how we're gonna be roomies for a while."

The Hydra was slow coming out of it. Fury reached down and encouraged wakefulness by carefully but firmly stepping on his head.

That brought the Hydra out of it. Reflexively, he grabbed Fury's calf, and attempted to throw him. Fury just stood there, as immobile as a sequoia tree.

The Hydra let go. "You feel like you're made out of iron," he breathed.

"Fifty years of daily excercise will do that," Fury said with a knowing smile.

The significance of that sunk in. The Hydra pulled himself together and put his back to one dripping wall.

"Where are we?" he asked, dull-voiced.

"Dungeon, it looks like," Fury told him. "About now, my

people will be getting themselves organized for the rescue mission. So we don't have a lot of time."

The Hydra made a contemptuous face. "Think again. Al-Bazinda planned to launch an air strike against your vaunted supercarrier."

"Best of luck to him. His air force is down to twenty-year-old MiGs held together by tin cans and bailing wire. S.H.I.E.L.D. flies top-of-the-line tactical fighters. Who do you think is gonna come out on top?"

"It does not matter. I would not look for a rescue until the battle is over."

"Either way, we need to debrief you."

The Hydra looked momentarily startled. He started to laugh.

Fury sank to one knee and fixed him with his solitary brown eye. The Hydra swallowed his outburst.

"This stealth missile strike al-Bazinda's boasting about. What's the skinny on that?"

The Hydra licked dry lips.

"Al-Bazinda double-crossed you," Fury reminded. "Not much percentage in holding back now."

"We are not allies," the Hydra said grudgingly.

"Fine. We're enemies. As one enemy to another, do you want to talk straight or do I haveta bounce you off these walls for five or six hours first?"

"I am Imperial Hydra, Middle East. How dare you speak to me that way?"

Fury reached down, took hold of the Imperial Hydra's shock of dark hair and lifted. The man's scalp bulged up, taking the rest of him with it.

Fury stood him against the wall, and leaned into him.

"Number one. You ain't Imperial Hydra no more. You are a blasted prisoner of war. Number two, you are outnumbered three to one."

The Hydra blinked. "Where do you get three?"

"I'm equal to two of you, then there's Starla here. You reading me so far?"

"Do not underestimate me. I am trained in Tae Kwon Do."

Fury looked interested. "Is that so? What color belt?"

"Red."

"Too bad. I'm a black. Got a brown belt in judo stuck in a drawer somewhere." Fury rubbed his unshaven chin reflectively. "Seems I was a heavyweight boxer back in my Army days, too. And that's not mentioning my Green and Black Beret Special Forces training. You gettin' my drift?"

The Hydra's healthy color drained of all blood.

"Now let's get back to the debriefing," Fury barked. "We're wasting time here."

The Hydra said morosely, "Empire Airlines is an arm of Hydra. I will tell you that much."

"Thanks. We figured that out already. Where does al-Bazinda fit in?"

The Hydra made a stubborn line with his lips.

Fury captured one wrist in one of his hands. He squeezed. The Hydra felt his wrist bones bending and buckling. The American's strength was prodigious. It was like a vise closing. Sweat popped out of his brow.

"We approached him a year ago," he gasped. "He was beleaguered and fighting off internal dissension and U.N. pounding. We offered to work with him toward mutual goals. The first goal was to rearm and reempower Quorak. Once that was achieved, Hydra ME would be allowed to set up operations in Gullahbad, where we could operate openly, but with impunity."

"Kinda like the setup Dr. Doom had in Latveria?" growled Fury.

"Yes. Precisely."

"But al-Bazinda double-crossed you good?"

The Hydra nodded.

"So what's the master plan?"

The Hydra clenched his teeth. "I am dedicated to the utter annihilation of S.H.I.E.L.D. and all it represents. You will get no more from me."

Fury increased the pressure. A low groan emerged

from between the Hydra's grinding teeth. Something broke.

Starla intervened. "Nick! I have a better way."

Fury let up on the pressure. "Let's hear it."

"I can interrogate him. Psychically."

If possible, the Hydra's expression grew even more fearful.

"You are an extrasensor?" he demanded.

Starla nodded. "We call ourselves telepaths."

The Hydra bared his teeth. "Do your worst."

"Sit him down," Starla told Fury. Fury gave the man a sample of Tae Kwon Do, and the Hydra found himself sitting down hard, a dazed expression on his face. That took the last of the fight out of him.

Starla took a seat before him. She assumed a lotus position, legs crossed, hands on her knees. She gave the Hydra the full benefit of her steady gaze.

"Your name is Anwar?" she asked after a few moments.

The Hydra flinched.

"Hit," said Starla. "This guy is so scared he's wide open."

"Go to it," Fury encouraged.

Starla closed her eyes.

"First, I'm seeing confirmation of what I sensed before. There are no missiles, as such. This is almost bizarre, but we've been too harried to put it all together. The Empire planes are the missiles. Al-Bazinda is planning a suicide strike using commercial passenger liners as the so-called stealth missiles."

"Not so bizarre," Fury said. "The first passenger jets started off as military transports. Over in Russia, Aeroflot's fleet are convertible for military purposes."

Her voice taking on a free-associational quality, Starla continued processing psychic information.

"They assume that no one would ever suspect aircraft displaying respected commercial livery as threatening.

The element of surprise is key to the operation. Feroze Dagius was Hydra ME, planted long before this operation was conceived. He was activated when he alerted this man that S.H.I.E.L.D. had created a Special Powers unit. The fear was the operation would be compromised by psychic means. This is why you were lured onto that Empire flight. This was also the trigger for the attack on the Helicarrier. They—"

The Hydra shouted. "Shut up! Shut up!"

Starla went on.

"The strike on Persopolis was a test of the system. This isn't necessarily psychic, but I think al-Bazinda chose to target it because of his hatred of the Niran government."

"That was an Air Carcassone flight," Fury pointed out.

"I can't explain that. Yet."

Horror rode the Hydra's pale features. "Enough. Enough. I will talk. Stop seeing into my mind. I cannot stand it."

Starla looked to Nick Fury.

"Monitor him for truthfulness," Fury told her. To the Hydra, he said, "Out with it. Start with Air Carcassone."

"The Air Carcassone incident was as the woman said," the Hydra said morosely. "It was both a test and a revenge. It was in truth not an Empire flight. But the copilot on that flight was one of Nadir al-Bazinda's people. It was his job to slay the pilot over Persopolis and plunge the aircraft into the heart of the city. Its cargo hold contained a sufficient quantity of . . . a certain explosive agent to demonstrate its power."

"Keep going," Fury urged. "What's Hydra's objective in all this?"

"The initial plan was to hit major Arab capitals, in one strike turning Gullahbad into the only functioning capital city in the Arab world. Thus setting the stage for the emergence of Quorak as the unchallenged leader of the Middle East."

Fury rubbed his jaw. "It might have worked at that," he mused.

"But al-Bazinda was too hungry for blood. He is a madman, a visionary who thinks he is destined to be the Anti-Christ foretold with the Millennium. He was not satisfied with this plan. He wanted to punish the U.S. at the same time. Washington. Boston. Philadelphia. New York. Los Angeles. Chicago. These cities and more were to be incinerated."

"You can't destroy a city by dropping a jumbo jet in the middle of it," Fury shot back. "Persopolis proved that."

"You can when the jet is filled with Inferno 42."

"Inferno 42?"

"A discovery of our brethren at Advanced Idea Mechanics. It is a synthesis of a meteoric element unknown to earthly science. A highly-combustible radioactive substance. Once ignited, it cannot be extinguished. It will rage out of control until it exhausts itself. This takes six to seven days. We refer to it as concentrated Hellfire."

Fury and Starla exchanged uneasy glances.

"When's Zero Hour?" Fury demanded.

"I'm getting that creepy Christmas tree again," Starla said.

"That right, Anwar?"

The Hydra winced.

"Christmas is the Zero Hour, yes," he admitted. "I am only telling you this because Nadir al-Bazinda has gone into a psychotic tailspin. The man is a true sociopath. His ego structure is fragmenting. He believes he is to die, so he is prepared to take as much of the world with him. This was too much for us. The goal of Hydra is world domination. For Hydra to rule, there must be a civilization worth dominating. If this multiple strike goes off on schedule, there is no predicting what the U.S. will do. Should the west mistake the Hellfire strikes as nuclear, retaliation would be blind, unfocused and overwhelming. Certainly Russia and China will be targeted. Once struck, they will retaliate as well. Where is the endgame? This is why Hydra wants nothing to do with al-Bazinda's ultimate plan."

"Who controls Empire now?" Fury demanded.

"It is a joint venture. Hydra ME created it. We oversee operations. Hired dupes actually conduct day-to-day operations. But the pilots are all al-Bazinda's. They are religious fanatics, prepared to die to fulfill their leader's mad goals. We do not control them."

"That it?"

"That is all you need to know for your purposes," the Hydra said morosely. He looked miserable.

Fury took Starla aside. "We gotta get out of here."

"What about waiting for rescue?"

"No time. Christmas is tomorrow. We got a lot to do between now and then."

Fury walked over to the single window. He slipped his eye patch off, broke the string and wrapped either end around the outer bars. The patch itself lay snug against the middle bar.

"Better stand clear," Fury warned.

Starla retreated to the door. The Hydra scrambled into a far corner.

Fury took a few paces back, judged the distance, then spit at the dangling eye patch.

He hit the floor. Not a moment too soon, either.

The iron bars jumped out of their concrete wells, sending blocks of hard stone flying in all directions.

When they looked up, the bars were nowhere to be seen.

Starla said, "I thought your eye patch was made of Nomex."

"The dress one is. For this mission, I went with Semtex with an H_2O detonator microchip."

Fury started for the window.

Starla called, "Nick! Wait! I sense danger."

Fury hesitated.

Scrambling to his feet, the Hydra leapt for the opening ahead of the S.H.I.E.L.D. director. He went out. And vanished as if entering an unseen dimension.

It was unbelievable. One moment he was poised to jump, the next he was gone. But not completely gone. They could still hear him.

His cry of frightened surprise was receding, as if down a well.

An ugly splat came to their ears, sounding like a pile of meat landing on stone.

Reaching the window, Fury looked out. Then down.

"I don't see him . . ."

"Nor do I. But there's something not right about this. I still feel that."

Starla tossed out a fragment of stone. It too vanished in midair, as if swallowed by the murk of night. A clink of rock hitting rock seemed to come from somewhere far below. But there was no far below. The ground was right below them, only inches away.

Fury reached his hand out. "This ain't real."

"A 3-D holographic projection," Starla said. "I knew what I was looking at wasn't right." She shivered. "Al-Bazinda is diabolically clever. He knew that if we got past the bars, we'd fall to our deaths. That way, he could claim we killed ourselves trying to escape as spies."

Fury climbed onto the ledge, saying, "We made a heck of a racket. Can't wait for the guards to come running."

"Be careful."

Fury's upper body slipped from view. It was a weird sight. From the waist down, he was still there. The rest of him faded off into the artificial scene before her eyes.

Fury came back, saying, "We're on the top floor. Come on. Time's wasting."

Starla hesitated. "Come on where?"

"The roof."

Fury's big muscular arm reached in and pulled her out. They were on the top floor, all right, Starla saw once her head passed through the hologram. The courtyard scene was far below. It was dark. Three Hydras lay sprawled in death eight stories below.

Fury guided Starla's hands to the roofline. He boosted her up. She went easily. The overhang gave her plenty of grip.

Once on top, she reached down and helped the S.H.I.E.L.D. director lever his big body to safety.

"Get down," Fury urged.

They lay flat, listening.

A complicated projector device sat on the roof's edge, pointing downward. Faint multicolored lights beamed down from a nest of bundled lenses.

"There's our answer," Fury said. "Hydra technology." He gave the projector a hard kick. Sizzling sparks sputtered and a low electronic humming died. The projector's multiple lenses faded.

"Now what?" hissed Starla.

Fury felt around the white hair at his right temple with a finger. He pressed down. Starla heard a soft click, like a tiny relay. She frowned.

"Sub-dermal transponder," Fury explained.

"What does it do?"

"Lie still."

Minutes later, a familiar whine greeted their ears.

The stealth-black Hummer was dropping down from the sky. Steel feet deploying, it landed with a clanking jar.

"Up!" Fury urged.

Starla exploded, "You called it!"

"And it came running like a faithful bloodhound."

They piled in. Fury took the yoke.

They took a few rounds to the undercarriage as they vectored away, but they got off safely.

The rattle of small-arms fire came dimly from below. But it was unfocused and ineffectual. By the time searchlights were sending up fingers of light, they were far out of range.

Fury found the winding Taurus River, which emptied out into the Gulf far to the south. He used it to calculate a flight path of escape.

"Next stop, the Helicarrier," Fury said.

"Didn't you say that once before?" Starla asked uneasily.

"This time we gotta make it home. I'm fresh out of cigars."

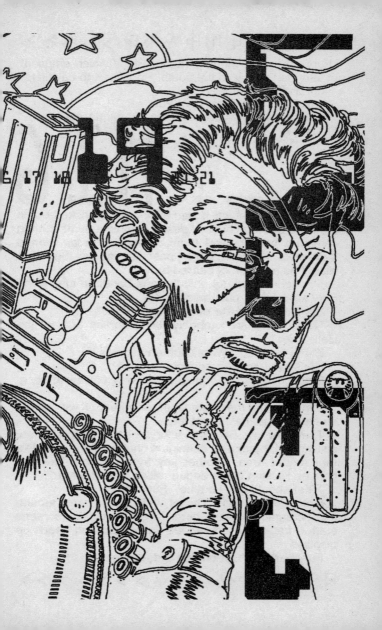

MIG

THEY PICKED UP A outside of Gullahbad. It was a Flogger-E, tricked out in the sand-and-dun hues of desert camouflage. Its roaring came up from behind them. On-board radar warned them of its approach. It blew past them so fast their eyes read it as a streak of blurred brown.

"I'm figuring we got only the one bandit to deal with," Fury said tightly, changing course.

Starla asked, "How do you figure that?"

"The others are probably flying sorties against the Helicarrier."

Starla frowned. "What's the good news?"

"He's too fast for a dogfight."

Starla blinked. "Is that another way of saying we're too slow?"

"I'm lookin' at the bright side," said Fury. "If we can get on his tailpipe, he's burnt toast."

They flew low. Starla hit a key. A hatch popped open, spilling radar-jamming aluminum chaff from the vehicle's rear fender area. Another key triggered the flare dispenser. Hissing flares began roiling from the rear.

"That should buy us time," Fury said.

It did. But very little. The jet circled back, came around low, screaming toward them. Target acquisition screens started tracking it on various dashboard and heads-up displays.

Fury barked, "Get on that Sidewinder."

"I'm on it," said Starla. She was looking at the FLIR—Forward Looking Infra Red—screen. It showed the undulating desert floor stretching before them as a stark high-contrast black and white image. The sands were light, the sky dark. Targeting symbology swept for the oncoming jet.

Breaking off evasive maneuvers, Fury returned to his original southerly course. The Flogger vectored after them.

"Got a tone?" he asked Starla.

Starla shook her head. "No. He doesn't seem to have armed his missiles, either."

"I'm betting he don't. Why waste an expensive air-to-air bird on a slow-moving target like us? That's our edge. He's going to try to chew us to pieces with his cannon."

Starla shivered. She wished Fury wouldn't paint such vivid word pictures. Half the time, she thought she was seeing their doom instead of her imagination.

Fury gave the Hummer altitude. The Flogger came up on their rear, jockeying for position. It was visible in the rearview mirror as a growing threat.

Fury shifted gaze to his heads-up display. "Bogey on gridline niner two-zero five-six-seven. Grid niner two-zero five-zero-seven."

"I have the 30mm cannon deployed," Starla was saying. "Oh, my God! It's empty!"

"Hit the reloader."

Starla did. The indicator light came up empty.

"The Quorakis must have rifled the ammo boxes," she said.

"The Sidewinders are concealed," Fury snapped. "They still gotta be there."

Starla closed her eyes. She perceived a dim image: a rattlesnake sleeping in a hole.

"They're there. Guaranteed."

"Good." Fury checked his rear-view mirror. The Flogger was coming on hard. "Hang on. I'm going to show you a little maneuver perfected by the Russians. It's called the cobra."

As Starla watched the FLIR screen nervously, the MiG continued closing. Sweat touched her upper lip.

"Starboard Sidewinder armed and extended," she called out.

Fury held the limping Hummer as level as possible, given the cold rear turbine.

A burst of greenish tracers raced over the roof, arcing like dying fireflies toward the desert floor ahead of them.

"He's getting our range!" Starla warned.

Fury gave the forward turbines full thrust.

The Hummer hiked up, caught a headwind and stalled. Like an errant kite, it hung in mid-air.

The MiG Flogger went hurtling by at an estimated 700 miles per hour—too fast for the pilot to change course.

Fury dropped in behind him, jammed the rear afterburner. The Hummer jumped ahead, slamming them back into their seats.

"The key to dogfighting is to get behind your opponent's tail," Fury growled. "You're there. Let 'em have it."

"I have a tone," Starla called out.

"Splash!"

The targeting display kept locking and unlocking on the Flogger's heat signature. "I can't get a fix! I can't get a fix!"

"Switch to black hot."

Starla pounded a key. The black and white screen reversed colors. The black turned white, the white became black and she got a lock-on signal.

"He's locked up." Starla tapped a hotkey. "Fox One!"

From the passenger side, a cutdown AIM-9l Sidewinder missile separated, its exhaust scorching Starla's window black. Soot smeared the windscreen. Fury hit a dash stud, saying, "Let me take care of that for you."

As chemical streams scoured the windscreen clear, the Sidewinder climbed after the hapless MiG. Jinking wildly, the Flogger attempted to escape. But the range was too short.

The Sidewinder arrowed into the tailpipe. The resulting eruption blew the aircraft into shards of boiling metal and fire.

The pilot ejected safely.

They flew past his descending parachute. Fury beeped the horn at him in passing. In return, the pilot shook his fist angrily.

Then Fury cruised as close to the desert floor as he dared and ran the length of the al-Quaquaa desert toward the Persian Gulf.

"I think we're home free," Starla said after awhile.

"That an observation or a prediction?" Fury asked.

"I think it's both."

The Helicarrier was in the center of a furball when they sighted it. Gold and white S.H.I.E.L.D. warplanes—a mix of F-14 Tomcats, F-15 Strike Eagles and Fighting Falcons—were chasing off a motley collection of Quoraki MiG-21 Fishbeds and MiG-23 Floggers. The MiGs were not doing well. Soon, they were in full retreat.

"Saint Nick to Hel-1. Copy."

Dum Dum's bellowing voice came back at them. *We're a little busy here. Where've you been, you old warhorse?*

"Getting captured. Getting uncaptured," Fury returned laconically. "How's your end?"

Al-Bazinda keeps sendin' 'em up, and we keep knockin' 'em down.

"Any get through?"

None so far. Recommend you come in hot.

"Understood. Saint Nick out."

Starla turned to Nick. "I don't like the way he said that: 'come in hot.'"

"Show you a trick."

Fury climbed to angels 4, found the localizer beam for the main runway and carefully laid the Hummer's nose into the groove.

"This is not a recommended procedure under any conditions," he told Starla.

Starla decided to close her eyes and snug her safety harness more tightly around her slim body.

It was probably a good thing that she did. Fury came in under full power. He was doing 40 knots when the flight deck bow came under his bumper. He skimmed along for a thousand feet with only a four-foot clearance. Dropping the rear takeoff-assist wheel, Fury killed the turbines, simultaneously retracting all four wheels.

The Hummer's tires had reoriented to their correct axes when they made contact with the centerline. Came a jolt. The Hummer bounced, settled and the vibration of solid-rubber runflat tires against non-skid steel made their teeth vibrate.

Fury let tire-and-air friction bleed off groundspeed.

A deck-edge lift rose to flight deck level. Fury steered into it without bothering to start the diesel. Dum Dum was waiting when he braked to a halt. He sent the lift whining down.

Fury got out. "What happened to the rescue mission?"

"What rescue mission?" Dum Dum wanted to know, handing him a cigar.

Fury stripped it. "When you lose a pair of agents in the field, you naturally send out a blasted rescue mission."

"Special Powers said you were in no immediate danger," Dum Dum retorted. "And we've been a little busy out here. Besides, it was only a little recon." Dum Dum grinned broadly in Starla's direction. Then he seemed to remember something.

"Oh, and the clairvoyants said you'd be needin' this," Dum Dum said, handing Fury a tangle of black material.

Fury snapped the fresh eye patch over his dull eye.

He looked like himself once again. "Casualties their side?" he asked.

"Eight bandits splashed."

"Casualties our side?"

"I have an earache from all the shootin'."

"Next time do better," Fury said, accepting a light from Dugan.

They stepped off on Deck 4. Fury led the way.

"What's the latest on the situation in Persopolis?" he asked Dum Dum.

"They're still tryin' to put out the blamed fire. But they can't seem to knock it down. Funny thing is that the Nirans are claimin' the jumbo jet struck a hospital, not a fuel depot like the media's been speculating. But no one can explain what's feedin' the fire."

"We can," Fury bit out.

Dum Dum looked interested. "Oh, yeah? I'm all ears."

"Save it for the briefing."

Director of Practical Intelligence Art Skindarian read his findings off a computer monitor in the conference room. Fury, Dum Dum Dugan and Starla Spacek were the only other persons present.

The director of S.H.I.E.L.D. was smoking furiously as he absorbed every word.

"We trace Empire Airlines back to a shadowy Egyptian consortium headed by a man named—"

"Anwar," Starla inserted.

"—Mohammed." Skindarian quirked a very black eyebrow in surprise. "How did you come by this information, may I ask?"

"We had the pleasure of meeting old Anwar in the flesh," Fury explained. "He's head of Hydra Middle East. Or was, I should say."

"Was?"

"He took a bad fall."

Skindarian continued. "Based on this information, it

may be possible to prevail on the FAA to ground all Empire planes in the United States. But of course, FAA jurisdiction stops at U.S. borders. Beyond that, we're helpless."

"What are the chances of a worldwide grounding?" Dum Dum asked.

"Slim. Empire routes cover most of Europe as well as the Middle East and parts of Africa. We will be dealing with a host of bureaucracies, not to mention foreign governments not exactly friendly to our interests."

"And we got no proof to show them," Fury said tightly. He laid a frustrated fist on the tabletop. "First things first. We got twenty-four hours to Christmas. Have all Empire jets grounded. Then I want every Empire aircraft we can find in the air or on the ground, located, IDed and tracked. I want to know where every damn bird in the Empire fleet is at any given time."

"We've got a good headstart on that already," Starla pointed out. "We have agents flying various carriers all over the mideast."

"I want every jet covered," Fury went on. "And I want every damn one of those birds disabled on the ground. I don't care how it's done. Slag their tires. Kidnap their pilots. Just do it. By Christmas Eve, I don't want a single Empire flight taking off. Is that clear?"

Skindarian said, "Yes, Colonel."

Starla frowned. "What role will Special Powers play?"

"None. Your people have done their job. The rest of this is a practical operational matter."

"But—"

"No buts," Fury snapped. "You done good, SPD Spacek. Take a well-deserved rest. If we need you, we'll call on you." Fury stood up. "Now get cracking, the rest of you. The doomsday clock is ticking. And I expect to spend Christmas Day opening presents, not counting airline casualties. Dismissed!"

Starla left the room feeling hollow inside.

Skindarian caught up to her and said, "We all have our parts to play, SPD Spacek. You've played yours. Leave the rest of the mission to more seasoned hands."

Which only made Starla fume inwardly.

Crunch time was coming, and she wanted to be part of the action. It wasn't glory. There were still loose ends, unanswered questions.

Questions whose answers might only be found in Alpha.

The first strikes were easy.

Empire's hub was in Phoenix, Arizona. They isolated more than a dozen aircraft there, ranging from Boeing 737s and 757s to a lone DC-10.

A S.H.I.E.L.D. strike team from Los Angeles descended on the planes, taking them out by the simple expedient of shooting out their tires. The craft were searched, the pilots taken into custody. None wore scorpion tattoos on their wrists. And none were Middle Eastern. Interrogations turned up nothing. They were legitimate pilots hired from other carriers. It was a dead end.

Other Empire jets were caught on the ground in other cities. Not many.

Nick Fury read the field reports as they came in.

"What was it al-Bazinda said about his stealth missiles?" he grumbled.

"Search me. I wasn't there," Dum Dum said.

They were on the Helicarrier Bridge. Another Quoraki sortie was being chased off by S.H.I.E.L.D. fighters. It was getting to be routine.

"He said the missiles will be launched from Quorak."

"Not much chance of that," Dum Dum said. "Air Quorak ain't allowed to fly outside of their own airspace as part of the U.N. sanctions. For that matter, they hardly fly within their own borders, anymore."

Fury paused. He seemed to gaze off into space.

"What is it?"

He shook his head. "I musta been hanging around Spacek too long. Something up and jumped into my head. Anybody ever get around to analyzing that gun-camera footage from our tracking plane in the Gulf?"

Dum Dum looked abashed. "In all the excitement, I plum forgot about it."

"Come on. I got me a hunch," said Fury, storming off.

The gun-camera footage was not the best quality. Rain smeared the lens, making for a watery image.

The silver-and-scarlet jetliner was also a smear. They watched it emerge from the storm cell, its scarlet Arabic corporate name completely indecipherable.

Fury said, "I'm betting when we match up this livery with one of the Middle Eastern carriers, we're gonna discover it's an Air Quorak jet."

Dum Dum scratched his head. "That don't exactly explain what happened to the missin' Empire bird."

Fury shut off the VCR. "Maybe it will, maybe it won't," he said cryptically.

Alone in her quarters, Starla Spacek sat before her personal computer, her tawny feline face splashed with color. All S.H.I.E.L.D. systems were tied together, she knew. Security might be monitoring her activities. That could be a problem. Not to mention embarrassing if Director Skindarian got wind of what she was doing.

During the final phase of Stargate, as more and more remote viewers crashed under the stress of too much time in Alpha, the CIA started recruiting fruitier psychics. Tarot card readers. Astrologers. Mediums. Virtually overnight, a serious program degenerated into a psychic circus.

Those unhappy memories made Starla's palm moist as she loaded an astrology program into the system and input Nadir al-Bazinda's birth data.

He came up Sun Scorpio with a Sagittarius rising.

Heavily Eighth House, with a Moon-Mars conjunction in Sagittarius. It was a chart full of war and anger, and a single-minded intransigence. Not a happy planetary picture.

She progressed it hour by hour, looking for death transits or violent squares.

A gasp came from her soft lips. She saw death in the turning wheel of planets. And it was closer than she ever dreamed.

"How on earth am I going to explain this to Colonel Fury?"

A low growl said, "You don't have to. He's standing right behind you."

Starla jumped out of her chair, tipping it over.

"You startled me!"

Calmly, Fury took an unlit cigar in his mouth. "Sometimes I gotta wonder how psychic you really are."

"I was engrossed in my . . ." Her voice trailed off.

Fury gestured to the screen. "Looks like a horoscope to me," he said thinly.

"Actually it's an astrological wheel. Al-Bazinda's chart. I—um—progressed it forward from today. Remember what he told us about his personal astrologer?"

"Yeah. His doom's right around the corner."

"Closer than we thought. The death angles go critical almost a day earlier than we imagined—"

"What are you trying to say, lady?"

Starla stood up. Her hands made tight, involuntary fists.

"Christmas Eve. He's going to strike on Christmas Eve, not Christmas Day. Tonight, Colonel. At exactly 8:48 P.M. local time."

Fury frowned. "And we ain't anywhere near done seizing his planes." He tapped the screen. "How much faith do you put in this stuff?"

Starla looked uncomfortable. "In my private practice, I dabbled in astrology," she admitted. "Put aside whatever prejudices you may have for a moment. Astrology is an operating system. The meanings of transits and conjunctions are fixed, according to astrological lore. According to this, al-Bazinda's Mars-Pluto conjunction will be transiting over his natal nodes."

"Say it in English," Fury suggested.

"This points to a violent death. The forces acting on him go critical in eight hours. This doesn't mean he's absolutely fated to die. He could survive. But Mars-Pluto points to an obsessive will. We know that Nadir al-Bazinda is extremely headstrong. He has free will, and forewarning of the time of his death. And he's a Scorpio. They tend to choose the time and place of their own demises."

Fury absorbed this in silence. "What's your gut say?"

"I haven't checked it yet," Starla admitted.

"I don't put much stock in the stars," Fury said thinly.

Starla held her breath.

"But then I'm a stubborn old Taurus." He grinned lopsidedly.

Starla grinned back. "Whatever your beliefs, this chart is identical to the one Nadir al-Bazinda's astrologer has cast. I'm certain it's been explained to him in detail."

Fury nodded. "That means he expects to die tonight."

Starla nodded. Her face was relaxing. "It follows that he will launch his so-called stealth missile strike tonight. Remember when I received that image of a Christmas tree? We assumed it meant Christmas Day. We assumed wrong."

"Kinda like not seeing the international dateline. That reminds me. A while ago I had a funny experience. I was thinking of that Empire jetliner than never came out of the clouds. I had me a brainstorm, I guess you could say. Remember you looked into it and got a picture of a scramble helmet?"

"I still can't explain that," Starla said ruefully.

"Maybe I can. I remembered it. And remembered how

that ESP helmet was rigged to shift colors, kinda like a chameleon. I kept seeing a chameleon in my head. It started me wondering. Could that technique be applied to the airframe of a jetliner?"

Starla brightened. "Sounds like you made an intuitive leap." She smiled broadly. "Maybe I was on the money when I suggested you showed extrasensory ability back in Colorado."

"Maybe we should take a closer look at that helmet," Fury returned.

Technical had the aft end of Deck 7 all to itself. The scramble helmet taken from the body of Hydra Remote Viper Feroze Dagius lay on a work table.

"A decal-like polymer skin has been applied to the helmet's shell," a Techno was explaining to Fury, Dum Dum and Starla Spacek. He lifted the cumbersome device, and stripped away a length of clear material that had been bonded to the burnished surface.

"We don't fully understand the technology," he went on, "but it might be an improvement on a new commercial pigment called electronic ink, which can be electronically manipulated to display specific images, and can be changed at will. This particular application causes the helmet's aluminum skin to take on the coloration of its surroundings, so that it blends into any environment."

"Like a chameleon," Dum Dum said.

"Exactly."

Fury asked, "Could this work on a 747 so that a jet in flight can convert from one carrier livery to another?"

The Techno considered. "It's basically a transparent polymer decal impregnated with electronically-sensitized pigments. Commercial jetliner livery is applied in decal form. Assuming multiple preprinted liveries imbedded in the material, a reliable power source and the ability to switch modes from the cockpit in midflight, yes, it's feasible."

Fury looked to the others. "I think our problems just went nuclear."

"This is bad," Dum Dum muttered. "Here we are tryin' to round up every Empire jet around the globe, and it turns out the stinkin' things are electronically camouflaged. Any bird in the air wearin' any carrier's colors could be Empire's. How are we gonna ground every commercial flight by Christmas Eve?"

"It's impossible," Starla said. "We still don't know how many planes constitutes Empire's worldwide fleet. Where would we begin?"

"Where to stop is the better question," Nick Fury said unhappily.

Art Skindarian was crunching numbers.

"Calculating the number of flights on three consecutive days, allowing for maintenance problems and downtimes, we have a total global fleet of approximately 86 aircraft. Against a total of 37 we've captured, there are at least 49 aircraft still out there."

"That don't count any Air Quorak flights that al-Bazinda can fill up with Inferno 42 any time he wants," Dum Dum added. "We might as well admit it. We'd have to ground every plane on the planet to get us through the next twelve to twenty-four hours—and here it is the busiest travel time of the year."

"Too bad we didn't interrogate that Imperial Hydra deeper," Fury growled.

Starla said, "What about the others?"

"What others?"

"Hydra ME couldn't consist of just the six men who died in Gullahbad. There has to be a cell somewhere, a headquarters."

Fury considered. "Maybe. Try finding it in under eight hours."

"There's a better way," Starla said.

"We're all ears," Dum Dum said.

Achmed Abdullah was scanning Quorak with his mind. He lay prone, stripped of his green Hydra thobe, staring at the cracked ceiling of an abandoned mosque outside of Karnopolis, Egypt.

There had been no word from Imperial Hydra. No word since he and a contingent of his trusted inner circle had journeyed to Gullahbad to lay down the true reality of their alliance before the mad leader of Quorak, Nadir al-Bazinda.

A full day, and no communication. As Hydra Middle East's sole surviving extrasensor, Achmed had been tasked to locate the missing envoys.

But they proved unfindable. Wherever their minds were, they could not be accessed remotely. Going deeper into trance, Achmed peered into the past.

It was there he found the truth. His own brother, Ali, had gone as part of the team. Finding Ali, he merged with him, becoming one with him, until he could see through his brother's very eyes. He beheld Nadir al-Bazinda. They stood in a courtyard. There were Quorakis brandishing scimitars. Tension filled the air. Ali was made to kneel. His head dropped to the ground. Ali saw the flags of the courtyard. Then his startled eyes saw a rolling confusion.

When the rolling stopped, there was enough life in them to spy his own neck spurting blood where it had crumpled, headless. And where the mind of Ali Abdullah had fled, his brother Achmed could not follow.

Achmed arose from his couch. Heavy of foot, he padded to the office of his superior.

"Hail Hydra. I have news."

The masked man behind the ornate desk invited, "Speak."

"You are the new Imperial Hydra. The others are dead. Truly, al-Bazinda betrayed them."

The new Imperial Hydra absorbed this news in silence.

"This can only mean the madman of Quorak has decided to pursue his own goals without regard for overriding Hydra interests."

Suddenly, Achmed stiffened.

"What is it?"

"I sense . . . a presence. Eyes stare at us."

The new Imperial Hydra jumped to his feet. "Whose? Quickly—speak!"

Achmed closed his dark eyes. "I see the accursed golden eagle of S.H.I.E.L.D."

"Bah! They cannot harm us now."

"I also see a flag. It is . . . white . . ."

"Surely they are not surrendering to us?"

"No. I think they are requesting a . . . truce."

The two Hydras stared at one another for a long minute.

The Attack Python was the top-of-the-line Hydra tactical attack aircraft. S.H.I.E.L.D. had engaged them in different theaters all throughout the world, shot a few down. None had ever been captured intact.

Thus, all eyes in the Helicarrier control tower were riveted on the single swept-wing black-and-scarlet Python as it came in for a landing on the main flight deck, bare of its usual complement of Copperhead air-to-air missiles.

"Vicious-looking thing, ain't it?" Dum Dum grumbled.

Nick Fury said nothing. Beneath a two-day growth of beard, his face was grim.

Val shivered slightly. "The thought of one of those butchers landing on my flight deck is enough to—"

"Stow it. We got bigger fish to fry."

It was a rough landing. The Python caught the third

arrestor cable and snapped backward. The fighter's tail-hook had been an add-on. It almost broke. The canopy popped and two green-robed figures climbed down, hands hanging loose and empty.

Fury met them in his personal Hummer. They submitted to a weapons search, which included a minute examination of their dental work.

"We had a little problem with one of your people a while back," Dum Dum explained. "He kinda blew his top."

The Hydra submitted to these indignities in silence. Then they were escorted to a secure conference room belowdecks.

Nick Fury addressed them.

"I'll give it to you straight. Nadir al-Bazinda plans to drop Empire jets filled with Inferno 42 all over the world on Christmas Eve. You probably know that much already. Here's what you don't know: Empire's been grounded in the U.S. and a few other countries. We've impounded maybe half of his planes. We need to know where the others are."

The Hydra exchanged uneasy glances.

"It's your hides as well as ours," Fury reminded. "You know that."

"We cannot help you. Operational control of the remaining aircraft have gone over to al-Bazinda's suicide pilots. He has aircraft secreted in several strategic locations."

"You gotta know where."

"We do not. But the former Imperial Hydra did, and now he is dead."

"So you're saying there's nothin' we can do," Dum Dum rumbled.

"You can shoot down all Empire flights. If you can."

"And blow a ton of innocent civilians out of the sky on Christmas Eve? No way."

"You have no choice. More will die on the ground if

you do not act to preserve your cities. Inferno 42 is virtually unquenchable. It can consume concrete, brick and most metals. Not to mention what it will do to human flesh."

Fury said, "Something's got to put it out."

"If you can deprive it of oxygen, it will die, of course. Just as you would cap a burning oil well. But how do you cap an entire city?"

Dum Dum drew Fury aside. "I think these guys are hopin' al-Bazinda's pilots take out a few Middle Eastern cities so they can proceed with their A plan."

"I concur," Starla undertoned.

Fury asked her, "They telling us the truth?"

"I'm afraid they are. My read is Hydra ME is very small. Al-Bazinda took their technology and pushed them out of the loop."

Fury nodded grimly. He returned to the waiting Hydras.

"Your cooperation is greatly appreciated," he said bitterly.

"We cannot help you with information we do not have," one Hydra said, showing helpless hands.

"But I can tell you're not about to go out of your way to stop what's about to go down, either," Fury growled.

The Hydra contingent were escorted back to their aircraft by armed Security Officers. Fury and Dum Dum went with them.

During the pre-flight walkaround, the Hydras discovered the Python fighter lay a little low in the nose.

"Well, look at that," Dum Dum clucked. "Tsk-tsk. Looks like you boys blew a tire on landing."

"Yeah. Musta been a slow leak," Fury added. "Too bad we don't have any spares."

The head Hydra said nervously, "We would appreciate being flown to a neutral safe location."

"Transportation home wasn't part of the deal," Dum Dum pointed out.

Nick Fury called over his shoulder, "Gabe, fetch these jokers a life ring and a set of parachutes. Looks like they're going home the hard way . . ."

And leaving the unhappy Hydras fuming on the wind-swept flight deck, Nick Fury got into his vehicle and peeled rubber.

WAR

THE WAR ROOM OF THE HELI-carrier was bustling with activity. Virtually every wall was jammed with computer screens and tactical displays. Data feeds were coming in from all over the globe. With each report, a gigantic Mercator projection map of the seven continents lit up with a white aircraft symbol, indicating a destroyed or confiscated Empire flight. A running numerical tally changed digits like a stock ticker.

Nick Fury stormed around, puffing furiously, barking orders. His voice was urgent and hoarse.

"Keep searching. Every plane we locate is another city that escapes Hellfire. We can't give up now. We're too close to knocking the Empire threat down to size."

The atmosphere was tense. The Helicarrier was still in the Gulf. There wasn't time to move her, and no strategically appropriate place to move her to. On the theory that the majority of surviving Empire aircraft were based in Africa and the Middle East, remaining in the Gulf seemed like the best course of action.

"Report coming in from Paris," Art Skindarian called out.

"Put it on the screen."

A S.H.I.E.L.D. agent's pale face came on the big four-sided Jumbotron hanging from the center of the ceiling.

"Reporting from S.H.I.E.L.D. Seoul. We've located a plane hangared where it shouldn't be. The livery says KAL, but KAL doesn't fly Fokkers."

"Stake it out. Capture the pilots. They ought to be showing up any minute now. And search it for Inferno 42. It might be a liquid, a gel or a solid. And whatever you do, don't ignite it!"

More reports filtered in. The well-oiled international machine that was the Strategic Hazard, Intelligence, Espionage and Logistics Directorate was operating with ferocious efficiency.

But the doomsday clock was ticking faster still. And everyone knew it.

Zero Hour approached and there were still an estimated fourteen aircraft not accounted for.

"Fourteen planes," Fury said bitterly. "Fourteen loose planes means fourteen doomed cities."

Dum Dum twisted one of his fiery mustaches tensely. "Yeah. And we got no inklin' of the cities targeted. It looks bad, Nick. We may have to shoot down some of them birds, passengers and all."

"I know," Fury said savagely. "And if we do, S.H.I.E.L.D. will bear the blame. They'll make scapegoats of us. Probably shut us down."

Absently, Dum Dum fingered the tinsel on a tabletop tree—the only hint of Christmas in the high-tech War Room.

"Some Christmas," he muttered half to himself.

As Fury watched, the big Irishman did a strange thing. He unhooked a cherry-red bulb from the tree and dropped it into his upended bowler hat. Then he put the bowler back on his head. His expression was perfectly blank.

Before Fury could question him, Art Skindarian stepped off the elevator.

Fury looked over—and his cigar dropped from his gaping mouth. Reflexively, he caught it in one hand.

"Where the heck are your shoes?"

Skindarian stopped, looked down. And found himself

staring at his naked toes. He looked up, his long face suffusing with a mounting embarrassment.

"I-I don't know," he sputtered helplessly. Touching his forehead, he said, "My mind is—foggy."

Nick Fury lifted his voice and addressed the room.

"I know we're under a lot of stress here, but I never thought I'd live to see the day my people started going barefoot and hiding Christmas ornaments in their derbys." His gaze went to Dum Dum Dugan.

The big Irishman blinked. "Are you referring to yours truly?"

"I don't see any other hats around here, do you?"

Cautiously, Dum Dum took his bowler off his head. Amid his disordered profusion of red hair sat a red bulb. He reached up, feeling the object with spatulate fingers. His blue eyes went strange.

Taking the ornament off his head, Dum Dum scrutinized it as if it might bite him.

"How the blankety-blank hell did *that* get there?" he thundered.

"You put it there," Fury told him. "I watched you."

"What the heck's going on here?" Dugan bellowed.

Fury's com link warbled. He lifted it to his face.

"Fury."

"SPD Spacek here, Colonel. I urgently need to speak to you." Before Fury could reply, she added, *"It's about the strange behaviors taking place in the War Room."*

"On my way," said Fury. Racing to the elevator, he threw a hard look to Dum Dum. "Stay on top of operations. And leave the decorations alone."

Dum Dum reached up and yanked his battered bowler down over his ears in sheer frustration.

Fury found Starla Spacek in her office on Deck 12.

"What the hell's going on, and how do you know about it?" he demanded.

"I have been monitoring the War Room, Colonel."

"I ain't gonna complain about that. What happened up there?"

Starla's voice turned grave. "Colonel, when I was with the CIA, we experimented with a number of operational methods. Some worked, others did not. One that showed promise was a technique we called remote influencing."

"What's that mean?"

"It means the power of one mind to psychically influence the other."

"Gimme a fer instance."

"For instance, suppose I wanted to demonstrate remote influence in a dramatic way. I might, for example, zero in on a certain red-haired Irishman, and induce him to take a bulb from a Christmas tree and place it under his hat. He would do this and not be consciously aware he was doing it. Or suggest that another subject leave his shoes in his office. If I did this correctly, staying with him, said subject would be oblivious to the feel of bare skin on metal floors until I released my mental control— or the discrepancy was pointed out to him."

"You did all that?"

Starla nodded soberly. "I did those things, yes."

"Why?"

"As a dramatic demonstration of remote influencing. Because in the heat of this crisis you might not otherwise accept my proposal. But mostly because human lives are at stake."

"I think I'm getting your drift. Out with it."

"I can do this," Starla said tensely. "A few of my people can, too."

"Keep talking," Fury invited.

"We'll never locate all those planes and pilots in time. Not through practical methods. You know that. You just won't admit it. Unless we find another line of attack, several cities will be incinerated."

"I know that only too well," Fury growled.

"Suppose Special Powers can locate the pilots. Influence them to land their planes intact and surrender. Or not take off in the first place."

Fury scratched his rough chin thoughtfully. "That would be useful, all right. If it works. How are you gonna find these people, when Practical Intel can't?"

"By the one thing that marks them all: their scorpion tattoos. All Special Powers needs to locate a person's energy signature in the universe is two coordinates. That's a pretty unique one."

"What's the other?"

"Their Nadir al-Bazinda mustaches. All Empire pilots have that feature in common."

Fury's solitary eye narrowed almost to a slit.

"You're pretty stubborn for a psychic," he said evenly. "But I can't put the entire operation in your hands. Too much is at stake."

"You can't afford not to let me try," Starla flung back. "It's the end of S.H.I.E.L.D. if you fail."

Starla fixed Nick Fury with her gray-green clairvoyant eyes. "Have I failed you yet?"

"You got me there. Okay, let's lay it out for the others."

Art Skindarian sat open-mouthed as Nick Fury summarized his plans. The War Room was growing dark. A sulken sun was setting over the waters of the Gulf.

"This—this is preposterous! You can't take this seriously. It smacks of voodoo and superstition. This is the twentieth century, for God's sake."

"That's tall talk for a guy sittin' with his bare tootsies grippin' the rug," Dum Dum suggested.

Skindarian blushed. "This entire operation is hanging on this woman's knowledge of astrology. Of all things. We aren't even certain that Zero Hour is tonight. It might be Christmas, or Christmas Eve. And when you factor in the international dateline, you have a pretty big window. For all we know, we still have forty-eight hours before the strike. At our present rate of success, we have an excellent chance of stopping Empire within the next twenty-four hours."

"Want to bet the population of Cairo on that, Art?" Nick Fury asked coolly.

Skindarian flinched. His voice dropped. "No."

Starla spoke up. "We know the exact Zero Hour because it's based on the planetary positions according to local Quorak time. And I want it on the record," she added, eyeing Skindarian, "that the timing of tonight's operation does not hinge on astrology. But on our knowledge of Nadir al-Bazinda's *belief* in astrology. He's been told that tonight marks his last hour on earth. He's a fatalist. If he believes he is to die, his warped psychology demands that it happen on his own terms."

"Noted," Skindarian said stiffly. "Make sure it goes into your report that way," he added.

Nick Fury jabbed his cigar in Starla's direction. "Spacek, you are sanctioned for this operation. Go to it. The rest of us will continue practical operations."

Starla left, saying, "You won't regret this, Colonel."

SPD Spacek requisitioned a computer room with six terminals. She had a scan of the scorpion tattoos taken off the dead Vinegaroon pilots uploaded onto each screen and sat her team before them.

"Find a subject, and make mental contact," she ordered.

One by one, her agents zoned out. She watched them go. And one by one, they began reporting back.

"Contact. Subject name Balid."

"Contact. Subject name Ibrahim."

"Contact. Subject name Ismeddin."

When everyone had locked in on a subject, Starla took a seat before her own terminal and fixed her eyes on the black scorpion painted there electronically.

Finding her way into her own personal Zone, she sent

her mind reaching out into the larger world whose time-and-space barriers were no barrier to her.

In Mexico City, two pilots sat before the controls of their Mexicana Airlines Boeing 737 as it rumbled along the taxiway toward the main runway. Their swarthy features were grim. They were almost indistinguishable from the faces of Mexican-born pilots. Even their thick mustaches seemed appropriate to their surroundings.

Not so the black scorpions that marked the inner wrists of their right hands.

When their turn came, the pilot turned onto the main runway and sent his lumbering aircraft forward. It gathered speed, and gear folding up, vaulted into the air, transforming from an ungainly ground machine into a mighty streamlined bird of flight.

Mexicana Flight 088 carried 128 passengers and a full load of fuel in both wing tanks. Its destination was Dallas, Texas.

It got as far as San Antonio, when the pilot reported engine trouble.

"Mayday. Mayday," the captain reported in his thick, difficult-to-understand accent. "Mexicana Flight 008 losing altitude. Emergency landing in progress."

Then all contact ceased.

Rescue aircraft were dispatched along its flight path. But no sign of the airliner was discovered.

During the frantic search, no pilot noticed—or paid much attention to—the Vinegaroon 737 that was vectoring northeast, on an unwavering course to Washington, D.C.

At Orly Airport in France, a S.H.I.E.L.D. Tactical Tiger Team surrounded an Airbus 320 as it backed away from its gate. It bore Empire Airlines livery. They blocked the jet with an Armored Personnel Carrier. The back door popped open and two armed Tigers raced to the starboard wheel assembly, frantically popped rivets with power tools. Through the open wheel well, they gained access to the cargo hold while their commander attempted to talk the Empire pilot and flight engineer into surrendering peacefully.

Working in studied silence, they unscrewed a floor plate and climbed up into the galley. One Tiger took up a position at the closed cockpit door while the other entered the passenger cabin.

The plan was simple: get the passengers down the escape chutes. Then take out the cockpit crew.

It might have worked, but for the fact that when Field Agent Guy Morrow showed his face, the passengers—a mix of men, women and children—reached up and touched their foreheads in an identical manner.

Their lifelike human faces lifted out and up like so many visors.

"Good Lord . . ." Morrow breathed as the unmasked LMDs' electronic inner visages began displaying red digits in countdown mode.

3 . . . 2 . . . 1 . . .

At zero, every LMD self-immolated. The aircraft burst like an aluminum sausage. The shock wave was composed of pure fire. It rolled outward, incinerating the S.H.I.E.L.D. APC, and all men and machines within a 5,000-yard radius.

Within three minutes, all of Orly Airport was involved in a new kind of earthly conflagration—fast-moving, voracious and utterly unquenchable.

At her terminal on the Helicarrier, Starla Spacek started in sympathetic shock.

"I just lost my subject," she said in horror. But there was no one listening. Her people were deep in Alpha. Swallowing a lump in her throat, she fixed her gaze on the evil-looking scorpion before her and attempted to find its counterpart in the real world.

The trouble was, she kept locking onto Nadir al-Bazinda himself—the one scorpion in the scheme of things she didn't need to connect with. . . .

Nick Fury received the report from a white-faced Art Skindarian.

"Orly Airport is a flaming crater, Colonel. We lost a Tac Tiger Team, and reports from the scene indicate firefighters are unable to knock down the blaze."

"This is only a little taste of what's to come," Fury said angrily. He glanced at the digital wall clock. "We still got three hours before Zero."

Val called up from the bridge. *"Another Quoraki sortie coming in, loaded for bear."*

"Don't they ever give up? Splash them good."

"Roger."

A flight of six F-16 Falcons roared off the main flight deck. Fury watched them climb, afterburners roaring. Three Quoraki MiG-21 Fishbeds raced to meet them.

It was no contest. While the MiGs were climbing, the Falcons launched AMRAAM air-to-air missiles from their wings. They sped true.

One, two, three flowers of smoke and burning debris blossomed over the Gulf. Fury turned away from the bank of windows. The Quoraki Air Force was just a side show. The main event was taking place in pockets all around the globe.

Art Skindarian called over from a satellite phone station. "Colonel, excellent news."

"Out with it."

"S.H.I.E.L.D. forces just captured an Empire jet on the ground in Chad. No casualties either side. Empire crew being interrogated. They're pretty dazed. It's as if they've been hypnotized." Skindarian's voice turned puzzled. "You don't suppose this has anything to do with the Special Powers' side of the operation?"

"What do you think?" Fury barked back. "I want every scrap of intel as it comes in. Nothing is too small."

Skindarian returned to his conversation.

Fury looked around the War Room. Everyone was focused. This is what made S.H.I.E.L.D. so important to the post–Cold War world, he thought with grim pride. The fierce dedication of its multinational force.

Whatever happens now, however things turned out for Nick Fury and his organization, countless lives were being saved.

But the director of S.H.I.E.L.D. took no satisfaction from that sure knowledge.

He would settle for nothing less than total success.

"The hour is almost nigh," a voice told Nadir al-Bazinda.

The dictator of Quorak, self-styled Fist of Allah and Scourge of the West, stood up in his ceremonial office in the Palace of Mysteries.

"My destiny is nigh," he said, his voice like that of a man long dead. His swarthy face was the color of old bread. His penetrating, intensely black eyes had the look of roadkill. It looked out at the world, but did not see.

"The bird that will convey you to Paradise awaits, *al-Ze'em.*"

Al-Bazinda straightened his emerald-and-ivory dress uniform, and checked his sidearm. "Before the sun rises on the Infidel, Omar, I will be with the *houris* in Paradise, where I will be feted as a hero."

Omar the astrologer closed his aging eyes. "I regret that after this fated day, we will speak no more, *al-Ze'em.*"

Al-Bazinda laid huge hands upon the frail shoulders of his servant. "You have been my faithful and loyal astrologer since I assumed power almost a revolution of Saturn ago. Now Saturn sits upon my shoulders like a great oppressive weight."

Omar nodded. "The stars impel us to our fates, they do not compel us. But the planets truly rule our destinies in ways we cannot brook. But I have been pleased to serve."

"And I have been pleased, O Omar, to be your ruler and protector. After such service, could I now turn my back on you and leave you to the cruel jackals who will seize all my worldly goods and snuff out my inner circle?"

Omar the astrologer looked into the eyes of Nadir al-Bazinda. He saw death mirrored there. He swallowed.

"I will fend for myself, be assured," he said.

"No, you must come with me," continued the Dictator of Quorak. "I insist."

"But I am not fated to perish for several years yet," Omar croaked.

"You obviously missed an important transit," said Nadir al-Bazinda. Taking his personal astrologer's spindly neck in his heavy hands, he throttled him until Omar's dangling feet ceased to kick blindly at the shins of his ruler and executor.

Twenty minutes later, a 747 jumbo jet decked out in the blood-red-and-silver livery of Air Quorak took off from Gullahbad International Airport.

Turning south, it took up a direct heading on the Persian Gulf.

The time was exactly 7:27 Gullahbad time.

Perspiration made Starla Spacek's features resemble a heavy moist sponge. Her back ached. Her eyes were red. She fought to keep them focused—focused on the hated symbol of death. The sign of Scorpio. The emblem of death to cultures all throughout the world.

On either side of her terminal, other Special Powers Officers had given up. Drained, exhausted, they'd gone to the brink of their psychic limits, and pushing beyond their operational limits, they had wilted.

Starla refused to wilt. Too many lives were at stake.

Clairvoyantly, she saw the electronic scorpion before her eyes swim, only to be replaced by a true-life image, on a human wrist, somewhere in the world.

Into her mind came a name clairaudiently: "Rafik."

That was all she needed now.

Rafik, she called. *Land your plane, Rafik, you do not want to kill. You do not wish to die. You want to live . . .*

It was hard. Starla first made the words in her mind, but words could not be transmitted mind-to-mind with clarity. She turned the thought into feelings and emotions, like a tight ball of knowledge. Rolling the ball across the unguessable distance between herself and her target subject, she could only hope Rafik the terrorist would accept the feelings.

She felt his anger. Felt it clearly. Feeling it dissolve like a sugar cube in the rain, she turned her attention to his copilot. The name she received was Abdul. This was the second Abdul she had contacted. It was a strain, keeping all these names straight. . . .

But she could not surrender to fatigue.

When Empire Flight 901 landed without incident in Cairo, Egypt, S.H.I.E.L.D. agents were there to meet it.

The pilots stepped off without incident. They were thrown to the ground and subdued. Faces dazed, they seemed unaware of what was happening to them.

A S.H.I.E.L.D. Tac Tiger Team rushed on board. They expected a passenger cabin full of Life Model Decoys. But these people were real. And frightened.

Evacuating them safely, they searched the Airbus for signs of Inferno 42.

But was it a liquid, a solid . . . or something else?

Art Skindarian called out the latest report.

"Empire Flight 901 just landed without incident at Cairo. That makes, what? Fifteen successful groundings." His face took on a peculiar expression. "Colonel, I'm starting to believe Special Powers is making a difference."

His phone buzzed. He picked it up.

"Make that sixteen, Colonel." His face was flushed with excitement. "Special Powers has done it again."

"Sounds like a convert," Dum Dum undertoned to Nick Fury.

Fury addressed the room. "We're doing great, people. But we still have another twenty minutes until Zero Hour. And just because we've exceeded our goal don't mean there aren't Empire flights still out there disguised as other carriers."

The reminder brought a momentary halt to the War Room celebration. A hush gripped them. It was dark outside. The sun had gone down completely. As yet, there was no moon to wash the Gulf with light.

Grimly, everyone returned to their duties.

If the Boeing 737 hadn't been painted with the sunset red and orange colors of Vinegaroon Air, S.H.I.E.L.D. Captain Kenneth "Doc" Drexel might not have noticed it.

His tasking was to patrol the airspace around Washington, D.C., determined by HQ to be the primary city on the Empire target list.

But it was a 737. He could tell by the distinctive flattened underside of the wing-engine nacelles. And Drexel knew from his pre-mission briefing that Vinegaroon did not fly 737s.

Rolling hard, he formed up beside the jetliner, his Fighting Falcon looking like a mere toy beside the huge aircraft.

"Unidentified Vinegaroon flight, ID at once," he called by radio.

The jetliner was silent.

"Vinegaroon flight, please state your destination."

A voice came back, throaty and cold.

"Hell," it said.

And suddenly, the aluminum skin of the jetliner began to shift and shimmer, changing color, going from flaming desert hues to a chameleon green.

On the side of the airliner, the red letters VINEGA-ROON changed, mutating electronically until they now read EMPIRE.

Swallowing hard, Drexel armed his missiles. His orders were clear. Even though Virginia's rolling and populated hills lay directly below.

Better Virgina than the nation's capital. . . .

Nick Fury paced the War Room as the digital wall chronometer ate into his margin of error.

"What's the latest? Dammit, I want answers!"

"Nothing out of Africa."

"No word from Europe in the last ten minutes."

"No news is good news, Nick," Dum Dum suggested.

"I ain't breathing easy until nine P.M. local time," Fury said savagely. "Maybe not even then."

Then came a call on the phone.

Art Skindarian took it. Already pale, his long funereal features went the color of bone.

"My God! No."

Fury reached him in three quick strides and snatched the heavy-duty receiver away.

"This is Fury. Report!"

"S.H.I.E.L.D. Washington, Colonel. One of our Falcons is tracking a suspicious Vinegaroon aircraft. It has just shed its camouflage."

"Let me guess. It's an Empire jet now. Where's it headed?"

"The nation's capital." Washington cleared his throat. "Colonel, I need your direct authorization to shoot it down."

"ETA D.C.?" Fury barked.

"Approximately fourteen minutes."

"Shoot it down before it crosses the Potomac. Got that?"

"Understood."

Nick Fury raced to the elevator, dropped the cage. It never seemed so slow. Reaching Deck 1, he grabbed his waiting Hummer and sent it careening wildly down a corridor.

Talking into his com link, he barked, "Spacek, where are you? Answer me!"

An unfamiliar voice came back. "She's in Alpha, Colonel."

"Snap her out of it. I need her."

When Fury reached the computer room, Starla Spacek was all but passed out on a couch. She looked like a pale towel that had been wrung dry.

"Did we succeed?" she asked weakly. "Is it over?"

"Almost. Listen, Spacek. We got an Empire flight heading for Washington. Loaded to the gills with Inferno 42. If we shoot it down, there goes a big chunk of Virginia."

Starla shook her head. "Help me to my terminal," she croaked.

Fury lugged to her chair and set her down.

Her head leaned forward until her brow touched the monitor's glass screen. Her eyes closed. For a minute, Fury thought she had passed out completely.

But her lips were moving. It sounded like a prayer. Maybe it was. Nick Fury didn't understand a word of the Cheyenne language. . . .

Captain Kenneth Drexel watched the miles reel past.

"ETA eight minutes," he called into his mike.

Silence from S.H.I.E.L.D. Washington.

"ETA, seven minutes, forty seconds," he repeated. His throat felt dry. At best, he was going to have to shoot down a planeload of innocent civilians. At worst, he was going to be responsible for the extinguishing of untold innocents on the ground, as well as the plane's passenger list.

"ETA six minutes," Drexel said tightly. "Is anyone reading me?"

"Doc," S.H.I.E.L.D. Washington came back. *"You are sanctioned to splash. Repeat, splash your target."*

"Damn."

Breaking off from the 737, the white-and-gold F-16 Falcon throttled back. The jetliner pulled away. Retreating, Drexel fell in behind it. Woodenly, he armed his AMRAAM missiles.

There was still time for a prayer. Drexel took those precious few seconds. He searched his memory for an appropriate one. . . .

It was fortunate that he did. Just as Drexel's targeting radar confirmed lock-on, a frantic voice screeched in his ear.

"Fire order rescinded immediately, Doc. Repeat: do not fire."

"Roger. Order rescinded. Copy."

An audible sigh of relief came through the radio.

As the Empire jetliner roared on, Drexel continued pacing it, wondering what could possibly avert the catastrophe now only three minutes away.

The jetliner overflew Washington. Its moon-made shadow passed briefly over the Potomac River Basin.

Then, over the Chesapeake Bay, the aircraft went into a steep dive.

"She's going down!" Drexel called.

"We know," came back the reply. *"The pilot has been ordered to ditch."*

"Ordered? By whom?"

"By a power greater than the people who sent him aloft."

That didn't make any sense to Kenneth Drexel, but as the jet dropped into the Atlantic, he executed a final flyby.

The flight crew were at their controls. Drexel caught just a glimpse. He could have sworn the captain's face was as blank and expressionless as a robot's.

The digital clock now read 8:40. In the Helicarrier War Room, Art Skindarian was speaking.

"S.H.I.E.L.D. Washington confirms the Empire 737

ditched in the Atlantic. No reports of fire. Rescue vessels are en route to pick up any passengers."

Dum Dum called into his com link. "Did you catch that, Nick?"

"Yeah. And inform rescue that all they'll find in the way of passengers are LMDs and a couple of Quoraki pilots who don't know what got into them . . ."

Belowdecks, Nick Fury looked to Starla Spacek. She managed a weak smile. Then she closed her eyes in utter fatigue.

Fury gave her tawny hair a paternal pat. "You done good, kid. You done real good."

Together, they entered into the War Room at exactly 8:44:32.

Applause rippled around the room. It quickly subsided. No one had much energy left.

Art Skindarian helped Starla Spacek into an empty seat. "I forgive you for that little barefoot prank," he said simply.

Starla gave him a weak nod in return.

"No further incidents," Dum Dum reported.

"I guess we just gotta wait," Fury said, eyeing the relentless march of numbers on the wall.

In the subdued hush of the War Room, they watched the countdown. They were starting to breathe more easily again. It was beginning to look like victory.

Then Val's uneasy voice came from the bridge below.

"Colonel Fury. Long range reports a flight of Quoraki MiGs en route to our position."

"Scramble a flight of Falcons and dust them," Fury growled back. He was stripping a fresh cigar. He had not smoked in three hours. For him, a long time.

"Colonel, radar shows one aircraft flying in the center of the MiG flight. We read it as a 747. And it's on a dead heading for the Helicarrier."

Fury and Dum Dum swapped wild glances.

"They tried to sink us once," Dum Dum exploded. "Stands to reason they'd give it one last try."

Fury barked, "Scramble that flight! And put every plane we have into the air." He turned to Starla. "I need a read on this."

Starla looked ready to collapse in her chair. Gamely, she closed her eyes.

"I see a face. Nadir al-Bazinda's. He's flying the 747 personally."

Dum Dum said, "Damn!"

"Intentions?"

"The destruction of the Helicarrier."

"We gotta shoot it down," Dum Dum said urgently.

"Not so fast." Fury knelt before his exhausted Director of Special Powers, taking her shoulders in his big hands. "Starla, I need one last favor from you. Then you can sleep for a month. Okay?"

"What is it?"

"Sweep the passenger cabin for me."

Starla nodded. Her eyes were glassy, almost without comprehension. She looked out of it.

Fury turned to Dum Dum. "Relay what she gets to me."

"Where are you goin'?"

Entering the elevator, Fury punched the Down button.

"Nadir al-Bazinda wants my hide. Well, I want his. So we're doing this the old-fashioned way: Man to man."

The elevator door closed on his resolute face.

The F-15E Strike Eagle was waiting for Fury on the flight deck. He climbed into the cockpit as deck officers hooked him up to the catapult.

The LSO popped Fury a salute and amid roaring clouds of steam, the Eagle was flung into space.

Fury rode the afterburners to Angels 6, picked up a northerly heading and called to the tower.

"ETA Bogies?"

"AWACS says you have five minutes."

"Then I'm gonna make 'em count."

By the time he reached the area of engagement, the MiGs and S.H.I.E.L.D. Falcons were embroiled in a nasty furball. In the growing dark, all that was visible were navigation lights and afterburner cones. It was enough to tell the story.

And in the center of it all, painted by cold moonlight, flew a big white Boeing 747.

Thundering in, Fury recognized the angular swept wings of a MiG 25 Foxbat spurting ahead to meet him. Quoraki's best. Obviously, al-Bazinda had saved his top fighters for the last ditch.

Fury lined him up in his gunsights. Uncapping the trigger of his 20mm MG1A-1 six-barrel machine gun, he fired a burst. Gold tracers showed the track. It flew true.

As he watched, the Foxbat blew apart. The pilot ejected, but fate pulled his descending chute into the path of the big jumbo jet. Its starboard wing sliced through the chute shroudlines. The pilot was flung about. He got sucked into a wing engine. The engine began laboring. Then smoking.

Other fighters saw Fury coming. Another Foxbat flying escort broke free and climbed toward him.

Fury armed his missiles, got a radar tone and fired.

The Foxbat was shooting upward. The green tracer-laced bullet track came up like angry fireflies. They fell short.

The missile did not. It went for the nose. Beak to beak, fighter and missile impacted. The result was spectacular. The Foxbat blew open in an expanding wall of superhot gasses. So hot they vaporized a passing MiG-21.

When the furball subsided, there was no trace of the MiG Foxbat Fury had killed.

"Inferno 42," Fury muttered. "Some of those Foxbats are loaded with Inferno 42."

Fury touched his mask microphone.

"What's the word on the passengers? Are they real, or not?"

Val said, "SPD Spacek's still working the problem."

"Not much time left," Fury warned.

"Hang on."

Fury made a close pass of the 747. He couldn't see much. The 747 pilot was just a dark shape in the illuminated cockpit. It could be anyone. But the scarlet and red livery was familiar. The same livery worn by the Airbus 320 that went into a storm cloud as an Empire plane only to emerge wearing the colors Nick Fury was now certain belonged to Air Quorak.

Coming around hard, he pulled level with the jumbo jet.

Pacing it, Fury had a clear view of the row of windows, portside. Faces were pressed to the Plexiglas. He saw men. Women. A few children. Their faces were twisted. They look scared.

Then, as the miles between the 747 and the Helicarrier narrowed, the skin of the jumbo jet rippled and wavered. Blood-red Arabic lettering wavered and swam. It started at the nose, worked its way back to the tail.

Red became green as unreadable Arabic script transformed into block green English letters.

They read EMPIRE.

Then, a further, more ominous transformation: EMPYRE.

And the moisture in Nick Fury's mouth dried up. This was it.

"Time's running out here," he complained.

Static hiss filled the air.

About to repeat, Fury felt something in his mind. A feeling. Then, in his mind's eye, he saw a traffic light. It was red. Then it switched to green. Green for go.

Val came came on, saying, "Special Powers reports the passengers read as LMDs. You are sanctioned, Colonel. Be cognizant of the fact that the LMDs are loaded with Inferno 42. Do not target the fuselage."

"Acknowledged. Thank Special Powers for me," Fury

said, rolling left. He armed his missiles. Targeting locked up the jumbo jet. It was now or never.

"Merry Christmas, al-Bazinda," Fury growled, "and to all a good night."

The AIM-9L Sidewinder spurted off its rail. The Eagle jerked with the release. Fury peeled way.

He didn't watch the kill. He didn't need to.

The jumbo jet took the hit in the outer starboard wing nacelle. It erupted. The wing screamed in pain, splintered, throwing aluminum fragments in its wake. It began to pull at the root. All along the cabin, the LMDs acted out a horrific pantomime of passengers in terror of their lives.

Slowly, inexorably, the wing-root gave it up. Abruptly, the entire wing folded back like a dragonfly's.

The great jetliner heeled, going into a slow flat spin.

Fury followed it down. It struck the cold, choppy waters of the Persian Gulf in a dark uprush of water.

The dolphin-shaped cranium disappeared under the dark waves, dragging the rest of the aircraft with it, like a monstrous fish returning to its natural habitat.

Nick Fury looked at his wristwatch. It was exactly 8:48:05.

He circled the regathering waters once, half expecting a delayed detonation of Inferno 42. There was none. The Gulf remained dark.

Fury climbed to Angels 5.

"Sing out. Where are those Foxbats?"

"Splashed. All splashed," Val reported.

"Casualties our side?"

Val sighed. *"I can remember more enjoyable Christmas Eves."*

"Next year will be better," Nick Fury promised, vectoring toward the imposing hull that was the mightiest weapons platform ever devised by the hand of man. "Count on it."

Fury sighed. The Christmas to come would be a day of

earthly peace and goodwill. A new year beckoned. It would be one of hope, not tragedy.

Once more, S.H.I.E.L.D. had triumphed. Once again, the world was safe.

But not for long, Nick Fury thought grimly. Not as long as Hydra still existed. Not as long as the monster remained intent on strangling the world in its spreading, tentacular limbs.

A major battle had been won. But the war against Hydra would continue.

Will Murray is a professional psychic, and the author of some fifty pseudonymous novels in series ranging from Doc Savage to the Executioner. He also scripted various versions of the Destroyer for Marvel Comics, and created the infamous Doreen Green, aka Squirrel Girl, for a memorable Iron Man story. On a more serious note, Murray has successfully executed most of the psychic functions depicted in this novel. Like one of the characters depicted herein, he's primarily clairvoyant/clairsentient, occasionally clairaudient and clairparlant, and demonstrably precognitive. Murray has received training in military-style coordinate remote viewing from a former U.S. Army remote viewer, but has never worked for any agency or government in that or any other capacity.

The author hastens to note that *Empyre* was written months before the Egypt Air 990 and Alaska Airlines 261 tragedies, both of which are eerily prefigured in its pages.

A Marvel reader since he purchased *Fantastic Four* #4 at a drugstore in 1962, Murray wonders if he was as psychic back then as he is now, would his younger self believe what his older self is doing for a living today? He doubts it. Nobody's *that* psychic.

Steranko is one of the most controversial figures in pop culture. As a writer, illustrator, magician, filmmaker, musician, escape artist, lecturer and designer, he has influenced the evolution of the entertainment world with a lifetime of innovative concepts. As one of Marvel's major superstars, he generated an international audience with his work on *Captain America, Nick Fury: Agent of S.H.I.E.L.D.,* and *The X-Men.* Recently, he was cover artist for the bestselling Marvel novel *Captain America: Liberty's Torch.*

CHRONOLOGY TO THE MARVEL NOVELS AND ANTHOLOGIES

What follows is a guide to the order in which the Marvel novels and short stories published by BP Books, Inc., and Berkley Boulevard Books take place in relation to each other. Please note that this is not a hard and fast chronology, but a guideline that is subject to change at authorial or editorial whim. This list covers all the novels and anthologies published from October 1994–October 2000.

The short stories are each given an abbreviation to indicate which anthology the story appeared in. USM=*The Ultimate Spider-Man,* USS=*The Ultimate Silver Surfer,* USV=*The Ultimate Super-Villains,* UXM=*The Ultimate X-Men,* UTS=*Untold Tales of Spider-Man,* UH=*The Ultimate Hulk,* and XML=*X-Men Legends.*

X-Men & Spider-Man: Time's Arrow Book 1: The Past [portions]
by Tom DeFalco & Jason Henderson
   Parts of this novel take place in prehistoric times, the sixth century, 1867, and 1944.

"Hiding"
by Nancy Holder & Christopher Golden [UH]
"Improper Procedure"
by Keith R.A. DeCandido [USS]
"The Ballad of Fancy Dan"
by Ken Grobe & Steven A. Roman [UTS]
"Welcome to the X-Men, Madrox . . ."
by Steve Lyons [XML]

These stories take place early in the careers of Spider-Man, the Silver Surfer, the Hulk, and the X-Men, after their origins and before the formation of the "new" X-Men.

"Here There Be Dragons"
by Sholly Fisch [UH]
"Peace Offering"
by Michael Stewart [XML]
"The Worst Prison of All"
by C.J. Henderson [XML]
"Poison in the Soul"
by Glenn Greenberg [UTS]
"Do You Dream in Silver?"
by James Dawson [USS]
"A Quiet, Normal Life"
by Thomas Deja [UH]
"Chasing Hairy"
by Glenn Hauman [XML]
"Livewires"
by Steve Lyons [UTS]
"Arms and the Man"
by Keith R.A. DeCandido [UTS]
"Incident on a Skyscraper"
by Dave Smeds [USS]
"One Night Only"
by Sholly Fisch [XML]
"A Green Snake in Paradise"
by Steve Lyons [UH]

<< < CHRONOLOGY > >>

These all take place after the formation of the "new" X-Men and before Spider-Man got married, the Silver Surfer ended his exile on Earth, and the reemergence of the gray Hulk.

These all take place just prior to Peter Parker's marriage to Mary Jane Watson and the Silver Surfer's release from imprisonment on Earth.

< < < < < < < 287 > > > > > > > >

"The Beast with Nine Bands"
by James A. Wolf [UH]
"Sambatyon"
by David M. Honigsberg [USS]
"A Fine Line"
by Dan Koogler [XML]
"Cold Blood"
by Greg Cox [USM]
"The Tarnished Soul"
by Katherine Lawrence [USS]
"Leveling Las Vegas"
by Stan Timmons [UH]
"Steel Dogs and Englishmen"
by Thomas Deja [XML]
"If Wishes Were Horses"
by Tony Isabella & Bob Ingersoll [USV]
"The Stranger Inside"
by Jennifer Heddle [XML]
"The Silver Surfer" [framing sequence]
by Tom DeFalco & Stan Lee [USS]
"The Samson Journals"
by Ken Grobe [UH]

These all take place after Peter Parker's marriage to Mary Jane Watson, after the Silver Surfer attained freedom from imprisonment on Earth, before the Hulk's personalities were merged, and before the formation of the X-Men "blue" and "gold" teams.

"The Deviant Ones"
by Glenn Greenberg [USV]
"An Evening in the Bronx with Venom"
by John Gregory Betancourt & Keith R.A. DeCandido [USM]

These two stories take place one after the other, and a few months prior to The Venom Factor.

The Incredible Hulk: What Savage Beast
by Peter David
   This novel takes place over a one-year period, starting here and ending just prior to Rampage.

"Once a Thief"
by Ashley McConnell [XML]
"On the Air"
by Glenn Hauman [UXM]
"Connect the Dots"
by Adam-Troy Castro [USV]
"Ice Prince"
by K.A. Kindya [XML]
"Summer Breeze"
by Jenn Saint-John & Tammy Lynne Dunn [UXM]
"Out of Place"
by Dave Smeds [UXM]
   These stories all take place prior to the Mutant Empire *trilogy.*

X-Men: Mutant Empire Book 1: **Siege**
by Christopher Golden
X-Men: Mutant Empire Book 2: **Sanctuary**
by Christopher Golden
X-Men: Mutant Empire Book 3: **Salvation**
by Christopher Golden
   These three novels take place within a three-day period.

Fantastic Four: To Free Atlantis
by Nancy A. Collins
"The Love of Death or the Death of Love"
by Craig Shaw Gardner [USS]
"Firetrap"
by Michael Jan Friedman [USV]

"What's Yer Poison?"
by Christopher Golden & José R. Nieto [USS]
"Sins of the Flesh"
by Steve Lyons [USV]
"Doom²"
by Joey Cavalieri [USV]
"Child's Play"
by Robert L. Washington III [USV]
"A Game of the Apocalypse"
by Dan Persons [USS]
"All Creatures Great and Skrull"
by Greg Cox [USV]
"Ripples"
by José R. Nieto [USV]
"Who Do You Want Me to Be?"
by Ann Nocenti [USV]
"One for the Road"
by James Dawson [USV]

These are more or less simultaneous, with "Doom²" taking place after To Free Atlantis, *"Child's Play" taking place shortly after "What's Yer Poison?" and "A Game of the Apocalypse" taking place shortly after "The Love of Death or the Death of Love."*

"Five Minutes"
by Peter David [USM]

This takes place on Peter Parker and Mary Jane Watson-Parker's first anniversary.

Spider-Man: The Venom Factor
by Diane Duane
Spider-Man: The Lizard Sanction
by Diane Duane
Spider-Man: The Octopus Agenda
by Diane Duane

These three novels take place within a six-week period.

"The Night I Almost Saved Silver Sable"
by Tom DeFalco [USV]
"Traps"
by Ken Grobe [USV]
These stories take place one right after the other.

Iron Man: The Armor Trap
by Greg Cox
Iron Man: Operation A.I.M.
by Greg Cox
"Private Exhibition"
by Pierce Askegren [USV]
Fantastic Four: Redemption of the Silver Surfer
by Michael Jan Friedman
Spider-Man & The Incredible Hulk: Rampage (Doom's Day Book 1)
by Danny Fingeroth & Eric Fein
Spider-Man & Iron Man: Sabotage (Doom's Day Book 2)
by Pierce Askegren & Danny Fingeroth
Spider-Man & Fantastic Four: Wreckage (Doom's Day Book 3)
by Eric Fein & Pierce Askegren
Operation A.I.M. *takes place about two weeks after* The Armor Trap. *The "Doom's Day" trilogy takes place within a three-month period. The events of* Operation A.I.M., *"Private Exhibition,"* Redemption of the Silver Surfer, *and* Rampage *happen more or less simultaneously.* Wreckage *is only a few months after* The Octopus Agenda.

"Such Stuff As Dreams Are Made Of"
by Robin Wayne Bailey [XML]
"It's a Wonderful Life"
by eluki bes shahar [UXM]
"Gift of the Silver Fox"
by Ashley McConnell [UXM]

"Stillborn in the Mist"
by Dean Wesley Smith [UXM]
"Order from Chaos"
by Evan Skolnick [UXM]
   These stories take place more or less simultane-ously, with "Such Stuff As Dreams Are Made Of" tak-ing place just prior to the others.

"X-Presso"
by Ken Grobe [UXM]
"Life Is But a Dream"
by Stan Timmons [UXM]
"Four Angry Mutants"
by Andy Lane & Rebecca Levene [UXM]
"Hostages"
by J. Steven York [UXM]
   These stories take place one right after the other.

Spider-Man: Carnage in New York
by David Michelinie & Dean Wesley Smith
Spider-Man: Goblin's Revenge
by Dean Wesley Smith
   These novels take place one right after the other.

X-Men: Smoke and Mirrors
by eluki bes shahar
   This novel takes place three-and-a-half months after "It's a Wonderful Life."

Generation X
by Scott Lobdell & Elliot S! Maggin
X-Men: The Jewels of Cyttorak
by Dean Wesley Smith
X-Men: Empire's End
by Diane Duane
X-Men: Law of the Jungle
by Dave Smeds

X-Men: Prisoner X
by Ann Nocenti
   These novels take place one right after the other.

The Incredible Hulk: Abominations
by Jason Henderson
Fantastic Four: Countdown to Chaos
by Pierce Askegren
"Playing It SAFE"
by Keith R.A. DeCandido [UH]
   These take place one right after the other, with Abominations *taking place a couple of weeks after* Wreckage.

"Mayhem Party"
by Robert Sheckley [USV]
   This story takes place after Goblin's Revenge.

X-Men & Spider-Man: Time's Arrow Book 1: **The Past**
by Tom DeFalco & Jason Henderson
X-Men & Spider-Man: Time's Arrow Book 2: **The Present**
by Tom DeFalco & Adam-Troy Castro
X-Men & Spider-Man: Time's Arrow Book 3: **The Future**
by Tom DeFalco & eluki bes shahar
   These novels take place within a twenty-four-hour period in the present, though it also involves traveling to four points in the past, to an alternate present, and to five different alternate futures.

X-Men: Soul Killer
by Richard Lee Byers

Spider-Man: Valley of the Lizard
by John Vornholt
Spider-Man: Venom's Wrath
by Keith R.A. DeCandido & José R. Nieto
Captain America: Liberty's Torch
by Tony Isabella & Bob Ingersoll
Daredevil: The Cutting Edge
by Madeleine E. Robins
Spider-Man: Wanted: Dead or Alive
by Craig Shaw Gardner
Spider-Man: Emerald Mystery
by Dean Wesley Smith
"Sidekick"
by Dennis Brabham [UH]
    These take place one after the other, with Soul
Killer *taking place right after the* Time's Arrow *trilogy,*
Venom's Wrath *taking place a month after* Valley of
the Lizard, *and* Wanted Dead or Alive *a couple of
months after* Venom's Wrath.

Spider-Man: The Gathering of the Sinister Six
by Adam-Troy Castro
Generation X: Crossroads
by J. Steven York
X-Men: Codename Wolverine ["now" portions]
by Christopher Golden
    *These novels take place one right after the other,
with the "now" portions of* Codename Wolverine *taking
place less than a week after* Crossroads.

The Avengers & the Thunderbolts
by Pierce Askegren
Spider-Man: Goblin Moon
by Kurt Busiek & Nathan Archer
Nick Fury, Agent of S.H.I.E.L.D.: Empyre
by Will Murray

Generation X: Genogoths
by J. Steven York
   These novels take place at approximately the same time and several months after "Playing It SAFE."

Spider-Man & the Silver Surfer: Skrull War
by Steven A. Roman & Ken Grobe
X-Men & the Avengers: Gamma Quest Book 1: **Lost and Found**
by Greg Cox
X-Men & the Avengers: Gamma Quest Book 2: **Search and Rescue**
by Greg Cox
X-Men & the Avengers: Gamma Quest Book 3: **Friend or Foe?**
by Greg Cox
   These books take place one right after the other.

X-Men & Spider-Man: Time's Arrow Book 3: **The Future [portions]**
by Tom DeFalco & eluki bes shahar
   Parts of this novel take place in five different alternate futures in 2020, 2035, 2099, 3000, and the fortieth century.

"The Last Titan"
by Peter David [UH]
   This takes place in a possible future.

Penguin Putnam Inc.
Online

Your Internet gateway to a virtual environment with
hundreds of entertaining and enlightening books
from Penguin Putnam Inc.

*While you're there, get the latest buzz on
the best authors and books around—*

Tom Clancy, Patricia Cornwell, W.E.B. Griffin,
Nora Roberts, William Gibson, Robin Cook,
Brian Jacques, Catherine Coulter, Stephen King,
Jacquelyn Mitchard, and many more!

**Penguin Putnam Online is located at
http://www.penguinputnam.com**

PENGUIN PUTNAM NEWS

Every month you'll get an inside look at our upcom-
ing books and new features on our site. This is an
ongoing effort to provide you with the most
up-to-date information about
our books and authors.

**Subscribe to Penguin Putnam News at
http://www.penguinputnam.com/ClubPPI**